Aaron Crash

Denver

Fury

American Dragons

Book One

Aaron Crash

Dedication

For Nikki, the Wednesdays, the Cons, and those
wicked, wicked egg rolls.

Aaron Crash

ONE

IT WAS GOING TO BE ONE OF THOSE NIGHTS AT THE Coffee Clutch. You'd think midnight in a Denver coffee shop would be pretty chill, and it was most of the time. But then things can get weird on the night before a guy's twentieth birthday.

Steven Whipp grabbed the mop out of the cleaning closet just as Bud came in and kicked the water bucket. "Oops," Bud sneered. "I just gave you more to mop up. Gotta earn that minimum wage, Cool Whipp."

Steven tried to ignore the guy. What was the point of getting in a fight and losing his job over some bully messing with him? The cleaning company job was the one job that Steven actually liked. His other two jobs—shelving books at the Denver Metro University's library and working in the cafeteria—were stupidly boring. Besides, there was no Tessa Ross there to make them bearable.

Bud swaggered back to the employee lockers to grab his jacket and backpack. He'd leave early and let

Tessa close down the latte machines and other equipment. It was unfair to Tessa, but Steven could relax once the jerk-off left.

Steven maneuvered the rolling bucket and mop out of the cleaning closet and into the main area of the coffee shop. Chairs crowned the tables, and while the bright overhead lights had been turned off, the neon signs cast a multicolored light like a buzzing rainbow. Tessa cleaned behind the bar, wiping off the machines with a rag and listening to music on her phone through one earbud. The other dangled free.

Even late on a Wednesday night, traffic still moved down Broadway in a parade of lights.

Before Steven started mopping, he inhaled and smelled the sweetly bitter coffee and Tessa's perfume. He so wanted to tell her how he felt about her, but she was light-years out of his league.

She was a hipster chick—tattoos, piercings, and one side of her dark hair shaved. She dressed in black and wasn't afraid of showing a vast valley of pale cleavage. She was a thicker girl, but Steven didn't mind a bit. He liked women with hips. While Tessa was ultra-cool and listened to music he'd never heard of, Steven was just an everyday average normal guy—medium height, medium weight, medium everything. He did like his hair, though, which was thick and inky. That was all he had going for him. He was too busy dealing with three jobs and working his way to a bachelor's degree to be cool. He'd never be able to afford even a single tattoo. He wasn't exactly shy, but he wasn't all that outgoing either.

He splashed the mop down and started in the far corner by the door. If he timed it right, he'd get to the coffee bar right when Tessa finished. On good nights, she'd stay, and they'd talk. On bad nights, she'd leave to hook up with someone, guy or girl. Tessa was pansexual and proud of it. On those nights, Steven wanted to burn the entire city down out of mad jealousy.

Bud walked out of the back room wearing what he called his extroverted bomber jacket and sunglasses, even though it was past midnight. He tossed Tessa a look and then did what he normally did. He pointed to a spot and said, "Hey, Cool Whipp, you missed a spot."

He laughed at his own joke. Instead of leaving, he paused. "What kind of a name is Whipp anyway?"

Steven felt Tessa watching them. He wanted to shove Bud, or come up with a snappy comeback, but his head was blank. Truthfully, he didn't much like his last name either.

"It's a name," Steven said. "Just leave, Bud."

The guy smirked. "That's the thing. You can't tell me what to do. You're just the cleaning guy. Tessa and I are baristas. We're important. You're not. We're the lords, and you're the servant, Cool Whipp."

Steven could picture himself slapping Bud across the face with the mop, but then Bud would contact the owners of the Coffee Clutch and there went that job. He'd have to spend a fortune on coffee just to spend time with Tessa.

He slapped the mop onto the floor. "Sure, Bud. I get it."

Bully Bud laughed, unlocked the door, and went out into the night.

Tessa returned to cleaning. Steven made his way across the floor, hating himself for being such a punk. The fact was, he didn't feel like a servant. He didn't think he'd be smelling like disinfectant when he was in his fifties, unlike his mom, who worked as a cleaner at the Denver airport. He knew that at some point, things would change. But when?

He had the floor shining when he reached Tessa, who sat on the counter, so he could get to the coffee stains and cast-off grounds on the tile floor.

He glanced up and saw she was watching him.

"He's wrong," Steven said suddenly. Well, that was certainly off script. He always let Tessa talk first. He didn't want to be the douche who talked her ears off.

"I know he is," Tessa said. "But come on, at some point, you are going to have to stand up to him. He messes with you because he can get away with it."

Steven leaned on his mop and dared to look into her face. She had a nose piercing and hazel eyes that changed color. Sometimes they were greener, and sometimes they were bluer, and sometimes they were even a brownish color. She obviously dyed her hair black, and he liked the combination. Always had. Dark hair with blue or green eyes was striking. There was a foreign exchange student at Metro University from India named Aria who had similar features. Steven thought Aria might be a model because she was kill-me-slow gorgeous. She sometimes studied in the coffee shop. She loved the caramel lattes there.

Yeah, the caramel lattes were good. Behind Tessa, the specials of the day, latte this, frap that, were written in her distinctive handwriting, full of loops and character. She'd also added little flourishes—cartoons of happy cups of coffee promising sweetness and caffeine.

"Guys like Bud don't matter in the long run," Steven said. "So what if he bullies me? I have a ton of stuff I want to do in this life, and I'm not going to let dicks like that get to me."

Tessa grinned at him. It was warm and welcoming. "What kind of stuff are you going to do?"

Steven felt a blush warm his face. "I have no idea. But … can I be honest with you?"

Tessa glanced at one of the many watches on her left wrist along with a bunch of brass bangles and plastic bracelets. "It's after midnight, early on a Thursday morning. If you can't be honest with me now, then when?"

Steven felt the fear in his belly like cold water. But he wasn't going to let that stop him. He was going to push forward and tell her something he'd never told anyone before in his entire life. And yet, every second of every moment he had felt it. "Tessa, this is going to sound stupid, but I feel like I'm going to do something great. It's just a feeling … I mean, I have no evidence to support it. I grew up in Thornton, I got Bs in school, and I knew I wasn't going to go to any big university. Hell, I'm lucky to be going to Metro. But at some point, something is going to happen, and it's going to make my entire life make sense."

He watched as the smile dimmed on her face. Her eyes went far away, and a hush filled the coffee shop. A car outside honked a horn and another car roared past on the street.

What was that look about? Why wasn't she saying anything? Steven had no idea. There was no way he could ask. He got the mop wet, swirled it into the wringer, drove the handle hard to wring it out, and then started on the floor behind the coffee bar. He'd been so stupid to open up like that. She must think he was such a moron.

He concentrated on wiping away the coffee grime and footprints from the day. In a few short hours he'd be twenty years old officially. According to his mom, he'd been born at exactly 6:16 a.m. But then, sometimes his mom said she'd brought him home at 6:16 a.m. His mom was a bit spacy even on her best days, so he had no idea what time he'd been born. And it was odd how she talked about it. Spacy and odd, that was his mother.

Why wasn't Tessa saying anything? Finally, he had to break the silence. "You know, today is my birthday. And maybe the big grand something that is going to happen will happen because of my superior mopping skills."

"You do mop well," Tessa finally said.

He risked glancing at her face. Instead of a smirk or sneer or any kind of disgust, he saw tears sparkling in her eyes.

Damn. Her silence was one thing, but tears were a whole other animal, a species he had no idea how to handle. It was time to try and back out of the trouble he'd got himself into. "Well, Tessa, you know, I bet most people think that they're special. Isn't that the point of humanitarianism? We're all special humans living special lives, when in fact we're just ants."

Tessa jumped off the counter, landing her trendy knee-high boots squarely onto the area he'd just mopped.

"Don't," she said viciously. "Don't do that." She grabbed his arm.

He found himself staring into her face. "Don't mop? You know, Mr. Slocum pays the Broadway Cleaners Incorporated like five hundred dollars a week to keep his coffee shop. Not to brag, but I get like five percent of that. A night. Cha-ching."

Tessa didn't smile, and those tears never left her eyes. "Don't do that either," she said. "Don't shit on your truth by avoiding it or by trying to be funny."

"Trying and failing," Steven murmured. "Obviously."

Tessa must've realized she had lost control of herself because she let go of his arm and stepped back. "Maybe we're all ants. Maybe nothing matters. But Steven, you work your ass off. You'll get home around two, but you have your cafeteria job at nine. You do that, then ace your classes, before you go to the library."

It was a shock that she knew his schedule as well as she did. Steven wisely stayed quiet.

She kept on talking, passion in her voice. "You're at least trying to make something of yourself. Me? I have this crappy job, and I write my crappy poetry and practice my crappy calligraphy, and that's my life. That's probably going to be my life for the duration. And yet …" She crossed her arms over her chest. "I've felt it too. On some nights, when I'm alone in my room, I know that someday, I'm going to rise above all this. For me, though, it's wishful thinking … For you …"

Steven couldn't stare into her eyes. They were too intense, too pretty. He slopped the mop back into the bucket.

"You're doing stuff to make your dreams come true," Tessa finished. "Unlike me."

"Give me a break, Tessa. You go out. You have boyfriends and girlfriends and you go dancing and you take care of your brother and you do stuff too. Yeah, I'm going to college, but you could too. I could help—"

Tessa flung out a hand. "It's all so empty, all that sex, and the newness wears off, and I'm with some hipster and his beard and there's nothing there. Yes, I have friends, and I love my family, especially my brother, but if some great thing is going to happen to us, we're going to have to work for it. You're doing that." She paused. "I'm not."

For a second, Steven thought about trying to argue against everything she'd just said. He thought about telling her he'd been in love with her for months. But then, he knew the friend zone well. And with someone like Tessa? It wasn't just a zone, it was a dungeon, and she'd thrown him into the friend dungeon long ago and thrown away the key. No way would she ever go for him.

Yet, she knew his schedule. She admired him for some strange reason even though he let Bud walk all over him. Could he escape the dungeon and into her heart?

He was about to say something when a guy in a lizard mask covering his entire head charged through the front door. In his hand was a black pistol.

Fuck! Bud hadn't locked the front door on his way out.

"Take the cash!" Tessa yelped in fear.

No, this guy hadn't just busted in to rob the place. Something about him, something about the way he moved, how he held the gun, and how his weird red eyes fixed on Steven said that he hadn't come for the money.

He raised the gun. He didn't aim for Steven, though. He fired at Tessa.

TWO

STEVEN DIDN'T EVEN PAUSE TO CONSIDER WHAT TO do. It was like every single movie he'd ever watched had taught him exactly what to do at that moment.

He flung his arms up and lunged in front of the bullet. He felt the punch of lead striking his chest and knocking him back. He wasn't dead yet, good. He didn't feel like he was bleeding, but he must've been.

"Tessa, get to the back room and call the police!" Steven whirled, grabbed his mop, and leapt over the counter. The guy in the lizard mask fired again. Steven dodged to the side on instinct. His heart hammered, and adrenaline gushed into his system, making it hard to think even as his senses came alive in a way he'd never known before. He could smell the guy's leather coat, the cleaner on the floor, the gun metal oil, even the exhaust of cars outside. Every detail screamed at him.

Another bullet hit him, this time in the arm, and it hurt, but that pain felt distant. He had to keep Tessa safe, and he had to get that gun away from the psycho. Why wear a mask that covered your entire head? It was green, scaly, and so realistic looking. He must've been a makeup artist since the mask melded seamlessly with the guy's face. His eyes were crimson and slitted horizontally like a serpent's. He must've bought cosplay contact lenses at a comic con to alter his eyes like that.

"There's a guy with a gun!" Tessa's panicked voice screamed from the back room. "He shot my friend. Please, get here quick!" That would be the 911 call.

Steven slammed the mop into the lizard mask. The gunman was driven back into a table. The stacked chairs came tumbling down in a crash of noise. Steven lowered his shoulder and drove it into the guy. He tripped back over the chair and went down. The pistol went sliding across the floor.

Dropping the mop, Steven bolted for the gun. The guy grabbed him and pulled him down. The masked man was strong and outweighed Steven by a lot. In fact, he was huge.

The guy scrambled over Steven, digging a knee into one of his kidneys.

The sharp pain made him gasp. That didn't seem right. How could a blow to the lower back hurt worse than a bullet wound? And where was the blood? Steven still didn't feel the blood. But he had other things to worry about.

Both he and the gunman were on the floor, reaching for the pistol.

"Why are you still human?" the gunman hissed into Steven's ear. "Why haven't you changed to fight me?"

Steven had no idea what that meant. He was human. The gunman was clearly insane. Too much time in front of the makeup mirror and too many comic cons.

Steven threw his head back and connected with the guy's face with a meaty *crunch*. The gunman grunted in pain. But he lunged forward and snatched up the pistol, rolling up onto his feet.

Steven recovered the mop and stood. The guy lifted the gun to shoot him a third time, but Steven swung the mop and knocked the pistol back to the floor. Instead of going for the weapon, he gave the masked man another bite of wet nastiness.

Sirens screamed. Lights flashed. A cop car skidded onto the sidewalk. Two cops stormed out of their cruiser. Pistols filled their fists.

The masked man's scarlet snake eyes glanced to the doors and then at Steven.

Steven sucked in oxygen, readying himself for another round, and while he might've felt ridiculous going up against an armed man with a mop, it was better than nothing. And help was twenty feet away and armed with 9mms.

"Enjoy your little victory. It's gonna be your last. Next time, nothing will save you. We fucking underestimated you. It won't happen again." The guy wheeled and took off through the coffee shop, past the bar, past the cleaning closet, into the back room, and out the rear door.

The cops burst in the front.

Steven yelled, "He's going out the back way!"

The cops dashed past him.

Steven felt at his chest and his arm. Both throbbed with pain. He wasn't bleeding, and he couldn't find the bullet wounds. What the hell?

Steven had to see the wounds. He peeled off his shirt and looked at the skin above his heart. It was red, and yeah, it was going to bruise up like storm clouds, but there wasn't a hole there. His left arm was the same, red and aching, but unpierced.

Tessa crept into the main room. "Steven, holy shit, are you okay?"

He turned. Embarrassed, he bent and picked up his shirt. There, on the floor, was a crushed bit of lead, the bullet that should've destroyed his heart.

Steven quickly pulled his shirt on. "Yeah, I thought he shot me. I mean, he was shooting at you, but then I got in the way. Not that I want you to thank me or anything. I wasn't a hero." He bent back down and retrieved the bullet and put it in his pocket.

Tessa crossed to him and hugged him close. "You were a total hero. You fought him off with a mop."

Her soft curves pressed up against him. The smell of her perfume—lavender dancing with cedarwood—and her body filled his senses. He wasn't just smelling her, it felt like he was *tasting* her as well. She felt so good in his arms, she smelled perfect, and he wanted to pull her tighter to him and run his hands through her hair and down her body, feeling her skin on his. His jeans grew uncomfortably tight. After the adrenaline of being shot and fighting off an attacker, he found himself incredibly turned on.

"I told you I have superior mop skills," he whispered.

The two cops came back in, looking perplexed. One was Hispanic with a big moustache while the other was African-American. Another police cruiser pulled up. The Hispanic officer walked to the door, talking into the radio on his chest.

The African-American had a smartphone out, and he walked over to Steven and Tessa. His last name, Potter, was on his badge. "You two okay? Do I need to call an ambulance?"

Steven wanted to ask Potter what it felt like to get shot, and if bullets ever didn't work. "I'm okay," Tessa said. "Steven?"

He blinked, trying to figure out what was going on. "Yeah, I'm okay. He must've missed me. I mean, if he would've shot me, I'd be bleeding and all messed up. But I'm not."

Potter's brows furrowed. "We chased him into the back alley, but then he was just … gone. He couldn't have climbed up the walls. And we would've seen him running. It was like he simply flew away. The stink back there was nasty. You guys keep rotting meat in the dumpster?"

"No, just coffee shop trash. Lots of grounds," Steven said.

Tessa moved from them. "I need coffee to calm my nerves. You guys want some?"

"Yeah, I'll take some," Potter said. "You?"

Steven shook his head. He didn't feel like eating or drinking anything. And he had to get up early for his cafeteria shift in a few hours. It was all so surreal. And it was Bud's fault. That dickhead should've locked the door behind him. Then the masked guy wouldn't have been able to just burst in like he did.

Steven went and replaced the chairs on the table. He saw the gun. "Officer Potter, I managed to knock his gun out of his hands. Maybe you can use that to figure out who he is."

Potter snapped on plastic gloves and got out a plastic bag. "Yeah, we can run it for prints and see if it's registered. I'd be surprised if it is, though. Most likely, I'm thinking this is a run-of-the-mill armed robbery. How much is in the register?"

Tessa answered. "There was a little under two thousand dollars, but we already cleared it and put it in the safe. I don't have the combination."

Steven mopped up the scuffles from his fight, which was kind of stupid, but it felt good to be doing something normal after such a fucked-up few minutes.

"What about your boyfriend?" Potter asked.

Steven turned.

"He's not my boyfriend," Tessa said. "But he doesn't have it either."

Ouch. Steven winced. Even though he had saved her life, he was clearly still in the friend dungeon, locked away.

The coffee machines chugged to life. Steam and screams of scorching milk filled the air.

Steven found the other bullet that had hit him. He slipped it into his pocket as well.

Potter got their names, checked their IDs, and took full statements.

The other police officer scoured the neighborhood, but the masked man had gotten away. No matter what they said, this hadn't been a typical robbery. The gunman had come in firing, and from what he had said, he'd come again. But was he aiming for Tessa or for him?

Steven had no idea.

It was a little after three a.m. when he and Tessa finally got the Coffee Clutch closed down. He unlocked his crappy thrift-store bike, then turned to her. "You don't have any enemies, do you?"

"Enemies?" Tessa shrugged. "There was this one psycho girl I had to dump because she was ultra-insane. But no, I'm pretty chill. How about you? When he came in, I thought for sure he was going to shoot you first. He was staring right at you!"

Steven nodded. "I thought so too. Maybe he thought he'd take you out first as a witness, and then he'd get to me. I don't know."

"Me neither," Tessa said.

Steven frowned. "He's probably just crazy. While we were fighting, he talked about me staying in my human form. And that mask? He'll probably get back on his meds, find someone else to bother, or get locked up."

"I hope so, Steven." She stepped up and gave him another wonderful hug. "But thank you for saving my life."

She went to move away, but Steven stopped her. "Let me …" He faltered. "I can walk you home … it's late. There might be …"

She grinned at him. "No, it's okay. You have farther to go, and you have to get up in a few hours. I only live a few doors down. I'll be okay."

She walked off down the empty sidewalk, and Steven watched her go. Well, that was a complete rejection if there ever was one. Still, he could go after her, tell her how he really felt.

19

As if that would help. Nope. He was going to be spending another night alone.

◇◇◇

Aria Khat transformed back into her human form. She crouched on the rooftop of the bar across from the coffee shop where Steven Whipp and Tessa Ross were talking. Their faces were painted by the neon lights. Cars flashed down the main avenue even though it was late.

Aria caught the odor of Tessa's perfume, Steven's aftershave, and the remnants of their adrenaline. She could also smell their arousal. But Tessa was walking away, and Steven was watching her with mournful eyes.

Was this really the presence she'd sensed? And she hadn't been the only one. The Prime had sensed it as well and had sent one of his vassals to take care of what could only become a problem for the power-hungry overlord. The vassal had failed. The boy still lived.

Something about this Steven Whipp was different. He reverberated with a power Aria had not felt before. Could this boy help her? Could he solve all her problems?

There was only one way to find out. She had to talk to him, test him, and see if he truly was as powerful as he seemed. It was the only way.

At least in his present state, he would be easy prey for her.

THREE

S TEVEN PEDALED HIS BIKE DOWN BROADWAY AND felt the back tire get squishy. He'd tried to patch the tire, but the slow leak told him he'd done a crappy job. He'd have to replace the tube, which shouldn't have been a big deal, but it would mean skipping a meal to afford it.

He turned onto his street, big houses, huge trees, an old neighborhood to be sure. Ancient cottonwoods sprouted from the cracked cement of sidewalks. Buds weighed down the branches, waiting for spring to get warmer before they burst open with new leaves. He found the biggest tree on the block, and that was his home.

He biked up to the rambling two-story house where he rented a room on the ground floor, right-side. A bizarre bunch of people lived in the dilapidated home: college students, old people, and half-homeless drug addicts on their way toward rock bottom. At nearly 4 a.m., lights were still on in half the rooms and the thump of music came from the basement, where the party was just beginning. The old people, on the other hand, were just waking up to watch the news.

Steven chained his bike up to the neighbor's fence. He inhaled the early morning air and wondered if getting three hours of sleep was worth it or if he should just power through the day with energy drinks. A question for the ages.

The smell of cinnamon filled the air, unmissable, warm and sweet. Odd. Were Old Man Yank and his wife making cinnamon rolls?

Footsteps ground on the gravel in the crack of an alley between houses. A slender figure emerged, tall and graceful.

It was Aria Khat, the gorgeous exchange student from his school, who also studied in the Coffee Clutch every now and then. She was wearing a black velvet dress, stockings, and heels. She had a glittering purple scarf capturing her lush hair.

Even in the dim glow of the streetlights, her eyes were emerald-green and gorgeous.

She approached, and her perfume hit him, part exotic scent and part cinnamon.

The amazing woman walked right up to him and took his hand. "Do you know who you are, Steven?" she asked. "Do you know what you are?"

Even at the best of times, Steven had trouble talking to beautiful women. Now, here Aria was asking him the weirdest questions, and his brain was already mush after a long night of violence and Tessa's complete rejection.

Steven blinked. Her hand was warm and soft in his. And her smell, sweet and sultry all at the same time, frazzled his brain. "Uh, yeah, I'm Steven Whipp. As to what I am?" He shrugged. "College student, poor bastard, and really sleepy."

Aria frowned at him. "You don't know. How can that be?" She leaned in closer. "What if I told you that you had almost infinite power in you?"

"Aria, what's going on?" Steven asked. He'd talked with her before, both in classes and at the coffee shop, and she had seemed normal. He didn't think she was crazy, but what was her deal?

"The vassal, he attacked you tonight at the Coffee Clutch, right? How did you survive?" she asked, eyes squinted.

Steven found himself looking at her lips while she talked. They were full, red, and kissable. He had to get ahold of himself. Weird shit was going down. "How do you know about that? Are you spying on me? And what's a vassal?"

Aria's frown deepened. Those burning green eyes turned sad, then desperate. "I need help, but you might not be able to help me. You don't know who you are. That, or you don't remember. But there is something … here." She pressed her hand against his chest, and the pendant he always wore grew hot on his skin.

It was a little chunk of topaz, hanging on a simple steel necklace. Mystic topaz, or that's what his mother said. It was one of those things he'd always had—in a cigar box, buried in a junk drawer, or hanging on his bed along with a badge from his most recent comic con and the one tie he had for special occasions. He'd started wearing the topaz pendant regularly after high school. He had no idea where he'd first gotten it. His mother's memory was terrible about such things, and his father had left town for good after Steven turned sixteen. If you're a gambler, and if you hit a losing streak, it's safer to become a moving target.

Aria drew the necklace out of his clothes and touched the pendant. It seemed to glow. No, couldn't be, just a trick of the light.

"Where did you get this?" Aria asked.

Steven moved back from the strange woman. Yes, she was amazingly beautiful, but she was also asking him odd questions he simply couldn't answer.

She turned on him and folded her arms across her chest, her hands on her shoulders. She wasn't pissed off. She was holding onto herself, so sad and so desperate. "You don't know. You don't know anything. Yes, I was spying on you, because I thought you were someone, something else. Now I understand you are a mystery, even to yourself." Tears spilled down her cheeks. "My fate is sealed. I'm lost. My masquerade as an American college student failed. And now my life will be as long and as loveless as my mother's back in Mumbai."

Anger flashed through Steven. He walked right up to her. "Aria, I have no idea what's going on, but I want to help. We could call the police, or there's the counseling office at Metro State. But first, tell me what's going and why you think I'm involved."

One good thing about the strange encounter with Aria, it made it clear he wasn't sleeping that night. Which was why God invented Red Bulls. He'd be okay. He'd done sleepless nights before. Plenty of them.

Aria gazed into his face. That intense look was back in her eyes. "I don't know where to start, Steven. So I will start with a kiss, to test you. But I must warn you, this kiss might destroy us both. This one kiss might change everything forever. If I am lucky. If you are damned."

Steven couldn't believe this was happening to him. A kiss from a beautiful woman? Yeah, that would change his life at least for a few weeks during his alone time with Mr. Fappy and his five-fingered dance-off.

But that wasn't what she was talking about, and deep down he knew it.

She stepped forward and took his hands in hers. "For whatever reason, you do not know what you are … You could live a normal life, you could be a normal person and avoid the battle and heartache that is the fate of our kind. So, I will give you a choice. You can go into your home and forget this ever happened. Or you can kiss me and embrace your destiny."

Steven grinned. "Aria, I've been a seemingly normal guy all my life. Kissing you, destiny or not, would be my pleasure. And damn the consequences."

He drew her to him, a bold move, probably the boldest of his life. He was normal, but he'd never felt normal. This was his chance to take a step in an entirely different direction. Yes, this woman was probably completely insane, but maybe she wasn't. After all, Steven had been shot twice and had the bullets in his pockets. Maybe he was more than just a college student in Denver.

Aria inhaled sharply.

Steven found his next breaths hard to take. His heart pounded, and his thoughts grew muddy. Their faces were so close. He could smell her skin and her breath, cinnamon and musky and deep and dark as chocolate.

She closed her eyes. He studied her face and then leaned in. His lips brushed hers and the sparks inside of him went off like fireworks. He felt electrified, breathless, insane. This was crazy. This kiss was crazy. He couldn't help but close his eyes at the power of it.

She grabbed his head and pushed his mouth harder onto hers. He tasted her mouth, feeling her wet lips and then her tongue. Bright, something bright enveloped them, and he wanted to look, but her body felt so good pressed up against him. He realized she was trembling, quaking, out of fear or lust or both.

She was gasping, and so was he. The light was getting brighter and brighter, and his skin grew warmer and warmer. There seemed to be a fire inside of him, not in his stomach, but filling his core with raw life. That wonderful heat and the pure pleasure of kissing this stunning, mysterious woman did seem like risking damnation.

She pressed herself harder against him, and while she had one hand on his head, the other went to his ass, and he found Aria straddling his leg while they kissed. She was rubbing herself on his thigh, and he'd never been harder in his life.

This was his first real kiss. The dare in the eighth grade with Kristen Pierce didn't count. Nor did the spin-the-bottle game with Maggie Maxwell or the two-week "dating" he'd tolerated with Taylor Houlihan, a gamer girl he'd met online.

No, those kisses had meant nothing, had been nothing.

This was a kiss that changed lives.

She was gasping into his mouth. Their bodies were entwined. But Steven knew they both wanted more, to fully join.

That bright light and heat, both inside him and without, was getting more and more intense. Sweat covered him. Every breath became painful, as did every heartbeat. It was like his chest was full of boiling gold.

Too much, too hot, too painful, and yet in that pain was such a wanton joy. It felt like a star about to go supernova, and it felt like a carnival of cotton candy. He wanted to pull back from the kiss even as he wanted to dive deeper into it, rip off her clothes, and take her on the ground under the cottonwood tree above.

The heat burned more, the light grew brighter, and the pain grew stronger until he felt himself consumed by them. He was falling, he was going to topple and bash his skull on the sidewalk. Didn't happen.

Aria grew in his arms. They weren't kissing anymore, but whatever she had started wasn't about to stop. He opened his eyes. All he could see was light exploding out of him. Before he knew it, he was blind, cradled in her arms, and then the sun inside of him exploded. He wanted to escape the pain. He never wanted to leave Aria's arms. Not ever.

He screamed. His consciousness was plucked away by forces far more powerful than he could ever hope to be.

He woke at some point later, and he knew time had passed, but he wasn't sure how much. He was in his bed with his fist around the pendant, clutching it tight. His clothes were on, but his shoes were off. He turned and saw Aria sitting in his desk chair by his bookcase and the reading lamp near it.

She was intently poring over a book, but he had no idea which one. He was hit with the desire to get up and at least grab his dirty clothes off the floor and throw them in the laundry basket. He winced. There was a pair of his underwear lying right on top of his jeans. And books, papers, mail, all were jumbled around his small room, which was basically a bed, a desk, a window, a bookcase, a lamp, and a bathroom not much bigger than a closet.

Steven wanted to rouse himself, get up, and ask Aria a bunch of questions, but he'd never been more tired in his entire life. The kiss had worn him out, but it had also awakened something inside of him. The pendant warmed his fist as the glowing started again. Then the pain, dammit, the pain…it felt like being burned from the inside out.

He twisted in the bed, kicked off the sheets, and flung out his hands. He was going to die, he knew it. This was what dying felt like.

"You poisoned me," he grunted. "Dammit, that kiss poisoned me, and now you're going to watch me die."

Aria came over, held his hand, and wiped sweat from his face with a damp cloth she'd grabbed from somewhere. "You haven't had Animus before, Steven. It's changing you. It's opening doors that you had no idea existed inside you."

Another wave of burning swept through his body, and the light, that light … Where was it coming from?

Then he knew in a flash of insight. The pendant. But why would the pendant be trying to kill him?

"I warned you," Aria said softly. "I warned you that the kiss could destroy us both."

She had. He didn't know what Animus was, but he did know that their kiss was killing him.

Thankfully, his mind snapped shut, fleeing the torture and the concern on Aria's face.

Before he lost consciousness again, he saw Aria's eyes had changed. They were greener, but that wasn't what was odd.

Her pupils had become long, horizontal slits, like the eyes of a deadly snake about to strike.

FOUR

EDGAR VALE WALKED TO THE WINDOWS OF THE secret penthouse suite and gazed out at the lights of Denver. Being up so high soothed him because he was a bird of prey. He had failed in the hunt that night, but he wouldn't rest until this Steven asshole was dead.

Tumbler in hand, he drank from the smooth single-malt scotch and enjoyed the bite. It was a Macallan, two thousand dollars a bottle, one of his Prime's cheaper liquors. He scratched at his long beard and then felt the stubble on his scalp with hands covered in tattoos. A lot of them were from high school, but some were from prison. He'd done time, a lot of it, and he swore he'd never be caged again.

The door to one of the bedrooms—there were six—opened and Mouse crept out.

She was a slight, petite woman, with platinum blonde hair and large blue eyes. Her black nightgown made her skin appear like flawless porcelain. That pile of platinum atop her head was mussed from sleep and those blue eyes were squinted even in the orange glow of the mood lighting in the suite. "Eddie, you need to sleep. You're not a full Skin yet."

He hated that he was still a Skinling. He hated that he had failed to kill the little shit. He'd even failed to take out that goth bitch. He'd thought he'd drill her first and then take out the little prick as the main event.

He hated that Mouse was beautiful and smelled so good and she was off-limits to him. And always would be, most likely. He hurled the tumbler to the floor and it shattered. "I know, Mouse. I know what I am, and I know that I'm nothing special. I'm weak."

"You didn't kill him, did you?" Mouse asked quietly. Yes, she seemed so shy and innocent, but Edgar knew what she could do, what she could be, when she transformed. She was a full Soul, an Escort to their Prime, and beyond reach.

"I shot him twice, once in the heart, and yeah, he didn't die. Goddamn bullets bounced off him. And then he hit me with a mop," Edgar growled.

Mouse raised a hand to cover her smile. "A mop?"

"And then the cops came," Edgar said. "I ran. The Prime hates dealing with the fucking human bureaucracy, though he's paid everyone off."

"He does hate dealing with the humans," Mouse agreed with a nod. "But he hates failure just as much. He will not be pleased. He will hurt us. He might kill you. You are just a Skinling, after all."

Edgar whirled on her. He charged across the room and grabbed her wrist. "You love throwing that in my face, don't you? You laugh at me, I know. But I don't care. When I become a full Skin, I'm going to ask the

Prime for you. It's been done before. If I serve him well …"

Mouse's arm grew scales and grew hot. The smell of her transformation hit him like a fist: a sharp almond smell, like if you threw almond extract onto hot coals. Edgar felt his palm sizzle. He gripped her harder, enjoying the burn and her odor. "Yeah, Mouse, I know what you are. And someday, you won't be able to hurt me. Someday, you'll be mine."

She smiled. "Why not take me now?"

Edgar shoved her away. He slammed his burned hand into an ice bucket sitting on the bar. "You know why. He put you here as a test. He's testing you, like he's testing me. Because he doesn't trust you. Otherwise, you'd be with him in the Cheyenne Aerie right now with the rest of his Escort."

That maddening smile widened on her face. Her eyes had become serpentine, blue sapphires slitted up the center. "If he's testing us, well, that's easy for me. I wouldn't fuck you even if you were a full Soul. You, however. You failed once. Our Prime comes back in three days to take on a new Escort. You had better have finished the job before then or else he'll take it out on both of us. You because you failed him. Me because he can."

"How can this little son of a bitch be bulletproof already?" Edgar asked. "He's not an adult Dragonsoul yet, and dammit, I don't even think he has access to his Animus. My gun should've put him down."

"He's special. I can feel it. The Prime is too arrogant to take him seriously. Which is why he assigned you the task of killing him." Mouse walked across the shattered glass to the window. The shards crunched under her feet without hurting them because of the tremendous power she'd been born with.

If only Edgar had been so lucky. He wouldn't have to go through the rituals, which were painful, but almost over. Soon, so soon, he would graduate from Skinling to full Dragonskin, and the leap in power would be amazing. He hadn't been born special, just some kid with a drunk mother and an ex-con father who had lived hard on the streets. He'd been born to die. Since God hadn't done shit for him, Edgar would do it. He'd make himself special or die trying.

"So, no bullets," Edgar growled. "But we have the blades. I know some men, bad men, who can help me. Next time, we'll take magic swords and chop him into fish bait and throw the pieces in Sloan's Lake. We'll let the goddamn carp clean up our mess for us."

Standing by the window, Mouse stretched. The lights of Denver shined on her skin and the silky fabric of her nightie. Her nipples were hard. Her hips looked so good.

Edgar felt himself stiffen. He licked his lips. "Yes, in the next three days, I will kill this Dragonling, even if I have to become a Skin a little early. The ritual might kill me, but then, what doesn't kill you makes you stronger."

"And you will need your strength," Mouse whispered. She drew the strings of her nightgown over her shoulders and let them drop. Standing there naked, she looked like sex personified. "To kill the boy. And to resist me."

Edgar swallowed hard. "And you just love teasing me."

She walked past him and pushed her nightgown into his face. It smelled like her. And it drove him insane. "I loathe my existence, Skinling," she said. "But I do love teasing you because in the end, you'll never have me. I'd rather join this Steven's Escort than ever sleep with you."

She moved past, and he watched her ass jiggle so enticingly.

"Fuck this new dragon," Edgar spat. "He'll never have an Escort, and I'm not going to let him acquire a Hoard or build even a single Aerie. This fucker is dead. Dead, you hear me!"

"He'd better be." Mouse paused at the door and turned her head, so Edgar could see both her ass and her face. "Or in three days, you'll be the dead fucker who never had the chance to fuck me."

She laughed and disappeared into the luxury of the master bedroom, the suite within the suite.

Goddamn her. Edgar hated her as much as he wanted her.

❀❀❀

Steven felt himself float off the bed, but then he was dreaming. It all had to be a dream because he stood in front of a huge dragon the size of a house. The thing was classic dragon, all right, with long wings sweeping from a muscled back armored with dark crimson scales. The serpentine face and long jaw sported teeth like spears. A silver-streaked black beard sprouted off the chin of the beast, and a long tail curled around the dragon. Both its feet and its strong, powerful arms were tipped with massive claws.

Steven stood in the middle of grasslands just as dawn broke over the horizon. The sweet smell of dew on grasses mixed with the scent of sagebrush. It was like he was on the Great Plains east of Denver, but in reality, he knew he was in his bedroom.

The yellow eyes of the beast opened, and the horizontal slits pulsed, capturing the light of the morning sun. The dragon spoke. "Stefan Drokharis, Dragonling, you will learn to know that name, and you will celebrate it. You were saved. All others were murdered, but you were saved. For two decades, you have remained hidden from the world. But lo, on this day, the day of your birth, you have tasted your first Animus."

Animus.

At the word, the ground broke open under his feet, and another dragon rose from the dirt, wings flapping away the dust and gasses. This dragon had dark blue scales and darker colored wings. It was bigger, and the blue beard on its chin waggled down its glittering chest.

It opened its great fanged mouth, and lightning shot from its maw and struck the red dragon, blasting off scales and charring the flesh underneath. Both the red and the blue creature took to the air. The red dragon opened its mouth and covered the blue dragon in flames even as the blue sent electricity to sizzle into the wing of the red.

The dragons crashed together, claws rending flesh, wings beating like hurricanes, tails lashing. The beasts smashed back to the ground, sending up clouds of debris that swept over Steven.

The two weren't done fighting, though. As the dust of their impact cleared, two human-shaped figures emerged. One wore crimson plate mail, edged in black. The visor on his helmet was drawn back to reveal a face, half dragon, half human. Crimson scales covered his face and neck. The other half-dragon, half-man hybrid was blue—blue scales, blue hair, and blue armor. Both gripped two-handed swords and rushed the other. Sparks flew as the blades met, flashing in the morning sun, until the red dragon knight cut the head off the blue.

Blood geysered out of the severed neck, and then, from the wound, flashed a brilliant blue light. The red knight reached out a mailed hand, and the blue radiance poured into his palm, swirling up his arm.

The red knight turned to the stunned Steven and spoke through a fanged serpentine mouth. "Animus gives us power. We gain Animus from the souls of our enemies and from the love of our Escort."

The dragon knight then shifted into being purely human, an older man, middle-aged with a white-streaked beard and salt-and-pepper hair. The armor fell away, and the guy was in jeans and a white linen shirt. Blood dripped down from a cut on his forehead, a wound he'd gotten from his battle with the blue dragon.

From behind Steven, because, yeah, dream logic, a gorgeous older woman slipped up to hold the dragon knight now standing there as a man.

She was in a flowing white dress, and she had a shock of bright white hair bursting over her forehead in her otherwise jet-black hair.

The two kissed and light flashed. More Animus flowed into the man. The woman stepped back and smiled at Steven, a warm, loving smile. His mother had given him similar gazes over the course of his life. He seemed to know these people, but how?

The man raised a hand and made a complicated gesture with his fingers. He spoke a word that contained soft vowels and hard consonants. Magically, the wound on his forehead closed, skin knitting together in a flash. He'd just cast a spell to heal himself using the Animus from his battle and the kiss.

The man caught Steven's gaze. "Yes, you are a Dragonsoul, Steven. All of this is within your reach. As you grow in power, you can use the Animus to transform into your True Form, into your partial form, and from there, you can add to your armor, or you can grow your strength, or you can increase your Exhalants. You can gain the ability to breathe fire, lightning, ice, acid, poisonous gas, or dark energy. And spells, Steven, you can cast spells to harness the power of the universe. In the Drokharis Grimoire, you will find all the answers. But you must first find it, write it, and then you will know your true destiny. The magic of three, Steven. Remember the magic of three."

Steven had played MMOs and D&D his whole life and couldn't help but think the man was describing a gaming system. The Animus was like experience points, and he could use it to level up, improve his abilities, and unlock new skills. That meant fighting, killing, or sex with women. Actual women. If he chose to go down this path, his life would be war and sex. Yeah, that second part would be great, but the first part?

The man took the hand of his wife—his Escort. That was the word he'd used. He went on. "You were hidden, Steven, but you can't hide anymore. And while it pains me to say it, you are not prepared to face the forces coming to kill you. Gain Animus, perfect your skills, gather your Escort, acquire your Hoard, and build your Aeries. Play the game of the Primes for now until you can bring … revolution!"

Steven gasped and woke. He really was levitating over his bed. He let out a yelp and went tumbling onto his mattress. He'd been high enough to bounce off his bed and onto the floor. Right in the middle of his dirty laundry.

The pendant glowed, getting brighter, and he felt the now familiar heat filling his chest, from his neck to his groin. The burn hurt, but he was getting used to the pain.

Aria was nowhere to be seen.

The curtains were closed, but from the edges, he knew it was well past dawn, probably around eight thirty, which meant even if he hurried, he'd be late for his cafeteria job doing dishes, wiping tables, and cleaning up after the breakfast rush.

The glow increased. The pendant sent a holographic map of Colorado in perfect 3-D shining in the air in front of Steven's eyes. Denver glowed brightly, all the streets, highways, and buildings. To the south was Colorado Springs, to the north, Fort Collins. Three bright flames flashed, one on the Great Plains, north of Denver and east of I-25 along the St. Vrain River. Another bundle of fire flashed on Lookout Mountain, near the edge of the western suburbs. Finally, right in the heart of downtown Colorado Springs, the last starburst of flame flickered.

"The magic of three," Steven whispered, though he had no idea what that meant.

He did know one thing—he had to get to work and start his day. He'd gotten a good, uh, two hours and fifty-seven minutes of sleep. That would have to do.

The pendant's light winked out.

Bulletproof or not, Dragonsoul or not, he had to tackle his day and try and get some normalcy back into the madness his life had become.

FIVE

IS BOSS AT THE CAFETERIA WAS PISSED THAT HE was late, but Steven was having a hard time taking anything seriously. Part of it was his brain, dipped in caffeine, pounded by lack of sleep, bored as he hosed oatmeal off bowls and old eggs off plates.

At the dishes station, he blazed through dishes and then hustled out to wipe off tables. What was he doing working this dumbass job when he could be out searching for the three flames?

He didn't know. Had he lost his mind? It felt like it.

Steven tried to make sense of the last twelve hours. He couldn't be this Dragonsoul thing. That whole thing had been a dream. And yet, it did explain why the bullets bounced off him, Aria's strange behavior, the magic of their kiss, and the glowing pendant.

He'd told Tessa that he thought he was special. He hadn't meant dragon special. At best, Steven figured he'd get rich running a successful business, get married, and have amazing children. He'd use his wealth and connections to help his family and other people live great

Denver Fury: American Dragons

lives. Where did shape-shifting come into play? And Escorts? Hoards? Aeries?

Manuel Rodriguez, a work friend, was in the office, fixing a computer. Steven had to talk to someone about what was going on. Manuel was a good guy.

Steven leaned in conspiratorially, arms crossed. "Hey, Manuel. What if you were bulletproof? I mean, what if you knew for a fact no one could shoot you? Would you keep going to work?"

Manuel screwed up his face. "Uh, how would you know for certain? That would be really hard to test. Like learning to fly. If someone told me I could fly, how could I prove it?"

What he said made a lot of sense. "Yeah, I guess. But what if someone shot you and the bullet bounced off? So you have proof."

Manuel thought for a minute, one hand on the mouse, other hand on the keyboard. "Okay, so I'm bulletproof. Like Luke Cage. I guess I'd fight crime, but that really doesn't pay the bills. And I wouldn't want to be a freakshow. Sooner or later, the government would come to study me." He paused and seesawed his head. "Maybe become a mercenary? You could go into any sort of bad situation without getting hurt."

"So I should quit my job, quit school, and go to Iraq?" Steven asked.

His friend laughed. "That doesn't sound like much fun. I don't know, man."

"What if you could change shape by killing people or having sex?"

"*Ese*! You're being super weird!" Manuel replied, rolling his eyes. "Seriously, you might be watching too many comic book movies. *But*, if I was an incubus, which is a male succubus, I'd find some lovely lady, work my magic, and get my sex on. Then, totally, I'd find someone to pay me to fight crime. Make the world a better place. You know, with great power comes great responsibility."

Steven nodded. "Thanks, man."

He thought Manuel might remember it was his birthday, but he didn't. Which was okay. Steven was too busy to really have close friends anyway.

Thinking about Manuel's answers to his weird questions didn't help him. Should he quit school and his jobs on such a risk? He wasn't sure yet. But he did know he had to finish up in the cafeteria, grab some lunch, and then get to his statistics class.

He had another energy drink, but he was starving. He got a burger, two hot dogs, and a big slice of pizza for lunch, but he still felt hungry. It was a feast he couldn't quite afford, but again, he wasn't thinking clearly.

On his way to class, he called his mom. He got her voicemail but didn't bother leaving a message. His mom couldn't figure out technology to save her life and that included voicemail. She didn't have a cell phone because the tech was beyond her. She was at work, cleaning the Denver airport, so he'd have to wait until she got home. At least she could work her old phone, still wired into the wall. Archaic.

He was dying to ask his mom about the pendant and about his childhood. Other than having a father with a gambling addiction, his childhood had been so normal. How could he be a Dragonsoul when he'd wet the bed until he was a third grader? Or there was that time Todd

Butch pantsed him in the seventh grade. Dragons didn't get pantsed, did they?

Thursday afternoon, he had statistics and his science for non-majors, which was actually a pretty cool class. But sitting in the auditorium, listening to the professors talk, didn't help him with his exhaustion or his spinning mind.

It was his twentieth birthday. And yet, it felt like a normal day, and nothing special was in store for him. But, fuck, man, everything was special now. He had a magical pendant that had showed him three places for him to explore. That and he was a dragon with experience points to grind in the form of Animus.

Or was he hallucinating the whole thing? Had he overworked himself into insanity? There was that whole Creepy Pasta story about the Russian sleep-deprivation experiment. After a month without sleeping, all the people had gone insane. Maybe that was happening to him.

Classes passed in a haze, and soon he found himself in the library. If anything would kill him, it was his library job. Shelving books was mind-destroying even on the best of days. Now, with his head whirling and his stomach growling, it felt like the minutes had turned into years, and he'd be able to clock out when he was thirty.

Eventually, he had a break, but that was filled up with studying. He had a paper to write about symbolism in the King Arthur legends.

The cheapest thing at the cafeteria was a baked potato, so he bought four and loaded them up. Okay, the amount he was eating was strange. Clearly, something had changed in his metabolism.

Still no call from his mom, and when he called her, the phone just rang and rang. He figured she might call him to wish him a happy birthday, but then, that would be relying on his mom's terrible memory. Not something he wanted to bet on. It wasn't her fault, and he knew she loved him, so he tried not to take it personally.

He was hungry again at 11:45 pm when he walked through the doors of the Coffee Clutch, ready to clean. However, he wasn't tired anymore. That was the nice thing about long days with no sleep: at some point, your body shifted, and your brain resigned itself to the fact that naps weren't gonna be a thing that day.

Sitting on the counter was a chocolate-chip muffin with a single candle burning in it.

Steven grinned, and Tessa grinned back. "Happy birthday, Steven." She was behind the bar, starting the cleanup early since the place was empty.

Steven locked the door to avoid any more bullshit like the night before. "Tessa, you're the best. You're the only one who remembered!"

"You saved my life last night," Tessa said, shooting him a wink. "It's the least I can do."

Bud came out to the main area to stack the chairs on the tables. "Hey Cool Whipp, I heard what you did last night. Sorry I left the door unlocked. But I heard you were a hero. I guess. If I would've been here, I would have totally kicked that guy's ass. He'd still be shitting out my boot leather."

Steven wasn't in the mood for Bud or his crap. "Shut up, Bud. And my name is Steven."

Bud, following the script all douchebag assholes kept in their pocket, threw out his chest and bustled up to Steven. "What if I keep calling you Cool Whipp? What are you doing to do about it?"

Steven shoved him back against the table. Fuck it, he had two other jobs. So what if he got fired from one? He was bulletproof, and if he could take a bullet, he could take a punch. He was tired, hungry, and confused. And Bud was a dickhead. Steven slapped him right in his stupid face. "This is what you want, right, Bud? If you want to fight me, well, let's go then. Yeah, my last name is stupid. So fucking what?"

Bud looked hurt, shocked, and he backed away. "Look, I was just messing with you. I'm sorry."

"Just leave," Steven said. "Then tomorrow night, when I come in, we can start over. You can treat me like a human being and not your personal punching bag."

Bud didn't move. He looked genuinely conflicted.

"Leave, Bud. And I'll get the door behind you."

Bud gulped. "I'll just leave through the back. Again, I'm sorry." He took off.

Steven stacked the chairs on the table. His head was buzzing, the adrenaline felt good coursing through him, and he felt strong. Powerful. It was almost like he'd gotten a dose of the Animus from the little tussle.

"Steven, come and blow out your candle," Tessa said after a long while.

"Oh, sorry," he said. "I didn't get much sleep last night." Idly, he considered telling her about Aria, and what happened, but he still wasn't sure that kiss or seeing her in his room had been real.

The candle dripped a colorful red shell of wax on the muffin.

Tessa sang him "Happy Birthday" in a nice, low, sultry voice, sexy as hell.

Steven was spellbound by her and her talent. "Wow," he said when she was finished. "You have an amazing voice, anyone ever tell you that?"

She blushed. "Oh, stop, now. Blow out your damn candle."

Steven did. Then she took the muffin, peeled the wax off the top, and gave it to him. She'd also whipped up a latte for him to go along with the sweet.

"You stood up to Bud," she said.

"I did," Steven admitted with a shrug. "I kinda feel bad now. He totally didn't see it coming."

They both laughed. He ate the muffin, but he had another type of hunger filling him. He thought about Manuel's suggestion, and if there were one person he wanted to bang, it was Tessa Ross. She stood there, so beautiful, so confident. She was wearing a cool leather skirt with tights, and she had a lacy blouse with a red embroidered vest over it. Her hair was swept back, showing the side she shaved.

He went around to where she stood behind the coffee machines. He had no idea what he was going to say, but he had stood up to Bud, and now he was going to go all-in with Tessa. "I really wanted to walk you home last night … Well, this morning. I've wanted to walk you home, make sure you were safe, since I first met you."

Her face grew serious. "But I'm not in school, and I'm kind of a loser," she said. "Why would someone like you want anything to do with me?"

Steven felt flabbergasted. *She thought she wasn't good enough for him? What?* "You're special," he said. "We both are. I'd like to kiss you, Tessa. And if you're interested, I'd like to do more. But we can start with a kiss." It was almost like what Aria had said to him without the talk of destiny and doom.

She crossed to Steven, he took her in his arms, and they kissed, hard. She smelled like coffee, perfume, and just her, Tessa Ross, the scent that made him want to take her right then and there.

She was breathing as hard as Steven was, and they both trembled at the power of their attraction. Energy filled his chest. His crotch throbbed. He knew the pendant was glowing like his own personal sun. The kiss was giving him Animus, he could feel it. Just like the fight with Bud had.

She broke away. He bent and tasted her neck. Her smell filled his nose, lighting up every single one of his senses. He loved how curvy she was, how her hips felt in his hands, and her breasts pressed up against his body.

"Oh, fuck, Steven. Oh, I can't believe it, how you are, how we are. What's happening? What changed in you? What changed?"

The truth? Aria had been dead right. Everything had changed with that one kiss.

He leaned back but kept her body tightly next to his. Feeling her against him felt so right. So natural. "Tessa, you won't believe me, and I'm not sure I can talk about it yet. How far do you want to go with me?"

"Here? Now?" Tessa asked, eyes widening. "Well, after that kiss, I want all of you, Steven. I've

47

fantasized about having sex here, at work, after hours. I've fantasized about you … us …"

Steven's hands went lower, and he touched her shapely ass for the first time.

She closed her eyes. He could feel the heat emanating from between her legs.

"Why didn't you ever give me any signals?" he asked.

She opened her eyes, and he felt trapped inside them. "I did. But you were too busy, too focused, and I figured you weren't interested in me."

"Holy shit, was I stupid," he breathed.

"Not anymore," she said, nipping at his lip.

"Not anymore," he agreed. He lifted her up and set her on the counter. The lights were on in the place, so anyone walking by could see them, but neither cared.

He was between her legs, kissing her, and she was peeling off her blouse. He unhooked her bra. It wasn't the first time he'd unlatched a brassiere, but all those other times had been childish and uncertain. He'd been scared of messing up, of being a dork, but not now. He wanted her. He didn't care anymore about what other people thought of him. He wasn't just some guy working and going to school.

He was more, and he felt it, down to his bones.

She got his pants off, and he pulled off his shirt. The pendant sent rainbows glowing down his skin. Had he lost weight? Was he more muscled? It seemed so.

She was bent down, on her knees, taking him into her mouth. He touched her hair and felt how soft it was. He touched her ears, and he brushed over her piercings— the metal as hot as her body. He wanted to lick every inch of her skin and take months to do it.

Glancing down, he saw her face, glowing with lust, and her bare chest, and he knew this was only the beginning.

He came close to exploding in her mouth, but he wanted to save it for the main event. He pulled her up, set her on the counter again, and then slid down her tights and her panties.

He spread her legs and returned the favor she'd given him.

She came quick, and then, he was inside her. He was having sex, real sex, for the first time in his life. She was a wonderland of skin and scents, a luscious woman who wanted him as much as he wanted her. Every part of him was on fire, and the burning sensation in his chest grew painful, and then it was beyond pain, into an ecstasy he'd never felt before.

It was heaven, and it was hell. It was lust, and it was love. He gave himself to Tessa, and she gave herself to him. Their friendship had melted like honey, and they were lovers now. Everything had changed.

"Steven, your necklace, the pendant," she gasped. "It's glowing. It's beautiful. You're beautiful."

They locked gazes, the light blinding them both, and then, staring into her accepting, loving eyes, he was pushed over into the first real orgasm of his life.

"Oh, it's happening, something is … Steven … I can feel it. I can feel you in me …" And then Tessa fell off the counter. He'd slipped out of her. Standing, they held each other, and Steven felt his body take in her energy, the Animus.

It was like before, with Aria, but this time, there was so much more of it. An endless river, it seemed. If he knew how to channel it, he knew he could do amazing things with that raw life force.

Tessa was weeping in his arms, crying softly, and he tilted her head up gently. They were back to staring into each other's faces. Tessa's eyes were no longer hazel. They glowed with a bright white light, and tears like liquid silver dripped down her cheeks.

"What is happening, Steven?" she asked.

He couldn't answer because, in the end, he wasn't sure how to explain it. Or anything.

SIX

CLOSING DOWN AND CLEANING UP THE COFFEE Clutch had never been more fun and never more flirty. Tessa kept smiling at him. Her eyes weren't blazing with light anymore, but they were still glowing with a mixture of love and lust.

Steven told Tessa every odd thing that was going on in his life, and she listened, enraptured, and when he was done, she said, "Let me think about some of this stuff. It's pretty wild, but come on, you're not crazy. This is happening. We just need to figure it out."

"Do you want to come back to my place?" Steven asked. It didn't feel like a bold move. No, it felt natural after what they had shared.

They got their work done and then went outside. She got on the back of his bike, taking the seat, while he peddled furiously standing up. His quads didn't mind because he felt so much stronger. A little rain pattered down. He only sped harder while Tessa gripped his waist. He spun in front of his house and bounced up the sidewalk before coming to a stop next to the cottonwood where he and Aria first kissed.

Where was Aria? What had happened to her? That kiss had triggered his change. Now she was gone.

Tessa stepped from the bike and held it while he locked it up to a fence post. Then they were up the steps, down the hall, and in his little bit of room in the great big house.

He got the door locked before Tessa was on him again, kissing him with a wet, wanton mouth, and if she smelled good before, now he was getting a double dose of her sweetness. His senses were heightening, he could feel it. Everything was changing inside him.

She stripped her vest, her blouse, and her bra off, and they fell to the floor to mix with his laundry. He liked the idea. Their lives were joining, syncing up. He tore his shirt, literally, ripping it at the seams.

She heard it, smiled, and shimmied out of her skirt. "Easy there, Tiger. We have all night. No need to destroy our clothes in the process."

"I don't care about any of that. I want you again, Tessa. I'd bring the entire house down to get to you." Steven found himself almost snarling those words. He'd never been more turned on in his life, and it wasn't just the sex, it was the sheer excitement over gaining more Animus.

It showed when he dropped his pants.

Both were naked, staring at each other. Steven couldn't believe he had a real naked woman in his room. She was curvy and hippy and breasty and beautiful. And real! Steven pounced. He pushed Tessa onto the bed, and her legs fell open.

It was heaven inside her, and when they kissed, the connection was complete. The energy transfer between them made the Animus pendant glow again.

"Oh, God, Steven, it's so beautiful!" Tessa gasped. "Maybe you're some kind of vampire. I feel you taking from me …"

That shocked him. He stopped moving but stayed inside her. "Does it hurt? Are you feeling weaker?" He thought about what Manuel had said, about an incubus drawing power from women through sex. Was that what he was?

His eyes traveled from where they were joined, up her soft belly to her breasts and then to her face and her eyes, which were glowing again.

"No. I feel it leave me, but then you give it back to me, like a circle. I've never felt better. I've never felt more connected to anyone during sex, and I love it, Steven. I feel safe, and sexy, and loved." More tears dripped down her face. "So loved and so powerful."

Steven kissed the tears off her cheeks, kissed her again, her wonderfully luscious mouth, and then he found himself lost in their passion as she screamed her pleasure. And he joined her seconds later, her cries of bliss triggering his own.

They stayed together, their sweat mingling, their breaths intertwined, and their hearts beating in unison.

Hours went by. Sleep was definitely not on the agenda. They rose and fell together, climbing up mountains of rapture and discovering valleys of complete ecstasy.

Finally, a little after four a.m., Steven collapsed, burying his face in Tessa's neck.

"I can feel the power flow into me," Steven said, finally, when he could breathe and think again. "It's the Animus Aria told me about."

"Aria?" Tessa asked. "That hot foreign exchange student?"

Steven had to grin. "Oh, so you find her hot too?"

Tessa rolled her eyes. "Of course. You'd have to be dead not to notice her. She's like the goddess of yummy."

"No, that's you," Steven said and licked the salt off her neck.

Tessa giggled. "Tickles!" She then sobered. "Steven, what's happening to us? From the little you told me, it seems like you get power from sex now. And I do too, in some weird way. Do you think I'm not exactly human either?"

Steven lifted his head to stare into those beautiful hazel eyes. "I really don't know anything. In my dream, the dragon mentioned Stefan Drokharis, and I Googled the name, but nothing came up. He said I was a Dragonsoul, but yeah, what does that mean exactly? I think with enough Animus, I can upgrade my abilities, but I have no idea how I actually do that."

"If this were a video game, you could get an ability tree and then divvy points. Maybe try imagining it and willing the points into your different abilities."

Steven quirked an eyebrow. "You like video games?"

"Sexist!" Tessa grinned. "More adult women over thirty play video games than boys under eighteen. I just read a report on video game demographics online."

Steven stammered and tried to apologize. "Sorry, it's just, you're so gorgeous, so sexy, and you go out so much, I figured you wouldn't be into gaming."

"Figured wrong, Steven. But try it. After our little bit of lovin', you should have Animus to spare. Try using that energy. Shaping it."

Steven recalled what the red dragon had said about strength, armor, the ability to shift his shape, and exhalants. He closed his eyes. He felt the energy in his chest, that terrible churning heat, which burned all the brighter as he focused. It quickly became painful, almost unbearable, but he pushed on, pressing his eyes shut tighter as he concentrated. An image bloomed in his mind's eye, brilliant strands of opalescent light churning and twisting, unfurling like a flower's petals, only to curl up and lash out like writhing tentacles of power.

Somehow, he knew he was looking at the raw life force, the Animus, filling him up. But he couldn't make sense of it. It was anarchy in motion.

Still, Tessa's words echoed in his mind: *"If this were a video game, you could get an ability tree ..."* That? That he could comprehend. So, he sharpened his thoughts like a knife, envisioning the various skill trees from a half-dozen different games he'd played, and forced the shifting, chaotic strands of Animus into a more familiar shape. His heart raced, sweat broke out across his brow, and his hands and arms trembled from the sheer effort.

But something was definitely happening. The twisting strands of opalescent light were pulsing, *throbbing* in time with his heart as they took on a new form. Slowly, *slowly*, a flickering image appeared, a skill tree, though not like anything he'd ever seen before. A skill tree in the form of an intricate black dragon, studded with glowing lights like burning stars. The image

55

wavered and danced, refusing to resolve long enough for him to get a good look. But he gritted his teeth and pushed ceaselessly against the mental resistance, determined to win this battle. This was his brain, dammit, and the Animus belonged to him, so it would do what he told it to do!

His brow furrowed, and his chest and back slickened with sweat. And then, just when it felt like he would collapse from the exertion, the image appeared again. Dim, vaguely translucent, but *there*:

Steven glanced over the strange image. The burning dots had to be different skills and abilities that he could unlock and utilize with the Animus flowing through him, but they were all blank save for the dot in the center, which read *Animus Absorption*. And then the image was gone, disappeared, as his concentration broke. He was panting hard and his mind felt weak from the effort. So instead of trying to force the tree back into view, he tried something a little different.

This time, he thought about how cool it was to be bulletproof. What if he could double down and really thicken his hide?

He imagined having scales like the red dragon knight had when he was in his partial state, part human and part dragon. He imagined being able to turn his arms into strong, scaled limbs with razor-sharp claws. He envisioned wings protruding from his back, wisps of smoke curling up from his nostrils. The smell of orange blossoms filled his nose, followed immediately by a smokier scent, like a roaring campfire in the heart of winter. And not just any campfire, but a campfire burning cedar—simultaneously sweet and spicy.

He cracked his eyes to find Tessa staring at him. "Do I look different?" he asked.

"No, but do you smell that? It's coming from you," she said and pulled him down to bury her face in his chest. "And it smells so good! It makes me want you again!"

"I can arrange that," Steven said.

Then hell struck his house. The entire building shook. The window in his room shattered, flinging glass.

Steven leapt from the bed, hit the floor, grabbed his jeans, and slid them on in one quick motion. Something huge hit his door. The wood shuddered and creaked in protest.

A figure appeared in the window, a huge man, with a bald head, dressed in leather. Across his back was

… no … couldn't be … but yes, he had a broadsword sheathed on his back. If he got to that weapon, he'd hack Steven to pieces.

Steven couldn't let that happen. Charging forward, he drove a shoulder into the guy climbing through the window. The man gripped Steven and hauled him outside. They fell onto a car in the driveway between houses. There were two cars and an SUV parked in a line.

"Steven!" Tessa screamed from inside. Another loud bang from whoever was trying to breach the door. If they got inside, they might hurt her.

Lights flickered on all over the house. People yelled out in alarm. Most likely, they would all call the police, or at least Old Man Yank would.

Steven clambered to his feet. The metal hood of the Subaru bent and crunched under his weight. The bald guy rose, standing on the hood, and yanked the broadsword from the sheath. He attacked.

Steven raised an arm and took the edge on his forearm. That sweet cedar-fire smell once again filled the air. The blade struck his arm in a shower of sparks. Steven's right arm had changed. His shoulder was white skin, but that skin ended in black scales covering a huge bicep. He could hardly believe it was his arm. Not only had his muscles grown, but his hands had elongated into dragon claws. Each finger was tipped with a three-inch obsidian talon as sharp as a switchblade knife.

His left arm was normal, but Steven's right hand had become a deadly weapon. Behind him on the ground there was movement, but unfortunately it was too late to turn. Another man—this one with long hair hanging greasily onto a crappy leather jacket—slashed his own broadsword down Steven's back.

No scales there. The blade carved through his skin. Pain exploded through his nerves, and blood gushed down his back and into his jeans. Steven whirled and pressed his back up against the house next door. Baldy was on his left now, Greasy on his right.

How long did he have until he bled out? He didn't know.

Two against one, not fair.

"Steven! Someone's coming in! Do you have a weapon, a gun, something?" Tessa called out from the window above.

"I don't!" Steven yelled.

Tessa, he had to get to her. He had to get past the two swordsmen and take care of the third guy inside. At least he thought it was a guy.

Greasy hacked at Steven, but he leapt over the blade. He came down on the car, spun, and clawed through Baldy's leather jacket, knocking him back.

Another sword stroke sliced into Steven's leg. Thankfully, the gash was shallow. He leapt on Baldy and swiped his sharp talons through the man's throat. Gore, dark in the night, bubbled up from the ruins of his neck. The severed carotid artery spurted out blood in rhythm to the doomed man's heart until both stopped.

Steven rolled off the hood and into the crevice between the car and the brick of his house.

Greasy raised his sword to split Steven's skull.

But Steven gave him his armored arm instead. The blade bounced off his scales, allowing Steven time to get to his feet. But the wounds were taking their toll. He was dizzy, feeling weak, his vision narrowing.

Tessa wailed. Sirens pierced the night. The police were coming, but if Steven didn't do something soon, Tessa would get hurt, and he might die by the time the cops arrived.

Light flashed from the corpse of the bald man Steven had already killed. The agony of the burning inside him made Steven wince, feeling like he was breathing lava. But then he felt the power fill him—Animus, from his kill.

So much power and where to put it? He wanted to end the fight and save Tessa. Stronger, he needed to be stronger. Muscles thickened, his whole body grew, and the seams on his jeans popped. New strength flowed through his body like his cells had become super-powered. He must've healed some because he felt so much better.

Steven shoved the swordsman back and clawed through an arm. The broadsword twirled, but Steven ducked. The blade chipped into the brick. He grabbed the man's wrist with his left hand. Adrenaline and his new power fueled him. He crushed the wrist, the bones audibly snapping.

Steven saw the fear in Greasy's eyes. Could he really kill this man? Baldy had been in the heat of the moment—almost an accident—but this was cold and calculated. Yes, yes he could. These men had come to slay him, but he was going to kill them first. Kill them and eat their Animus. He squeezed harder, and the sword clattered to the ground in a metallic ringing.

Steven flexed his dagger-like fingers and slashed the man's face, slicing through his eyes and cutting off his nose. Bending, Steven grabbed the sword and drove it into the man's chest. Blinding light erupted from the pierced heart, and Steven breathed it into his body.

More armor, better armor—he focused on improving that skill, and his left arm scaled over and his hand turned into a claw. Now he had two black dragon arms and a fistful of claws.

From inside the house, fire alarms took up an incessant buzzing that blocked out all other noise. His housemates from upstairs descended the fire escape on the side of the building.

Home invaders and now a fire? What else could go wrong?

Steven jumped back onto the crumpled hood of the Subaru. Broadsword in hand, he hurled himself back into his room through the torn-out window.

The door lay in splinters on the floor. Tessa had managed to get her skirt and top back on before they'd smashed through the door. But now she wrestled with one man, some thick thug with a muscled neck, stubbled face, and a stubbled head. Thug #3.

And at the door stood the guy in the lizard mask from the Coffee Clutch. But this time, with clearer eyes and more understanding, Steven saw that it wasn't a mask. The guy had green scales, a leering mouth, and a ridge of spines going up and over his head and crimson eyes. Like the dragons Steven had seen in his dream, this one had a thick beard drooping from its scales.

The dragon man gripped a broadsword in one clawed fist. This weapon, though, was different from the other rough-hewn claymores. A green gem in the pommel glowed and green flames flickered over the blade. The sword might be green, but the fire alarms painted the villain in a hellish scarlet light.

Steven raced forward and drove his sword into the gut of the stubbled thug, driving him back into the hallway. The dragon man cut through the thug and into Steven's arm. That green sword was magical, must've been, because it cut through his scales and sank into his flesh underneath.

The dragon man leered.

Steven growled and clawed through his attacker's face, driving him back into the hallway. The dragon man laughed even as blood dripped down his cheeks like red tears. "Tough guy. Didn't see that coming. Well, the Slayer Blade will take care of you. Like it's taken care of so many."

Steven raised his sword to defend himself. He couldn't let the Slayer Blade hit him again. Blood dripped down his arm and onto the floor. It was his main concern because that wound he felt. The slash on his back and the one on his leg were strangely quiet.

The bearded dragon man waded forward to end Steven.

Steven braced himself for the attack, but it wasn't necessary. A stream of fire struck the dragon man, pushing him down the hall. In seconds, everything was fire and smoke and chaos. The fire detectors in the hallway were silenced, consumed in the blast.

What the hell just happened?

The scene flashed through Steven's head, and it clicked into place: a fire-breathing dragon, obviously.

But were they friendly? Or would Steven have to slay his first dragon while his home burned?

SEVEN

FIRST THINGS FIRST, WHEN YOUR BUILDING IS ON fire, you grab your precious shit and get the hell out. Steven whirled and pushed the broadsword into Tessa's hands.

"Hold this while I get my things," he told her.

Tessa nodded, speechless, shocked, as she should be.

Steven felt strangely calm. He'd just killed three men. Three. They were dead, they were gone, their families would weep for them, and they would never again drink coffee or eat another meal. Gone. Death was one permanent state of affairs.

Tessa went to the window, dragging the sword behind her.

"Don't go out yet," Steven cautioned. "There's a dragon out there. Not sure if it's on our side or not, so better to be safe than sorry."

"Burning, house, smoke," Tessa sputtered. "We have to leave. Dragon or not."

"In a second." Steven glanced around. Nice thing about being poor, he didn't have much to rescue from the flames. The only thing he had that was worth anything was the laptop in his backpack, which he slung over his shoulder. He slipped his phone into his pocket. It hardly worked, but it was better than nothing.

The heat from the fire in the hallway washed into his room along with choking smoke. The heat from the fire didn't bother Steven. In fact, it felt good, like a sauna. It was far better than the hot-coal burning inside of him. The fact that the outside air matched the terrible agony inside him made him feel better.

He grabbed a few books, including his copy of *The Hobbit*, and threw them in a box of important papers. He tossed the cardboard box outside. Then he helped Tessa, who was crouched near the floor to escape the smoke. She tossed the broadsword out. He helped her out the window then followed her, dropping down onto the Subaru.

Tessa crawled across the blood-spattered hood to stand on the asphalt of the driveway. She held the broadsword like a broom. She was pale white, and her eyes were wide and frightened. Then again, she was near two dead men, both of whom Steven had killed.

That seemed like such an impossible thing … that Steven Whipp could've killed anyone. But what choice had he had? They had come to murder him.

But why? Why? He shook his head, confused and uncertain. *The magic of three*, he thought. Maybe there would be some answers once he tracked down the clues offered by the pendant.

Steven crawled off the Subaru and stole a look around. There wasn't any sign of the dragon that had breathed the inferno through his house nor the dragon man with the Slayer Blade. Good news on both accounts.

Steven went to retrieve his box, but he didn't have to.

Aria Khat held it in steady hands. "We need to go," she said simply. "Now."

"What about the police?" Steven asked. "The bodies? I need to fill out a report. I need to tell them it was self-defense. I can't just flee the scene of a crime."

Smoke plumed from every window of the old house. Out front, a fire engine pulled up, and men clambered out. Sirens were everywhere, flashing, screaming, hardly audible over the sounds of the house burning. The odor of the smoke was stifling.

But Steven liked the smell, which shocked him. How could he like the overpowering stench of burning destruction when all his housemates were losing all their possessions? Poor Old Man Yank and his wife. All their memories, gone.

Aria raced forward. "No police. No report. If the assassins are working for who I think they are, you'd be killed in a jail cell."

She herded Steven and Aria around the Subaru, through a gate, through a backyard, and then through an alley that ran next to a house, adjacent to the street. Steven knew the gravel and glass on the asphalt should be killing his feet, but he didn't feel a thing.

Neighbors were out, watching the tongues of the fire leap into the early morning sky. The fire engines were already in action, three of them at least. High on extension ladders, firefighters soaked the houses around the blaze while two worked on the main conflagration.

A Mercedes AMG roadster *chirped* to life, lights flashing. Aria popped the trunk, stuck Steven's box in the back, and headed for the driver's side. "Get in. Now. Fast."

Steven opened the passenger door. Tessa tossed the broadsword in, then pulled the seat forward and squeezed into the back seat. Steven got into the front, backpack on his lap. Before he even had a chance to close the door, Aria was speeding away.

They were all quiet for a time.

Steven breathed in the scent of cinnamon, which mixed nicely with the rich smell of the expensive car's soft leather. A Mercedes. The car was probably worth his entire education plus an extra hundred thousand dollars easy. He could sell the car and buy a house in his mom's neighborhood and use cash to do it.

Police cruisers raced by them in the opposite direction, but none pursued them.

Steven hugged his backpack to him and started to catalog everything he'd lost: his favorite clothes, that one pair of boots he got in high school, birthday cards from his dad, most of his schoolbooks, his TV, and his PlayStation. Ouch.

Gone. Up in smoke. Burned away in dragon fire.

Now that Steven was sitting—the adrenaline fading from his system—a myriad of injuries and pains he'd ignored before began to creep up on him. His jeans were stiff from his own congealed blood. His back and his leg ached like mad, but worst of all was his arm. He checked it, thinking he'd see black scales, but his skin was human again. When had he lost his scales and claws? No idea. There had been fighting, running, fire, Aria—what the hell? What was she doing back? He pushed a palm over the ragged wound he'd received from the Slayer Blade. It had already scabbed over, which was good news, but it hurt. Bad.

Aria turned onto Colorado Boulevard and pulled off to the side as more police cars sped by, lights flashing red and blue. Their sirens blared loudly then were gone, hushed, as quiet as the three in the Mercedes.

Finally, Tessa said, "I don't have any underwear on. I didn't have time to put on underwear." She laughed, loudly, clashingly, tittering until she was guffawing.

The laughter made Steven smile, then he was laughing too, and it felt so good. He laughed because he was wounded, and he laughed because he'd lost all his stuff, and he let loose cackles at the fact that he had killed three men. Boom, boom, boom. One with his own claws, then two with a fucking broadsword. Seriously. What the hell? What had happened to his life?

And sleep, damn, he was on his second day without any real sleep.

Aria drove on as the two laughed like loons until they got themselves under control.

"Are you quite finished?" Aria asked.

A long, tense beat. Tessa didn't say anything. But then Steven burst out, "I'm not wearing underwear either!"

That brought on more hilarity. Ha, fucking, ha.

Aria whipped the Mercedes into a U-turn, heading back down Colorado Boulevard. Where was she going?

She hit Colfax, turned right, turned right again, then hung a left back on the main street and headed south.

Steven took in a big, shuddery breath and ran a hand through his sweat-soaked hair. His heart burned like a furnace, and his lungs felt like they were full of soot. His arm throbbed. But he wasn't bleeding anymore, he didn't think. Even if he was bleeding out, though, it didn't really matter. He'd had the best sex of his life, he'd protected Tessa, and he was riding around in a heaven of leather, wheels, and the best of German automotive engineering. There were worse ways to go.

His head seemed to be floating above his body. Was he going to pass out? He realized that Tessa had gone from laughing to crying. He reached back, and she seized his hand with both of hers.

He turned to Aria and something slid into place. "That was you. You're the dragon. You breathed fire down the hall. You ruined my home, my life, everything."

"That is certainly *one* way to look at it," Aria murmured. "Another way is that I saved you and saved everything else in the process. He would've cut you in half with that sword, you know." She paused, gaze distant. "It was magical, but where would a Skinling get a sword like that?" That last bit seemed more for her than for Steven.

"It's not like we can ask him, right?" Steven asked. "He couldn't have survived your fire."

"He might've, depending on how far along he is in the rituals," Aria replied. "We would be very fortunate if I killed him, since he must be connected to a Prime. If we're lucky, it's some foreign Prime coming to dick with us. Most likely, however, he's one of Rhaegen Mulk's vassals. And in three days, he'll find you and kill whoever is with you. Except for me. He won't kill me. He has other plans for me."

Finally, the chaos of the night got to Steven. Tessa cried. He got pissed. "Where were you, Aria? Dammit, you kissed me, and then you took off. And here I am, trying to do my normal life like an idiot when I have fucking assassins with broadswords coming after me like it's a Highlander sequel only with more dragon people. That guy with the dragon head, is he a Dragonsoul?"

"No, he is a Skinling, on his way to becoming a Dragonskin. Humans who want to become dragons can become Dragonskins. They can shift into a partial form, at first, but when they complete the rituals, they can transform into a full dragon, but their abilities are limited. They must serve a Prime." Aria sighed. "A Prime like Rhaegen Mulk."

It was a lot of information to process, and Steven was having a hard time keeping up.

"What's a Prime?" Tessa asked in a weepy voice, wiping away her tears with the back of her hand.

He didn't blame her for crying. The stress they'd been under would've made anyone emotionally unstable.

Aria stopped at a stoplight. The streets were basically deserted. It was 4:28 a.m. on a Friday morning. "A Dragonlord Prime rules a Primacy." She faltered, lips pressed into a thin line. "Look at it this way, the world is divided up among the dragon kings, and each one jealously guards his kingdom. He has vassals—servants —who fight for him and serve him unquestioningly. Denver is part of the Great Plains Primacy, which stretches from the Rocky Mountains east to the American Farmlands Primacy, which starts in Kansas."

Tessa put some of it together. "And this Rhaegen Mulk is the Dragonlord Prime of the Great Plains Primacy."

"He is," Aria said.

"So, who are you?" Steven asked.

"I'm the daughter Rhakshor Khat, the Dragonlord Prime of Maharashtra Primacy in India. But who I am is not the great mystery here. What Steven is … who he is … that is what I don't understand. After our kiss, I read through your books, your journals, to discover more about your true identity. I left, and I've been making calls and studying ancient texts, trying to unlock your secret ever since. You are a Dragonsoul, clearly, but raised by humans. Such a thing has never happened. You were hidden, obviously, but why?"

"Uh, not sure," Steven said. "My parents, though, my mom and dad, they would have to be Dragonsouls, wouldn't they?"

"Yes, they would," Aria said. "But if they didn't show you your power, raise you as a Dragonsoul, perhaps they are human. Perhaps they are not your real biological parents at all. That is my best guess at this point."

"Uh, Steven, are you pissed she went through your stuff while you were asleep?" Tessa asked.

"I think we're beyond that now," he answered. "My stuff is gone, and Aria can do whatever, as long as it helps me figure out who I really am."

Aria had a question of her own. "Are you going to be angry I kissed your boyfriend?"

"No," Tessa said with a casual chuckle. "He wasn't my boyfriend yesterday, and I'm not sure he's my boyfriend now. Even if he was, I don't own him. Besides, I'm not what you would call the jealous kind anyway."

Steven knew for a fact that Tessa was polyamorous. She liked to date lots of different types of people—men *and* women—at one time. For a minute, Steven thought about the possibilities in that luxury automobile. But he shook the thought off, as tantalizing as it was, since he had other things to worry about.

Now, more than ever, he wanted to talk to his mom. He fished his phone out of his pocket and called the house phone. It rang and rang and rang. No one picked up.

"Aria," he said, "we need to get to my mom's house. If my life is in danger, they might go after her."

"Perhaps," she said. "But it could be, they know nothing about her. I was drawn to you because last night you turned twenty, two decades, and that is a powerful time in a Dragonsoul's existence. That is why the Skinling tried to kill you. If your mother isn't a dragon, she is safe. If we drive to her house, we could accidentally lead the Skinling and other assassins to her. We should stay away."

Steven let out a frustrated breath. "I keep calling. She doesn't answer. And she's not good with voicemail. Like, she can't do it at all."

"Can't do voicemail? Ouch," Tessa said with a wince.

"If I'm such a baby dragon," Steven said, "why would anyone want me dead?"

"You are a male, and you have great power," Aria replied. "You see, Primes must fight to keep the Primacies. Very few males are born—most Dragonsouls are women—and so any new male birth is seen as a potential rival. Dragonsoul laws are strict about

71

murdering male dragonlings, and yet most of the Primes see themselves as above the law."

"So this Rhaegen Mulk sent his lackeys to kill me the minute he realized I existed." Steven shook his head. "That's just great."

"But not just once, twice," Aria said. "If you were a typical male, Rhaegen Mulk might not care. He might see you as a Ronin, a Dragonsoul male without a Primacy. There have been powerful Ronins before and they went unmolested. You, though, you are different. I know it, and so does whoever wants you dead."

"So what do we do now?" Steven asked.

"That is why I keep driving in circles," Aria said. "I have no idea."

"I'd like some underwear and a bra. If we have to fight again, I don't want to be flopping all around," Tessa said. "Why don't we start there?"

"Sorry, Tessa," Steven said, "but I think I know what we have to do." He corrected himself. "No, I know *exactly* what we have to do."

Steven lifted the mystic topaz pendant on his chest. As if prompted, the pendant gleamed and the map of Colorado was superimposed on the windshield. The three blinking flames flickered in the north, the west, and the south.

The pendant map was the one key Steven had to unlock his mysterious past, and he intended to use it.

EIGHT

STEVEN REACHED OUT AND TOUCHED THE FLAMES burning to the north along the St. Vrain river. He felt himself called to the north first.

"Fuckin' A," Tessa cursed. "That's like a hologram. That's like fucking *Star Wars*. Or *Harry Potter*. Maybe *Lord of the Rings*. Moon letters or some Hobbit shit. That map ... how does it work?"

"It's magic," Aria whispered. "I asked about such a pendant, and from my sources, they said that it might be ancient sorcery. Such artifacts were popular a thousand years ago, but today, we have so much technology, they aren't needed by Magicians and Dragonlords. Are you sure you don't know where you got it?"

Steven shook his head. "You know that junk drawer in your house where odds and ends wind up? I swear, I pulled this out of a junk drawer when I was thirteen. I wore it on and off until I graduated from high school, and then I really liked it for some reason. I've worn it very day since."

"I believe it is from your parents. Your real parents," Aria said. "The man and woman who raised you —kind and loving as they may be—are not your kin."

Steven felt his heart shrink. That was hard to take. He'd hoped his mom was blood-related because he really loved her, and he knew she really loved him. They'd been through a lot together. As for his dad? Screw that guy. He'd taken off, trying to outrun gambling debts. "Maybe I'm half Dragonsoul. Maybe because of my dad. I always knew he was such a snake, but maybe he was really a dragon. My mom, though? She's awesome."

"She didn't call you on your birthday," Tessa murmured. She'd scooted up between the seats to talk to them and to admire the map.

"Her memory is terrible," Steven said, waving away the statement.

"Or she has been ensorcelled. Or she is dead," Aria said. Then she caught herself. "Oh, Steven, I'm sorry. I shouldn't have said that out loud."

Steven let the pendant rest against his bare chest. "It's okay, Aria. I think she's okay. There haven't been any news stories about anyone missing or murdered in Thornton. I have the neighbor's phone number. I'll call it in a few hours, when it's not, you know, still dark. Speaking of which, I either need sleep or breakfast. Both, preferably."

"Steven," Tessa said, touching his hair. "We can't go to a diner dressed like this." She eyed his pants, ruined and bloody, then ran a finger across his uncovered shoulders. The shirt hadn't made it. "And I'm not sure where we can go shopping before dawn. We could always hit my apartment, I suppose."

"No. That would be dangerous," Aria said. "The Skinling might be alive and telling Mulk about Tessa. She was in the coffee shop with you when you were shot. They could use her to get to you."

Tessa grimaced. "Not cool. I'm total fridge material—as in the bad guys chop up the girlfriend and stick her in a fridge. That sucks, but also kinda rules." She shrugged. "Guess my life will never be the same either."

"I have to call in sick tomorrow, uh, today," Steven muttered as the full impact of Aria's critical kiss became crystal clear. "Or maybe I should just call in dead. I won't be getting to my jobs or my classes until we figure all this out, right?"

Aria didn't respond. Instead, she flipped another U-turn.

"Going in circles is making me dizzy," Tessa said. "Please, let's chance hitting my place. I can go in the back door, grab some stuff, a hoodie for Steven, maybe find him shoes. I can steal some from my roommate's boyfriend. He'll be sleeping over. That guy is so loud and derpy when he has sex. He's all like …" She deepened her voice and imitated a man. "Oh, baby. Take all my love, baby, take it.'" She rolled her eyes and let out a long breath. "I feel crazy. Sorry. I'm talking way too much. I'd be less of a chatterbox if I could get some underwear on my nether regions."

All Steven wanted to do was eat. And he couldn't do it shoeless and shirtless. If they could grab some clothes, they could hit the Village Inn on Mexico and

Colorado Boulevard, get a bunch of food, and then figure out what to do next.

Aria gripped the wheel in both hands. "I would take you to my house, but my own apartment has been compromised. The Skinling saw me, recognized me." Her voice faded away. Her jaw muscles clenched. Determination sparkled in her green eyes. She did another U-turn on Colorado Boulevard. "Okay, Tessa, tell me where you live. We'll risk it."

Fear knifed into Steven's belly, mingling with the burning sensations in his chest. His glands sucked in a fresh dose of adrenaline at the prospect of another fight and more Animus. He could feel the power ready to be used, but he wasn't sure how to really use it. He breathed in deeply through his nose and exhaled through his mouth, closing his eyes just as he'd done back in his room prior to the attack. Once more the shimmering, twisting, opalescent strands of light appeared in his mind.

Once more he focused on the dragon-shaped skill tree he'd envisioned before, and this time it coalesced with surprising ease, far more solid than the last time he'd glimpsed it. Even more surprising, the tree had changed:

Interesting. This time around there was both an experience bar and an Animus gauge, not to mention the glowing orb above *Animus Absorption* was now labeled *Partial Transformation*. Steven hadn't invested any points, which meant he must've somehow unlocked the ability naturally during his tussle with the Skinling and his hired muscle. But he had no idea how exactly it had happened or how he was supposed to unlock the rest. Hopefully, the clues from the pendant would shed more light on the situation.

He opened his eyes, and the image disappeared in a flash. Gone as quickly as it had come.

Tessa lived in an apartment complex off Evans, close to where they were. Tessa directed Aria to drive around the back and she did, parking the Mercedes next to a dumpster. "I'll be right back," the barista said.

"I'm going with you," Steven said, popping the door and sliding out.

"And if he's going, I'm going," Aria insisted. "I can't let anything happen to him. I can't ... my ... life ..." Again, her voice faded, and she offered no further explanation.

Of course, Aria had secrets, but she wasn't being too forward about sharing them. She wore a colorful knee-length dress with a cut that showed one knee and kept the other hidden. Steven reached in and grabbed the broadsword.

All three of them walked across the parking lot to the back door of the complex. Tessa punched a code into a bulky metal panel above the knob, then pulled the building door open with a soft *squeal*. Aria reached down, pulled up one side of her dress, and retrieved a small semiautomatic pistol. "I'll go first. Stay behind me. If we have any trouble, Tessa, you run. Steven, stay by me."

"I'm so not liking this gun thing," Tessa whispered, eyeing the weapon.

Steven, however, felt better. He had his sword, which felt right though *odd*—seriously, walking around half-naked in Denver with a sword? What the hell?—but a gun was far less showy and bulky. Far more practical.

They made their way down a short hallway and walked silently up the staircase to the second floor. The building was quiet, the halls empty. Tessa walked halfway down the hall and keyed into her apartment. Again, Aria went first, pistol in her hand. Tessa went next, followed closely by Steven and his sword.

Was this really his life? After spending the night having sex, he'd found himself in a battle, and now he was on the run with not one but two beautiful women.

Inside, the apartment was messy, lived in. A bed squeaked rhythmically at the end of a short hallway on the right. A man's muffled voice filled the air. "Oh, baby, you feel so good, baby. Take it, baby, take it."

Yeah, he sounded so derpy.

All three moved quietly through the living room, where the TV sat in tangles of wires, Blu-Ray players, and video game components. A bottle of Jack Daniels was on a crowded coffee table next to a tottering pile of pizza boxes.

Tessa's room was off to the left and smelled like candles and incense. Steven was relieved to see that she had her own collection of dirty laundry on the floor. Gauzy fabric covered the window, giving the space a Bohemian feel. Her bed was a heap of blankets and pillows.

Tessa opened a drawer and retrieved underwear. Instead of excusing herself, she pushed her skirt down and pulled her top off. She was naked, curvy, and beautiful. But what really stood out was Tessa's complete and total confidence. She had no problem getting naked in front of him or the strange woman who had a pistol in her fist and could breathe fire.

Despite the danger, seeing Tessa naked ignited Steven's libido again.

Aria was taking in the sight as well. Her eyes were glued to the naked girl in front of them. Sexual energy filled the room for a minute, and then Aria glanced away, rubbing at the back of her neck. Yeah, it was in poor taste to stare at people while they dressed, and yet, she hadn't been able to stop herself.

With bra and panties in place, Tessa dressed in jeans, a T-shirt, and a blouse over that. She threw Steven a gray hoodie, which he put on to cover his new muscles. She also rummaged around and found a pair of pants, which she tossed to him.

Uh, what was she doing with random denim around? Oh yeah, she had a past. Thankfully she did because he couldn't very well walk around in blood-splattered pants. The ripped jeans covered him, though they were tight and a little short. He rolled up his old clothes into a tight ball. He'd toss them in the dumpster outside.

Tessa pulled a duffel bag out from under her bed and started to pack, but Aria stopped her. "We don't have time for that. We can buy you new clothes, new everything. We have to go now."

The headboard in the room next door banged into the wall.

It made them all jump. Then the loud boyfriend was at it again, spouting off, "Baby, I'm about there, baby. So close! So close!"

Steven covered his eyes with the grimy ball of denim in his free hand. That was just so embarrassing.

"Fine," Tessa said before glancing at Steven's bare feet. "But let's steal Barry's shoes while he's going at it with Katrina."

They snuck out of the room, through the apartment, and into the kitchen. Steven plucked a banana out of a bowl, his stomach growling in protest. At the front door, Tessa grabbed a pair of big Adidas. They'd be huge on Steven, but at least he'd be able to get into a restaurant.

They closed the door behind them with a soft *click*. The roommate and the boyfriend hadn't seemed to notice their intrusion, and no one had attacked them.

Steven threw his battle-torn clothes into the dumpster. He was leaving his old life behind. What would his new life bring?

Back in the Mercedes, they drove off. Steven peeled the banana and ate, but it was like trying to stop a forest fire with a cup of water. The hunger was terrible. Almost like a living thing inside him.

"Much better!" Tessa said, adjusting her hair. "I feel almost human again. Next up on my wish list, though, is a shower. And then let the adventure continue!"

Twenty minutes later, they pulled into the parking lot of a Village Inn. Steven left his broadsword in the car, and Aria holstered her pistol. In a booth, an hour before dawn, Steven almost felt normal. Not that sitting in a VI with two stupidly attractive women was normal. As he waited patiently for his meal to arrive, he eyed his traveling companions.

Tessa and Aria couldn't have been more different. Tessa was shorter and curvier, with pale skin, and her hair was dyed dark, shaved on one side. That and her piercings and tattoos gave her a certain look. Aria, on the other hand, was tall and slender, with darker skin and naturally black hair. She had a classic beauty to her, while Tessa was more on the alternative side.

He thought about how Aria's eyes had traveled up and down Tessa's body. Steven couldn't help but envision both girls wrapped around him, even though he knew that a threesome was probably never going to happen. Things like that happened in porn, but in real life, people became couples and tried to avoid the drama and conflict of multiple sex partners.

The waitress—a doleful-eyed woman of fifty with stringy blonde hair—dropped off his plate. He shook off his horniness as best he could and tackled the omelet, hash browns, pancakes, green chili, and coffee with gusto. He'd have to use his credit card, which he hated to do, but money seemed silly to think about at that point. This was their victory meal after their fight to the death with the Skinling and his cronies.

As he ate, Tessa and Aria chatted about school, the coffee shop, and family life. Tessa's brother had multiple sclerosis, really serious, and she helped him and their mother out a lot with the day-to-day stuff. Aria had grown up in a wealthy family in Mumbai. She referred to her Aerie, which made Steven remember his dream. An Escort, a Hoard, an Aerie. He was still wrestling to figure out all the new terminology.

He took out his phone, got on the restaurant's Wi-Fi, and saw news reports about the fire in south Denver. It took forever. His cell phone was prehistoric.

There wasn't any mention of bodies. Not a one. And there had been three. The corpse inside might've cooked away to nothing—though he imagined there'd be bones, at least—but the two outside should've attracted attention.

Tessa knocked him with an elbow and gestured to the mound of plates, empty of the food he'd hoovered down. "Hungry much?"

"Yeah," Steven said seriously. "I'm starving. I'm thinking about ordering their breakfast burrito. It's pretty good. And big."

"That would be your fifth breakfast," Tessa said, smiling.

Steven nodded and drained his fifth cup of coffee. "Yeah, I don't know what's wrong with me." He touched his chest. "I'm hungry, and I have this burning in my chest. It hurt at first, but I'm getting used to it."

Aria frowned. "You were never shown how to handle the Animus. If you had been raised as a Dragonsoul from birth, this all would've been different. We just don't know how this will work in the long run, and there are dangers. From my research, children who are not trained to handle the power die when they transition from human adolescent to Dragonsoul adult." A look of worry flashed across her face. "I'm sorry. I shouldn't have said that so bluntly. I'm sure that won't happen to you."

Aria was funny. She didn't have much of a filter for some things, like death and destruction, but for other things, she'd clam up.

Tessa took Steven's hand and squeezed it out of concern.

"I'll be fine," Steven said, shrugging one shoulder. "Or I hope I will. Maybe whatever we find on the pendant map will help me with this process. My, uh, real parents might've seen this coming. I just wish I knew more about them." That was a difficult thing to consider. His *real parents*. His whole life, who he was, had suddenly become such a mystery.

"Before we seek out the first fire marker, we should rest," Aria said. From her purse, she removed a wallet and then an American Express card. "From here on out, I will be paying for everything. Believe me, my father can afford it. And he hasn't cut me off yet."

Another clue to Aria's situation. Why would her father cut her off?

Tessa smiled. "I was thinking I'd have to shower at a truck stop on I-25, but we'll be staying in style somewhere, won't we, Aria?"

Aria smiled. "Yes, Tessa," she said. "I believe we will."

The women shared a moment, gazing into each other's eyes.

Steven felt their mutual attraction and suddenly a world of possibilities seemed to open up for him. *Maybe a threesome isn't so farfetched after all*, he thought.

NINE

E DGAR VALE PICKED HIMSELF UP OFF THE BACK lawn of the house as it exploded in flames. Smoke stank up the air. Sparks and half-burning swirling pieces of paper settled down on him, but that little bit of fire didn't hurt. He'd just had that foreign dragon bitch blast him full on with Dragon Flame. His clothes were nothing but soot. Every bit of his hair was gone, too. He was lucky to be alive, but he was badly burned.

He could fix that, though. While the fire engines got to work with their hoses, he slunk away, climbed a fence, limped through another yard, and ducked behind a brick wall as a police cruiser rushed by, lights flashing and sirens wailing.

The last thing he wanted was to get taken in by the cops. His Prime could fix it all with bribe money and promises of future favors, so that wasn't the problem. The issue was with how his Prime saw him. Edgar had fucked up twice. He'd let that weaselly Dragonling slip through his hands twice. Mulk would already be furious with him, and if he had to dick around with the local law enforcement, he'd finish roasting Edgar himself.

Edgar managed to make it to Broadway without being spotted. The pain was blinding. It was like someone had heated needles up over a stove and then shoved them into every inch of his skin—between his toes, into his taint, through his nipples. Edgar huffed and gasped at the pain, but he had to keep moving. He needed to fix himself before he died.

It was early morning and all the legit businesses were closed. But growing up as the son of a hope-to-die alcoholic, Edgar knew how bars worked. For the civilians, 2 a.m. meant going home. But for those bottle-soldiers marching toward an early whiskey-soaked grave, 2 a.m. meant going underground.

Max's Bar, Grill, and Shithole would still be throwing around drinks to a certain low class of booze hounds.

Edgar ran, naked, blackened, and burned, up to the door. The place looked closed. He knew better. He shoved a shoulder into the wood. Using his dragon powers, he broke the lock and staggered inside.

The shades were drawn, and the place was dark, but it was full of people sitting at stools and congregating around circular tables, getting shitfaced. Mostly men, though there were a few glammed-up women who were riding that wrinkly borderline between young slut and old skank.

Some big-bellied, big-bearded good ol' boy got up to his feet to save the day. Or maybe he'd been looking for a fight all night and finally found one. There was always that kind of drunk, soused and wanting violence. If they could justify it as heroism, fine, but sadism would do just as well.

Like a martini with vodka or a martini with gin, both would get you there.

"Max's is closed!" the big man said.

Edgar didn't have time for pleasantries. He shifted his right arm into dragon form, but he was so weak, his chest and head also transformed into his partial appearance. Mulk said his control was iffy, and that was when he wasn't fighting to stay conscious.

The big man's eyes widened. "Fuckin'…"

That was the last time the big man would curse. Edgar drove his claw into his chest, squeezed his heart to pulp, then ripped it out and dropped it on the floor. The light of the Animus exploded out from the ruined man's body and filled Edgar, repairing his skin and regrowing his beard, healing the damage that foreign bitch had caused him. She thought she could get out of the deal she had with Mulk by joining the Escort of another Dragonsoul male. She was stupid, but then, most foreigners were stupid.

Steven Whipp was a child. He'd gotten lucky. He would be dead soon and then Edgar could watch Mulk take that bitch apart. The idea got Edgar hard.

And there were no clothes to hide his erection.

He let the corpse collapse to the floor. The jagged tips of the big man's ribs poked from his caved-in chest.

Edgar turned and showed the skanks his hard-on.

The drunks blinked stupidly at the death of their friend. Or maybe they were glad to be rid of the loudmouthed good ol' boy. Drunks were as funny as they were antisocial.

Edgar stretched and flexed his new skin. His muscles popped, rippled. He was back to being his old self and there was Animus to be had. But first, he needed clothes. He bent and stripped the jeans off the big guy. They'd be baggy, but the guy had a belt. Perfect. He dressed.

The bar room was silent except for the *drip, drip, drip* of the corpse's blood hitting the floor.

Edgar went around to the cash register, broke it open, and collected up a fistful of hundreds. "Any of you fine ladies want to spend the night with a murderer?"

Two of the skanks rose to their feet. He knew why. It was partly due to his display of strength and partly because of the money, but mostly it was his dragon powers. He wasn't a full Dragonskin yet, and he wouldn't get serious about starting his Escort until then, but even now women were drawn to him.

Edgar grinned. There was a trashy motel down the way that catered to drunks, hookers, and druggies. He'd take these two there, get some more Animus, get a shower, and then bring in the big guns. Literally. There were ex-special forces mercenaries on Mulk's payroll that Edgar had called in. He had positioned them across Colorado, in places where he knew this Dragonling would go.

And if the cold-blooded mercs failed?

His Prime didn't know it, but Edgar had met some Dragonsoul Ronins—males without a Primacy of their own. He knew at least three that would love to get in Mulk's good graces. Edgar could help with that, provided they helped him first.

Together, they'd put down Steven Whipp, the foreign bitch, and that other slut, too stupid to know that she was with Steven not because he was a good guy, but because she didn't have a choice.

But first, he had to clear their minds. Mulk had taught him the Mind Wipe spell for just such occasions. It was how the Dragonsouls stayed hidden. Edgar splayed out the fingers on his left hand and said the word. His hand burned electric-blue. Every straight-up human in the joint would not remember what they'd seen.

Edgar laughed and tucked a skank under each arm. He kissed one; she tasted like Jägermeister and puke. He kissed the other, and it was like lapping beer out of an ashtray.

Oh well. He figured other parts of them would taste better.

☼☼☼

Steven convinced Aria that just driving by his house in Thornton couldn't hurt. And they could let the morning commuter traffic die down a bit. Like before, Aria drove, and Steven rode shotgun. Tessa, in the back seat, had fallen asleep.

Steven's mom still lived in the lower middle-class suburban house Steven had grown up in. The lawn was mostly weeds, the juniper bushes were overgrown, and the paint was peeling off the siding. Sections of the roof filled the gutters. It was the worst house on the block, hands down. Steven blamed himself. If only he had more time to come over and fix some of the stuff. Or if he had more money. His mom worked all the time at the airport, but that barely covered her bills.

In fact, even though it was before 8 a.m., her beat-up Chevy, thirty years old and still ticking, was gone. The lights in the Robertsons' house next door were on, and Dave Robertson was heading out to work in his truck.

"Keep driving," he told Aria.

He dialed up Kathy Robertson and she answered with a, "Hi, Stevie."

Ugh, he hated when people called him Stevie. He wanted to correct her, but he always felt douchey doing that. Besides, it was the old neighbor lady who had watched him grow up. He could let her slide.

The conversation went quick. Steven asked Mrs. Robertson about his mom. She said she was fine, and the mystery deepened. Why wasn't his mom answering her phone if she was okay? He'd just have to try her at work later.

Aria used GPS to thread her way through the neighborhood until she found a way back to I-25 heading north.

"Okay," Steven said, "we need new clothes, a place to rest up, and then we're off to St. Vrain."

"There's the Orchard Town Center," Aria said. "Check your phone to see what time the Macy's opens."

"Uh, my phone's internet is terrible. Like so slow, it's not even worth trying."

"Nine. I bet it's nine." Tessa rose and rubbed sleep out of her eyes. "I hate sleeping in cars. I lived in one for a couple of months. It's terrible. I need a bed, guys. Sorry to be the weak link."

"Not weak at all," Aria said, glancing over one shoulder before returning her eyes to the road. "You both survived last night. Many wouldn't have."

Turned out, the Macy's opened at ten, so they had some time to kill. Aria got coffee from a Starbucks—a full twenty dollars for three people. An utter outrage, but she just used her American Express to pay. It was like magic.

Outside, leaning against the Mercedes, Tessa sipped her latte and frowned. "They got the grind all wrong. This is why you go to local coffee shops, so you don't have muggles making your brew."

"So you're part wizardess, part barista?" Steven asked, cocking an eyebrow.

"Don't you know it." Tessa gently knocked him with a swing of her hip.

Steven excused himself, called in sick to his jobs, and called a friend to take notes for him in his Western Civilization class that afternoon. He couldn't reach his mom directly at work, so he left a message with her boss. That was a good sign at least: his mom was at work. Still, he really wanted to talk to her directly. He said it was urgent. It was a fifty-fifty proposition that the distracted supervisor would actually give it to her. How much did his mom know about him, the pendant, and his past? Those were his biggest questions.

His biggest concern, though? Was she okay? Had anyone come around to hurt her?

Normally, Steven thought his mom was better off without his dad. But at times like this, he wished she had someone to take care of her. To watch her back.

They were the first ones inside the Macy's.

"Get whatever you want," Aria directed them, "and don't worry about price. We have far more money than time. As long as we're on the move, we should be safe. Don't forget to buy a warm coat because this is spring in Colorado. Anything can happen. And for the suitcase, don't scrimp. A good bag can last decades."

Steven had never, ever shopped without worrying about cost. He went to the men's section, and he couldn't help but look at price tags. It all became so real. This stranger he hardly knew was going to buy him a wardrobe and a suitcase to put it in.

It was wrong. Surrounded by the expensive clothes, in an actual Macy's, he shook his head and remembered the crappy house he'd grown up in. Getting jeans from the local Ross had been a big deal. Mostly, he got secondhand clothes from garage sales and thrift stores. It had been fine, he hadn't cared, and having to buy the cheap store brand of mac 'n' cheese seemed like a bigger deal.

Did he really need new clothes? He was fine in the used jeans, the old hoodie, and the loud sex guy's Adidas.

Maybe it was all just a misunderstanding. Maybe he'd gone insane. He touched the mystic topaz pendant. That was real. He'd seen the map. This was his life now.

Okay, he could go to the police. He could tell them about the men who wanted to kill them. He could get them to protect him and his mom.

But why hadn't there been any news on the dead men—the men he'd killed? Aria had said something about the Prime owning the cops.

Steven found a pair of jeans that were really cool. He checked the price tag and nearly choked. A hundred bucks. How could he make Aria spend so much?

Aria found him dithering. She had a bag and a pile of clothes in her arms. "Hurry, Steven, we have to figure things out before Sunday night."

"Why Sunday?" Steven asked.

Aria glanced away. "I don't know. I ... we just need to hurry. We're all tired and need to rest. If that

Skinling or another of Mulk's vassals find us compromised, we could get hurt, and people could die. Just buy them."

She rushed off. Yeah, Aria had totally just lied to him. She was involved in this deeper than she was letting on. What would happen on Sunday?

Steven took the jeans off the rack. He sighed. Buying jeans shouldn't be this hard. But it was. For the first time in his life, he was going to accept charity, he was going to get exactly what he wanted, and he wasn't going to care about the price. He needed new clothes for the adventure he found himself on. Aria was rich. The evidence was clear. Exhibit A? Her fucking Mercedes.

He didn't look at another price tag. He bought clothes using the mannikins as a model for what might look cool. He grabbed a suitcase, and he met up with Aria and Tessa at the cash register. Tessa had embraced the free fashion.

Three thousand dollars later, they were out the door and back in the Mercedes, driving off. They found a Courtyard Marriott, and Aria didn't get them normal rooms but booked a suite. The amount of money was staggering.

They took the elevator up to the top floor. Aria and Tessa went in first.

Steven sighed, standing out in the hallway. This was his life? Macy's and suites and expensive cars? Could he handle it? He wasn't sure. It was like he'd lived his life in a desert, sipping from an old canteen, afraid at any minute he'd die of thirst. And now, he was standing in a lake of fresh water. No, not just water—*sparkling* water.

He strode into the suite. This wasn't a hotel room, it was a small house. Two bedrooms, a main living room, a bathroom the size of the Coffee Clutch, and when Aria pulled open the curtains, they were given a view of the freeway and the Rocky Mountains in the distance. Everything was new, beautiful, and smelled fresh and clean.

"I was so tired in the car," Tessa said, "but now after the coffee and shopping and this room, I'm wired! How can I sleep?"

Aria smiled and gently took Tessa's hand. "I know what we can do to help us sleep."

TEN

ARIA STOOD WITH TESSA IN FRONT OF THE window that showcased the Rocky Mountains in the distance. The suite wasn't as lush as most of the rooms Aria had stayed in over the years. In India, she had grown accustomed to staying in palaces rented out to Dragonsouls. And her father had built Aeries in the former residences of rich princes.

But the room was warm, there was a view, and there was a large bed. It would do.

Aria brushed a strand of hair out of Tessa's face. She'd always liked going to the Coffee Clutch because of this beautiful, witty woman. She loved the way she dressed, how quick she was to laugh and flirt, and how free Tessa seemed. Aria admired her for changing her makeup, changing her outfits, and changing her hair on an almost daily basis. The fact that she had been brought into Steven's Escort made it all seem inevitable. Of course they would come together to laugh, to love, to fight.

It was destiny.

Growing up as a Dragonsoul, Aria didn't have the same sexual ethics that most people had. She was far more open-minded and had experienced a wide array of lovers. This, though, felt different.

It was ironic. Steven had no idea of the work in front of him: gathering an Escort, acquiring his Hoard, and building his Aeries. He'd healed his wounds because of the Animus he'd gained from the fight and his night making love to Tessa. Aria knew they'd been at it for hours ... that much was clear from their energy.

Aria knew the rules even if Steven and Tessa didn't. If she had sex with Steven, she would be linked to him forever. For Dragonsouls, especially young ones, mating created bonds that were extremely hard to break. Steven's power was off the charts, true, but he was still so innocent. So clueless. So weak. If Aria gave herself to him and he was slain, she'd never recover from the wound. She wasn't ready yet to commit.

But, she was all too willing to explore the beautiful barista, Tessa Ross. It would relax her like nothing else.

"Can I kiss you?" Aria asked her.

"If you don't, I might die," Tessa said breathlessly, eyes wide.

Lust radiated off Steven like a hot wind. She could almost hear him get an erection.

Aria drank in Tessa for the first time. She slipped forward and tasted her sweet mouth, breathing in her scent. Their bodies pressed together. Aria was lean and muscled, while Tessa was curvy and pliant. This was a woman Aria could play with for a long time. Maybe even for a lifetime.

Their kiss became wilder, more passionate, and Aria felt the thrill of Tessa losing control. The barista grabbed her long hair in a fist. Aria took hold of her ass and pulled her in tighter.

Steven came up and put his hands on their backs.

Tessa broke the kiss. She was breathing hard, her eyes were sparkling, and Aria found herself in the same situation, tingling and wet.

The barista turned to the Dragonling. "Is this okay, Steven? It feels right to me, but I know how these things can turn sideways. This won't be my first threesome. We have to talk, a lot, about everything, or someone is likely to get hurt. Even then, it can still get …" She faltered. "Complicated," she finished after a moment.

Aria studied the woman closely. Part of her attraction to the Dragonling was because of his power as a Dragonsoul, but there was more to it than that. Tessa had true feelings for Steven, and she was a very sexual person, that was clear. The Indian woman had to smile. Again, it felt like fate had brought the three together.

Both women waited for the Dragonling to answer Tessa's question.

Steven finally exhaled. "Tessa, this is every man's fantasy. You both are gorgeous. You both already have given me the best kisses of my life. Doing anything more with the two of you is kind of hard to imagine. It's like me trying to picture heaven after I die."

Tessa squeezed Aria's hand and then moved over to Steven. "I want this." Aria watched the two kiss, man and woman. With her supernatural eyes, she watched the pair trade Animus. Tessa's skin glowed a golden hue and so did the pendant. Normally, a Dragonsoul didn't need any kind of amulet or artifact to help them process Animus, but Steven was different. The pendant seemed to act as a kind of battery, so his cells weren't damaged by the influx of the powerful energy.

And Tessa was special. She wasn't a Dragonsoul, but she *was* something else. Something not strictly human, though she wasn't sure what. Not yet.

The barista gave Steven's mouth a last lick and then she pulled back. "I want this. And I think Aria does too. Aria?"

The Indian woman found herself speechless for a moment. She felt so full of emotion: fear, lust, and love. Already the pull to become part of a Dragonsoul's Escort was nearly overwhelming. "Steven, Tessa, I want us all three to be together. But I can't have sex with Steven yet. It's complicated, like you said. Is it okay if I watch? Help? Kiss you both and get you ready? I'm sorry, it's just … I can't …"

Tessa pulled Aria close to Steven. "You don't have to explain. Sex is weird and powerful. We'll honor your boundaries. We'll accept how far you want to go. Let's just go to the bed. If I don't come soon, I think I might explode."

Aria found herself laughing. She knew how that felt.

They all went to the bed; Tessa stripped off the bedspread and started to undress.

Aria took that opportunity to kiss Steven for the second time. That first time, he'd been uncertain of who he was and what he wanted. It had been a test. And it had triggered the Dragonling to begin his long journey toward ultimate power.

This time, Aria touched the stubble on his face. She gazed into his dark eyes. She smelled his scent and the fragrance of his shifting power—hints of orange blossom, musky cedar, and the char of a fresh campfire. She knew when she shifted she gave off a powerful cinnamon spice odor. His scent was utterly unique and made her heart quicken and her breath catch in her lungs.

He was stronger now, taller, and surer of himself. His hands rested on the swell of her hips. Her hands were around his neck, and she played with the soft hair on the back of his head. Their mouths grew closer until Steven closed the distance and brushed his lips against hers. The sizzling power of their connection made Aria growl. Had she really made that sound? She wanted this dragon man inside her. She wanted to join his Escort and fight by his side until the entire world worshipped them.

But no. Not yet. She resisted, needing to hold that desire back, at least for now.

Tessa was on her knees between them, helping them out of their clothes, pleasuring first Steven and then Aria.

Aria found herself on the bed, her legs spread. While Tessa gave her the gifts of her mouth, Steven kissed her and held her breast in a gentle hand. The heat of their bodies made her sweat, and then she was falling over the edge and into an ocean of bliss. Animus filled her from the wonder of this man and woman. She felt the familiar flow of power, and she felt her muscles thicken even as they relaxed.

Then it was Tessa's turn. She was beyond ready for sex, and when Steven slipped inside her, she cried out into Aria's mouth. The barista's eyes glowed with a bright light that filled the room. Definitely not human, but what?

Another mystery Aria would delight in exploring.

"My chest, Aria," Tessa gasped. "I get so turned on …"

The Indian woman gave her a last kiss and then moved to her breasts.

Steven had quickened his pace. Aria reached down and felt where they were connected. A gentle touch and Tessa was coming. Not a second later, Steven sank deep inside the woman, stiffened, and let out a cry.

Then all three were kissing and laughing in the light of the glowing pendant. Steven's hands felt so wonderful on Aria's skin, as did Tessa's. They curled up together and fell fast asleep.

Aria knew that fighting her desire for Steven was futile. But before she could give herself fully to him, she needed to know more. She needed to know that, in the end, he was a Dragonsoul worth dying for. While Tessa might be able to leave his Escort, being Dragonsoul, Aria couldn't.

Dragonsouls mated for life.

◇◇◇

Steven woke up and felt like he was overheating. Sleeping between two women—one a fire-breathing dragon, no less—was a sweaty proposition.

They hadn't set a specific time, but he wanted to get to the mysterious destination before dark. It was late afternoon and the light was fading in the curtains. He pulled himself off the bed and immediately felt cooler. But not comfortable. The burning sensation still filled his chest. It was like someone had shoved a kerosene heater between his lungs. Every breath made the heater burn brighter, and it felt like his heart was smoldering.

He didn't know how, but he knew the pendant was helping him. Without it, he might have already cooked from the inside out.

Water, he needed water. He went and grabbed the big bottle of mineral water from the fridge and drank the entire liter. Then he saw the price tag. Shit, it was ten fucking dollars. Why would anyone on earth spend ten dollars when water from the tap was free?

Rich people were crazy. Definitely.

After he'd guzzled down the water, hunger hit him. Eating from the minibar would bankrupt them. No, that wasn't right. Aria said money wasn't a problem. She was swiping her American Express card like it was directly connected to Fort Knox.

Either way, Steven couldn't stop himself. While what he really wanted was steak, he'd settle for the huge Snickers bar and the trail mix with chocolate-covered almonds. Fancy. He'd eaten half the minibar before he realized it. There went another two hundred dollars. Shit.

At the window, he stood and watched the sun drifting toward the tops of the mountain peaks. I-25 was a river of traffic. They might see him in the window, naked as he was, but he didn't care. Just like he didn't really care about the three men he'd killed earlier that day.

How could he be so callous?

And he'd just had a threesome with his two crushes. It had seemed so normal, though. It was like he could anticipate what they wanted and how it would work out, and he'd been just fine when Aria said she wasn't ready for sex with him just yet. It felt right. Should it?

Steven crunched through the trial mix, thinking.

He realized he'd held himself in check his entire life. He'd had to. Being a poor kid, the son of a single mother, every one of his actions had consequences, not just for him, but also for his mom.

Get in a fight at school? His mom would have to leave work early to pick him up. There went money for groceries. Get a girl pregnant? That would mean bills and added responsibility for his mom. Even with that bully Bud from the coffee shop, Steven had held back because he hadn't wanted to lose that job. When you're working every minute of your life, you want to keep things simple. Be a good guy, follow the rules, act like society wants you to, and things flow a lot more smoothly.

And once you're used to holding back, acting out, going for what you want, and breaking rules all get harder to do.

When those guys tried to murder him, all of society's rules had gone out the window. It was kill or be killed. And he'd had to protect Tessa. Those guys would've killed her as well. The lizard-masked man had shot at her first.

Those fuckers deserved to die. Steven felt rage fill him. He relived the battle, and he felt how wrong it was for them to try and take his life. Especially now that he had something to live for.

So that explained the violence. As for the sex? Aria had started the threesome. Tessa had dived in with both feet. And who was Steven to ruin anyone's good time? The time for playing it safe was over. Holding back now just might get him and his girlfriends killed.

He found himself holding the pendant. It was warm, glowing, filled with Animus. He thought about the map, and that triggered it. He saw the flames flickering by the St. Vrain river, not that far away. He saw himself southwest of the fire. His icon was a black dragon.

That was his birthright, maybe from his father, maybe not.

Could he really become a dragon?

Only one way to find out.

He went into the bathroom and gazed into the mirror.

It was time to unleash the beast.

ELEVEN

S TEVEN WENT INTO THE SPACIOUS BATHROOM AND gazed into the mirror. Normal guy, dark hair, gray eyes, just his own face that he didn't really think about. The burning power inside him flared, and he wished he had an antacid or an ocean of milk to soothe the burn. Were those flames building so he could breathe fire? Or did it have something to do with the Animus he'd collected while having sex with Tessa and Aria?

He sighed. He'd only been in this mixed-up world for a few days and already all the damn questions were getting old.

Concentrating, he pulled up the dragon-shaped skill tree, and again it appeared blurry in his vision, wavering, indistinct. It was getting easier to access it, but it was still far from being a crisp image. He could see the skill markers, but he couldn't focus on them enough to read what they were. It didn't matter, though. He knew what he wanted. He gritted his teeth. The *Animus Absorption* skill had been the first skill he'd managed to unlock—triggered when Aria had kissed him. The memory of that kiss still got him excited.

No, no time for that. He had to focus.

During his throw down with the Skinling, he'd somehow unlocked a second ability called *Partial Transformation*. In his mind he replayed the battle, envisioning his arm, thick with muscle, covered in black scales, fingers capped by wicked talons. If he were going to tangle with the Skinling and his ilk again, he needed to be able to transform more than just an arm. He stared at the skill tree and intuitively seemed to understand that the neck and head of the tree represented his transformations.

He focused on the second circle on the neck of the dragon, gaze like a laser as he pumped his plentiful supply of Animus into the glowing orb.

The Animus bar plunged, and a new tag flickered and appeared on his skill tree: Homo Draconis ...

The results were immediate. And painful.

His arms scaled over and thickened; three-inch black talons sprouted from his reptilian hands. This was not so different from the Partial Transformation he'd mastered during his fight with the goons, but the changes didn't end there. Oh no. Black scales emerged from his stomach. He wanted to scratch his skin off completely as the itching overtook him, but with his razor-sharp claws, he'd have shredded his body.

Agony assailed him. His bones—*creaking, cracking, twisting*—grew. His joints popped as they expanded. Steven gasped. It felt like someone had taken a hammer to the inside of his skull. His mouth elongated, and slits appeared where his nostrils had been. He stretched his new jaws and found he had rows of jagged fangs. He lashed out with a forked tongue. Holy shit. He had the snout of a fucking dragon. His eyes gleamed. The stink of orange blossoms and campfire became overpowering, like someone was burning down a Florida orchard.

His tail burst from his spine, and he smacked the wall with it. He'd grown at least two feet—now just under eight feet—and he had to crouch to keep from bashing into the ceiling. He lifted a clawed foot at the bottom of a powerful leg. Half human, half dragon, he was wingless, but damn, he had claws, fangs, and a tail, and he knew he was stronger. It felt like he could easily break through walls or upend a car if the need called for it.

He glanced back to the skill tree, still hovering before him, and noticed that keeping this form burned through his available supply of Animus. He could feel it draining from him by the second.

Tessa screamed from the doorway, naked except for his hoodie.

When Steven turned, she backed away into the main room.

Steven tromped toward her. He had to be careful as he slipped out of the bathroom. He towered over Tessa.

Aria rushed out of the bedroom, pistol in one hand, broadsword in the other, totally naked. "What is happening?"

Tessa backed up, hit the coffee table, and landed on her butt. She pointed. "That. It. Thing. There." Her wide eyes radiated fear. Her mouth trembled. Her finger shook like a leaf in a stiff breeze.

"That 'it' is our Steven." Aria walked up to him and put a hand on his massive, scaled arm. "So, you have already mastered your partial form and moved on to bigger and better things. Very impressive. Would you like to see my Homo Draconis?" She arched an eyebrow.

"Yesss ... I ... would ... like ... to see," Steven said in a loud, rough whisper. Talking was hard, but he could manage it. His vocal chords had changed in the process, but the bigger issue was his mouth. The new tongue, fangs, and lips made communicating difficult, to say the least.

Aria put the gun and sword next to the TV. She raised her arms, and the smell of cinnamon mixed with that of orange blossoms floating in the air. Red scales flipped over themselves, covering her body as she grew bigger, taller. It was a good thing they had a suite because a normal hotel room with normal ceilings would never accommodate both of their draconian bodies.

Aria, too, had black claws, striking against her crimson scales. Her small breasts all but disappeared into the muscles of her chest. She was a little more than half his size and far more slender. She touched his arm and growled. "Your appearance improves as you near your true shape, Steven," she hissed. Her words came slowly, but she could talk far better than he could.

Steven imagined what Tessa was seeing … two giant dragon people, one huge and black, the other smaller and colored a striking firestorm red.

Unfortunately, Steven's Animus was running out. Holding the Homo Draconis shape was taxing him, and his reservoirs of the energy weren't as deep as Aria's. Perhaps as he gained levels that would change.

With a gasp, he changed back to being human, the scales and claws drawing into his body as his limbs shrunk. He fell to his hands and knees, trying to catch his breath. Aria, still half dragon, crouched next to him and traced her claws up and down his back. They felt so good, easing the terrible itching. There was less pain from his bones reshaping, and he could see how he could get used to it in time.

He glanced up and gazed into Aria's bright green eyes. Somehow, she managed a very lizard-like smile. "You are stronger than I thought." She changed back into her human shape. The effects were almost immediate. Claws retracted into fingernails, skin replaced scales, and hair grew over her head as her face flattened until she regained her human beauty.

She continued to caress his back. "You are doing well, Steven. I can't imagine what you are feeling. I spent my entire life growing accustomed to the Animus and using it to change my shape. As children, our kind derive Animus from our parents, through their love and caring—though only in small doses. It's not until we can fight and mate that we truly seize power." Her eyes flashed as she spoke.

Steven rose and took Aria in his arms and kissed her. The electricity between them sparked up at once and her energy filled him, but it wasn't going to be good enough. He'd depleted himself, and there was only one surefire way to get more back without any enemies to face.

Steven picked her up and took her to the bed. He kissed her as he laid her on the bed. He found himself between her legs, brushing his sex against hers. He wanted her.

But Aria stopped him. "Not yet, Steven. I can't … not with you. Well, not until …" She trailed off, face flushed. Instead, she slid down, kissing her way down his chest and belly. On her back, with him over her, she took his stiff member inside her warm, wet mouth.

Tessa came around and got on the bed with them. Kissing Steven, touching him, she gave him her Animus as well. Steven's hands drifted down Tessa's body to the patch of hair between her legs. She was soft and wet there.

Tessa in front of him, Aria under him, Steven never had a chance. Both the women pushed him over the edge. The pendant glowed as, breathing hard, his mind whirling from the intense pleasure, he collected more Animus from their sexual energy.

Both of the women were hot as well, so Steven gave up on leaving the hotel room right away. He had to take care of their needs, first Aria's, then Tessa's.

After more sex and showers, they dressed in their new clothes.

Steven felt clean and powerful, and he buzzed with curiosity. He was close to finding the first clue about who he truly was and where he'd come from.

To the west, the peaks of the Rocky Mountains touched the sun as it slowly set, leaving a chill. Luckily, they had bought warm coats at Macy's. Aria wore another colorful dress but accented it with a black camisole and a leather jacket. Tessa was in ripped blinged-out jeans, boots that came up to her knees, and a black sweater with one sleeve longer than the other. As for Steven, he wore jeans and a white linen shirt, just like the man from his dream.

Aria drove like she wanted to outrun the sunbeams that gave the passing farms and fields a soft glow. They buzzed down a back road, and the Indian woman deftly avoided potholes and passed the few cars on the road. The narrow strip of asphalt ran parallel to the shining waters of the St. Vrain River. Tessa, in the back, chattered nervously about this and that, mostly about the fact that she couldn't believe that dragon people existed. And—maybe even more importantly—that she was having sex with them.

Steven could understand; it blew his mind as well. He had to concentrate, though, on the pendant map. It glowed in front of them. His black dragon icon drew closer and closer to the flames burning next to the river.

Steven tried his mother again. Most likely, her supervisor hadn't given her his message. The home phone rang and rang, but no one picked up. Dammit, his nagging worry was turning into cold fear.

"We should expect trouble," Aria said during one of Tessa's lulls. "Whoever is trying to kill you will only be upping the ante. They might not know where we are, but then again, they might. So keep your heads about you."

"Roger that, General," Tessa said nervously. "I'm not really the fighting type, but I can warn you guys if I see anything." Then she went quiet for so long, Steven turned and made sure she was okay.

"Are you good?" he asked.

She nodded, chewing on a fingernail. "Yeah, I … just … you guys know what you are. But me? What am I? I can feel the Animus in me, and when we have sex, my eyes glow. I'm kind of torn. Part of me wants to be normal so I can go back to a regular life when this is all over. But then … maybe some part of me wants to be special too."

"You are not simply human," Aria said in confirmation of Tessa's suspicions. "I expect all of our questions will be answered in time. Ah, we've arrived at last." She pointed.

A tower rose from yellow fields of dead grasses and the ancient cottonwoods hugging the banks of the St. Vrain River.

Aria turned and drove to a gate at the end of a weedy dirt driveway.

All of them got out. Their boots crunched on the gravel. They smelled cold sage and the dank odor of the riverbank. The wrought-iron gate was as rusted as it was ornate. Spiderwebs, old and new, covered the scrolling metal. The gate was attached to a thick cinderblock wall topped with razor wire.

The grounds around the tower had become a tangle of undergrowth, though at one time they would've been beautiful. Lost in the grasses, weeds, and sagebrush were dry fountains and crumbling retaining walls. The round citadel dwarfed most of the bare-limbed cottonwoods around it. Three trees, however, stood taller. The fortress was six stories, at least, and was mostly concrete, but near the top were the remains of stained-glass windows, most broken, though a few were still intact.

The very top of the tower was flat but had four animal heads carved out of marble facing the four cardinal directions.

"Marble and stained glass?" Steven asked in wonder. "Who in the hell lived here?"

"Yeah, if this is a grain elevator, it's the fanciest fucking grain elevator in all of creation," Tessa agreed with a bob of her head.

"It's an Aerie," Aria whispered. A chill wind blew, and she grasped her coat tighter around her. Then she drew her pistol, disengaged the safety, and quickly checked the chamber for a round. Cool, practiced, efficient.

Steven gripped the broadsword in a sweating fist. He pointed to a sign on the front gate obscured with weeds. He went forward and used the blade to clear off the yellow-and-gray tangle.

A single word in the scrollwork made him shiver.
Drokharis.

TWELVE

THE SUN WAS GONE. THE WIND WAS COLD. THE light was gray and growing dimmer.

Steven pointed at the word. "What does this mean, Aria? In my dream ... my vision, I guess it was ... I heard a name, Stefan Drokharis."

Aria stepped forward, frowning. "It's an old Dragonsoul family now gone. I remember the name Drokharis from my studies, but I can't recall specifics. The Drokharis lineage had a grand tradition like the Tudors in England or the Medicis in Italy. The last of the Drokharis clan died out mysteriously." She paused, gaze flashing toward him. "None remain."

A sadness filled Steven, and he wasn't sure why. Imagining his dad as some kind of king made him smile. Joe Whipp was a lot of things—gambler, asshole, absentee father—but he wasn't royalty. As for Steven's mom? Florence Whipp? Yeah, Joe and Flo Whipp, not exactly the stuff legends were made of.

Thick chains kept the gates closed, blocking their way.

Tessa stepped forward and picked up the giant lock in a small hand, her chipped and chewed fingernails painted black. "So, I'm guessing neither of you have a key."

"I can help with that." Aria raised her muscular arm; her skin became scales and her fingernails claws. A dark energy surrounded her hand as she brought her three-inch talons down through the lock. She ripped the lock into pieces that tumbled to the dirt. Normal claws wouldn't have been able to do that, but that shadow energy had imbued her with a powerful force.

Aria grinned. "Soon, you will master your skills, Steven, and you will be able to do that. That and more."

Steven blinked.

"Come on, my dragon-y friends," Tessa said, pushing the gate open. The hinges creaked loudly in the chill hush of twilight.

"Friends or lovers?" Steven asked, a quirk of a smile on his lips.

"My dragon lovers?" Aria rolled her eyes. "Sounds like a bad erotica novel."

"An awesome erotica novel!" Tessa protested.

The three stopped bantering as they walked through the gates and past the sage and weeds of the courtyard. Huge double doors blocked their way into the tower. Big iron rings hung from fittings in the central panels, and the entrance would've felt at home protecting a Bavarian castle. What was such a fortress doing in the boonies of Colorado?

Aria tried her shadowy claw trick again, but her nails only left deep scars in the wood.

"The place is magically protected." She squinted her eyes as she studied the door.

Steven fished the pendant out of his shirt and held it aloft. A *click* echoed through the courtyard. Bolts slid from behind the wood, and the doors creaked open on rusted hinges, revealing the darkness of the hallway beyond. It felt like a haunted house ride at an amusement park. Classic and creepy.

Steven gulped. The whole place had gone quiet—no birds, no wind, a preternatural hush surrounded them. He gripped the broadsword tighter.

"Don't suppose you brought a flashlight," he said.

"As a matter of fact, I did." Aria reached into her coat and came out with a mini Maglite. She clicked it on, and the beam cut through the gloom, showing granite tiles dusty with time.

This was it. This was the next stop on his grand adventure. And, fortunately, no one was trying to kill him. Yet.

He stepped in, breathing hard. Sweat dripped off his face.

Lights winked on. Not torches, light bulbs. The hallway led to a round living room with a kitchen off to the side and a bathroom. The place had furniture: a big sectional sofa, dark wood bookcases, a dining room set with twelve chairs around a mahogany table. But everything was slashed apart, the books ripped open like dead birds, the walls burned. One section of bookcases was melted as if someone had splashed it with acid.

Skeletons, long moldered away, lay on their stomachs, arms outstretched as if they were trying to crawl to safety. The place was in ruins, the leftovers of a battle, decades old.

"What happened here?" Tessa squeaked.

"The downfall of the American Drokharis Primacy it looks like," Aria replied in a whisper. "Though in the histories I read, the Drokharis Dragonsouls preferred to be Ronins. A few had Primacies, but they were a clan more interested in sorcery than conquest."

Steven cupped a hand around his mouth and called out, "Stefan Drokharis! Stefan Drokharis! Are you here?"

Nothing answered them, though ceiling lights above the stone staircase winked on, spiraling upwards. Steven's pendant radiated light and heat. It grew so hot that Steven had to keep it off his skin.

"Looks like we go up," Tessa said. She put a foot on the first step, then retreated behind Steven. "Uh, Dragonsouls go first. Baristas go last. So we're around to make coffee at the funerals."

Steven laughed at that one. Even though the place gave him the creeps, he couldn't stop now. And he wasn't going to let Aria go first. While she had her secrets, he didn't think this was about her. No, this was about him and his past.

And his future.

The second, third, and fourth floors were bedrooms and bathrooms and pantries with small kitchenettes connected to them—all as sumptuous as the suite they were staying in at the Marriott. But like the living room below, these rooms were torn to pieces. A wide brown stain marked one Persian carpet under a small skeleton, probably the remains of a woman, given the size of the body. And that stain? That stain was long-congealed blood without a doubt.

The sixth level had been a library with two studies attached to it. The bookcases were bare, the papers scattered and mixed with leaves. The stained-glass windows were only jagged bits of glass in the window frames. More of the acid had eaten away the stone walls. A desk lay like a BBQ briquette in the middle of a burned-out study.

Dragon fire, certainly.

As they walked up through the levels of the tower, lights flashed on as if by magic. Or maybe they were connected to motion detectors, which was probably more realistic. Then again, his sense of what was realistic had changed drastically in the last couple of days. The lights of the library were small recessed bulbs scattered in a pattern across the ceiling, but not a pattern Steven recognized. A lopsided polygon led to a line that circled around the ceiling but not in a spiral. The line of lights just kind of meandered.

He'd hoped to find answers in the tower, but they'd explored every room, and all they had found was the signs of a violent struggle that had taken the lives of dozens of people decades ago.

Standing by the barbecued desk, Steven turned to Aria. "There's nothing here." He pulled up the map, and his black dragon icon was standing right in the middle of the flames by the St. Vrain River. He pointed. "See, I'm right here. Maybe my real parents just wanted me to see where they were killed." He paused, taking a long look around. "Maybe we should just go."

Tessa screwed up her face. "Dude, give up much? Haven't you seen *National Treasure*? Or like any movie ever? No, it's going to be a puzzle. We just have to figure it out."

Aria walked under the pattern of the ceiling lights. "Wait, that's a constellation. Draco."

Tessa sighed. "I wish I knew my stars. That would be so cool. Did it take you long to memorize the night sky, Aria?"

The Dragonsoul smiled impishly. "I hardly know the sky. But as a dragon, we are required to at least know that one constellation."

An idea hit Steven between the eyes. "We're not done yet. The top of the tower. We have to get to the top."

They went back to the staircase, but there seemed to be no way up. They returned to the damaged library

"I bet you a million dollars there's a secret door," Tessa said. "We just have to trigger it."

Steven walked quickly to the only bookcase that hadn't been destroyed. The carpet had long burned away, revealing a scorched hardwood floor covered with leaves. He brushed some of the debris away with his boot, and he saw a half-circle marked into the floor. It was from the bookcase swinging out. But how to activate it?

A metal sconce for a candle jutted out from the stone.

He and Tessa exchanged glances. "You don't think …" she started.

"Well, I've seen that movie," Steven said. "Or was it a Scooby-Doo episode?" Either way, he pulled the sconce down, a mechanism behind the wall *groaned*, and the bookcase swung open, revealing a set of stone stairs leading upward.

Tessa suppressed a giggle. "Can I just say that this is the greatest moment of my life? We found a secret passageway."

"Total cliché," Steven said. "The candleholder? The bookcase? Duh."

"Lucky for us it was cliché," Aria said. "I would not want to be here all night trying to find a way to the top of the tower. I would imagine we have a more difficult puzzle ahead of us. We do not have any idea of why we are here or what we are looking for."

"I think we'll know when we find it." Steven started up the stone steps. The passageway was narrow but thankfully short. They came out of a doorway and found themselves on the flat top of the tower. A four-foot parapet wall ran around the roof, and the marble creatures he'd seen from below each sat in their own corner. Up close, even in the dark, Steven could see what the animals were.

There was a dragon, of course, a kind of wolf creature, an eagle with is wings back, and a cat with one paw out as if to scratch someone. Each statue was about five feet wide and ten feet long and extended outward from the wall. Each had a door in the back. They'd come out of the dragon door.

His pendant glowed, giving them light, so they didn't need Aria's Maglite. Steven headed across the tower and tried the other doors; each was made of heavy wood with a brass handle, tarnished and weatherworn.

"Do you think there are other secret passageways?" Steven asked.

Tessa shrugged. "Could be. But I think this is where we need to be."

Eyes glittering, Aria nodded but didn't say anything. Her face was serious.

Night had fallen. In the distance, they heard a car whoosh by on the highway. Mostly, though, all they could hear was the St. Vrain River trickling, running shallow since it was only early April, and the snow in the Rockies hadn't melted that much. Another car rushed by. This one seemed to stop, or at least slow down.

They went to the edge of the tower and looked down. Steven expected to see police cruisers, or black government Humvees, or a truckload of thugs with broadswords. But all they saw was Aria's car in the driveway, lots of grass and sage, and an empty road. The vehicle must've kept on going.

Steven turned and walked to the middle of the rooftop. Tiles made up a mosaic, but the sun, rain, and snow had washed out their colors. Maybe that was the key?

If so, that clue was so gone.

He took the pendant off and held it up. Then he saw it, sparkling on the floor: certain tiles in the mosaic gleamed in a polygon connected to a meandering line. Draco, the constellation.

"Look!" Tessa called out. She was pointing up at the sky.

The constellation of Draco, in the northern night sky, was shining brightly. It was next to the Big Dipper. Steven knew that one at least.

The mystic topaz pendant glowed so much it was a like a second sun on the Drokharis fortress. Shadows around the cottonwoods lengthened, and yet, something was different. The night sky shimmered like it was a pool of water with diamonds shining in its depths, but all other stars were dim compared to the Draco constellation.

So close … the liquid night seemed close enough Steven could touch it. He bent and placed the broadsword on the rooftop. Then he stood and reached out a hand, and it felt like dipping his fingers into a warm pool—so warm and comforting on his skin. His hand disappeared into the stars of Draco's head. Something was there, something square. He gripped it and tugged, pulling the mystery item out of the night sky itself.

Suddenly, he found himself holding a book, a huge leather-bound thing with a blank cover. Wasn't blank for long, though. As the light from the pendant streamed down, words appeared on the front.

The Drokharis Grimoire.

Aria hissed, "It's a Prime's spell book … the family's spell book. Could you be part of that family, Steven?"

He shrugged. He just didn't know.

Tessa crept over to stand next to Steven. She reached out a hand and touched the night; it sent ripples across the sky. Her eyes shined as brightly as the pendant and the Draco stars. "It's so warm," she breathed. "I would've thought it would be cold because, well space, right?"

"Could you also be a part of the Drokharis family?" Aria asked.

Tessa made a face. "Uh, I hope not because, yeah, that would mean Steven and I were related. Which would be both illegal and, more importantly, *gross*. We can't have that."

Steven ignored their chatter. The book became heavier in his hand, so heavy he had to put it on the ground. The minute leather touched the tiles, new color flooded into the mosaic, creating a picture of a black dragon, surrounded by other dragons, smaller, more slender. *Females.* There were also men and women standing with the black dragon, most likely a powerful Prime with at least one if not many Primacies under his control. The dragon in the mural had his arms out. Swirls of energy smoked out of his claws and crossed the roof to end at the three closed doors. The dragon's tail reached to the door they'd come out of.

What did it mean? Steven didn't know.

He opened the book but didn't get a chance to read it.

Six men in black combat gear burst through the door and out onto the rooftop. They were special-ops guys, some armed with assault rifles and some with swords—the blades all glowing neon green. Those blades were enchanted, without a doubt, and probably able to cut through dragon scale. Black body armor covered their arms, chests, and legs. Black paint made their faces disappear in the night.

Aria turned, sprinted to the edge of the tower, and threw herself off, leaving Steven and Tessa alone.

Oh shit. Had she led them into a trap?

THIRTEEN

THE SWORDSMEN STOPPED WHILE THE RIFLEMEN crouched, aimed, and fired.

Steven whirled, grabbing Tessa and pulling her in against him as he activated the Homo Draconis ability. His entire body expanded upward and outward. In a blink, he became eight feet tall and three feet wide. His new clothes burst at the seams to accommodate his muscles, scales, and the spines rising out of his vertebrae. He crouched over Tessa, hugging her to his chest, sheltering her from the gunfire with his armor-plated back.

The bullets thudded into Steven's shoulders and spine, each one a hammer blow. But Tessa was safe, that was the important thing.

"Get the book!" he growled at her through jaws ill-equipped for speaking.

Then Steven spun and lashed out with his tail on instinct. It had to be instinct because he'd spent twenty years with only four major appendages. He drove the thick coil into the face of a man, crunching through bone. The thug fell, screaming, clutching at his ruined face. Animus burst out of his crushed skull and swept into the glowing pendant still hanging around Steven's neck.

One guy with a rifle kept firing. The muzzle flashed brightly on the rooftop and bullets struck Steven, but like before, they bounced off—though they still hurt like a bitch; each felt like a mallet-blow of fiery pain. Another soldier dropped his gun and drew a long knife, the blade etched with glimmering runes. Meanwhile the three men with magic swords advanced, spreading out in a semicircle, death and determination etched into their faces.

Steven was outnumbered five to one. Didn't matter. He was close to finding out the truth of his past, and he wasn't about to let these assholes get in the way.

He waded forward and clawed the rifleman's face off with a single strike. Without the constant pounding of the bullets, Steven felt much better. More Animus flowed into him through the pendant.

The knife guy lunged, driving his rune-etched blade into Steven's side. It snapped off. Wheeling, Steven batted him off the roof with a sweep of his tail. The knife guy went screaming to his death, arms pinwheeling on the way down.

A glowing sword carved through the air, but Steven was ready. He ducked the blow, then dodged another strike from an assailant on his right, his speed increased, his reflexes supernaturally quick. But how? Then he knew. The Animus. He had three kills, and their energy now filled him. He couldn't harness it well, but the energy was there, fueling him, helping him.

A swordsman slipped left and shot in, sinking his blade into Steve's shoulder. As expected, the neon-green blade parted scale and found the flesh and muscle beneath. Steven grunted, but pushed away the surge of pain. He picked up the attacker with one hand, then twirled like a top and slammed him against another armor-clad swordsman. Both rolled across the tiles, slamming into rock of the parapet.

The third swordsman rushed forward without missing a beat. He had his sword, glowing green, poised to impale Steven's heart. A blow that would end him.

Something crimson and deadly streaked out of the sky, snatching the attacker up with such force he dropped his weapon. The glowing sword clattered across the mosaic as the man screamed. The deadly creature carried the man up, great wings pumping, then released him with a flick of powerful arms. He struck a hulking cottonwood with a meaty thud and the crack of breaking bone. His crushed corpse tumbled, his limbs clearly fractured, his neck twisted in an unnatural direction.

Aria! She'd taken on her True Form: a scarlet dragon fifteen feet long, winged, tailed, and clawed. She flashed overhead in the darkness, trailing inky smoke from her jaws.

By that time, the first two swordsmen had regained their feet. Behind them, through the door, came three more Kevlar-clad men, all armed with assault rifles. Laser targets found Tessa's chest. They fired.

Steven was fast enough to intercept the rounds, taking another pounding on his chest. He huffed as each bullet struck home. His blood from the sword wound dripped onto the mosaic. He couldn't use his right arm, not a chance. Could he fight the five men with only his tail and his left claw? He wasn't exactly spoiled for options, so he had to.

Steven whirled and caught a swordsman by the arm before the man could cut into him again.

The other swordsman attacked with his magic blade, slashing into Steven's side. More black blood gushed onto the tiles.

One of the newcomers bent to retrieve the third magic sword, which lay on the tiles.

Laser spots appeared on Tessa's head. The thunder of gunfire followed, those bullets heading toward the barista's brain. Steven lifted his tail and saved her. His tail took the damage, and the sheer force of the impact spun him around.

Another sword landed, this time on his right arm. He howled and tried to raise the arm, but it hung limp from his body due to the shoulder wound he'd suffered earlier.

In that instant, he knew he couldn't fight all five men at the same time, keep Tessa safe, and keep himself alive. They had to get off the rooftop. There was no other way.

A hot wind smelling of cinnamon filled the air. Aria, beating her wings, soared by overhead, banking sharply right, then circling again. Steven knew exactly what she was waiting for. He turned his back on the attackers and was promptly rewarded with the bite of more sword blades, but they would soon be gone. He wrapped Tessa up in his arms, loped across the rooftop with his powerful reptilian legs, and leapt onto the lip of the tower. He wavered there for a moment before leaping off; the wind whipped around them as they plummeted, down, down, down.

He turned into the fall so his back would land first, his body absorbing the brunt of the impact. He had some armor, but it was a six-story drop onto unforgiving ground. He hoped this suicidal move worked or it would be the last reckless thing he ever did.

The instant he left the roof, Aria unleashed a powerful burst of flame. She covered the top of the tower in an inferno, breathing an intense fire that engulfed the remaining armored attackers. Their screams ripped through the night. Their skin hissed and spit as the intense heat flash-fried them. The dragon fire was so hot that it made Tessa's skin grow slippery from sweat, and Steven felt it blast his face even as they hurtled toward the ground.

The smell of smoke and meat cooking mixed with the cinnamon-spice of Aria's dragon form. That sweet scent grew more intense, and then he felt Aria's claws latch onto his left arm, slowing them down. She beat her wings furiously, but Steven in his Homo Draconis form was too heavy to support.

Still, Aria managed to slow them down enough to survive the fall. Steven and Tessa struck the ground, and they bounced through weeds and sagebrush before smashing into the basin of a fountain. Sweeping through the air, Aria banked, narrowly missed a cottonwood, and then came around to land on the ground. She towered over them in her True Form, green eyes glimmering in the flickering firelight from the tower above.

She brought her huge head forward and smiled. Seeing a dragon smile made Steven grin using his own reptilian mouth. But he had been wounded, and he felt light-headed. Something bounced into the dirt in front of them. At first, Steven thought it was debris from the top of the tower, but then he saw the familiar shape of a grenade.

Aria bustled forward, pushing Steven and Tessa to the ground. She slammed a clawed foot down on the grenade. *Boom.* The explosion lifted her off her feet and blasted her back against the tower. But dragons, apparently, were even tougher than grenades. She recovered in a heartbeat, then turned and let out a geyser of fire at another six soldiers hustling out of the trees.

Reinforcements. Great.

The soldiers dove behind cottonwoods, but the dry grasses caught and soon smoke swirled upward into the night sky. Machine gun fire erupted in staccato bursts. Muzzle flashes gave away their positions. Aria drove her body forward to either burn them or eat them. Something streaked across the ground, slamming into Aria's chest with a violent explosion of light and heat. An RPG. Like an actual missile. The blast threw the dragon to the ground, a plume of smoke rising from her body.

"Aria!" Tessa screamed in worry.

Fury reddened Steven's vision. These special-ops assholes had hurt his friend, and they were going to pay. They might have advanced weapons, big shit, but they didn't have any magic swords, and he was bulletproof.

"Find cover," he growled at Tessa.

He raced across the ground, jumped over Aria, and landed in the middle of the six mercenaries. Bullets punched into his scales, but though they hurt, the blows weren't lethal. Not even close. He spun his tail around and took three down to their knees. He lunged forward and ripped the throat out of another with his jaws. For the first time in his life, he tasted the life blood of someone else. It was salty, warm, and awful, and yet the burst of Animus filled him with vital power.

Steven kept moving. He clawed through the belly of another soldier, leaving butchered flesh in his wake. The guy went to his knees as his guts hit the dirt, and then he keeled over.

Steven was surrounded by fire, but the flames didn't hurt. In fact, the heat felt good on his scales. Then a wind came sweeping through, so strong and powerful, the grassfire was extinguished, blown out like the candles on a birthday cake. That hurricane breeze smelled like cinnamon ... Aria was still alive and putting out the fire she'd caused with her breath. Steven spun and saw her silhouetted in the night, a real live dragon, standing over them, working her huge wings.

It was as beautiful as it was strange.

Another rocket-propelled grenade struck her in the chest, and the explosion left her shrieking in pain. She stumbled, reeled, tripped, and fell to the ground again. This time, she didn't get up.

Steven went for the guy with the RPG. He was quick, strong. The mercenary drove the butt end of the rocket launcher into Steven's jaw, cracking loose a tooth. Steven responded by leaping onto the guy, grabbing his skull, and squeezing. The added strength of his Homo Draconis form threatened to pop the soldier's head right off his shoulders.

The three mercenaries Steven had dropped with his initial tail swipe had scuttled off into the darkness in full retreat.

"Mercy!" the RPG soldier cried out. "Don't kill me! No paycheck is worth this!"

Steven pushed his reptilian snout into the face of the man. "Who hired you?" His voice came out in a bestial growl.

"I can't tell you!"

Steven increased the pressure, and the mercenary cried out in fear and pain. "You're going to tell me," Steven snarled, "or I'm going to crush your skull like an egg."

More pressure. The white eyes in the black-painted face went wide.

"Okay, okay, okay … I'm a hired gun for Rhaegen Mulk. His Skinling dispatched us to this old Aerie. He thought you'd come here."

"Give me a name," Steven ordered. "What is the Skinling's name?"

"Edgar Vale," the mercenary said. "If you let me go, I'll run. You won't see me again. Rhaegen Mulk might come for me, but I'll do my best to disappear. Just please don't kill me."

A stick snapped to Steven's left. He glanced up to see Tessa helping Aria limp across the ground. She was back in her human form, naked, wounded. The skin over her heart was blackened from the rocket-propelled grenade.

"You have to kill him," Aria said. "He is your enemy, and you could use the Animus."

She seemed so calm, but then, the Indian woman had a different perspective about life and death. She had grown up with Dragonsoul Primes warring, and in war, there were casualties.

Steven was losing track of his kills, and the thought disturbed him. Taking lives should mean something. And while he hadn't promised to let the mercenary go free for information, a deal had been implied.

"You run," Steven grunted. "And don't come after me again. Tell everyone you know. Tell all of Rhaegen Mulk's vassals. If you mess with me and my Escort, you die. Understand?"

His Escort. The word had come out of his mouth so easily. *Naturally*. He'd fought so well. He'd been so brave. The pendant was helping him; it was the only explanation. He was coming into his own, and the gemstone was easing the way.

He let go of the man's skull, and the mercenary fled into the darkness.

Steven rose, his head dizzy, and he felt his grip on his Homo Draconis form slip. He took a step and suddenly his legs were human. His arms followed a second later, and then he was on his hands and knees, gasping. Blood, human blood, dripped into the weeds and dirt of the courtyard. He'd been hacked with magical swords numerous times. And now he was feeling it. The adrenaline was fading, the pain encroaching with vicious glee.

He swayed and then fell to his side. Naked like Aria, he curled up in a ball of hurt. Three blinks later, he was unconscious.

He woke with Tessa trying to get him to his feet, pleading with him to walk. "Come on, Steven, work with me."

"Aria … is she okay?" Steven asked in a mumble.

"Yes, in the car. She's less bloody than you are, but she's also hurt." Tessa helped him into the passenger's seat, then climbed in the driver's seat and started the engine. Aria was in the back, unconscious.

Tessa dropped the car into gear and pulled out, gravel crunching under the tires. Steven thought to ask about the book, but his thoughts were fuzzy, and everything just hurt so damned much. He leaned his head back. He was out the second his head touched the seat.

He woke to the smell of cigarette smoke. He was covered in a blanket, as was Aria, and they were in the Mercedes, in the parking lot of the Marriott. Every inch of Steven ached. He touched the wound on his shoulder and found he wasn't bleeding anymore. Like before, he was healing at an accelerated rate. That was good. But his head felt like a junked-out car in a demolition derby.

Hunger and thirst fought it out in the rest of his body. He managed to choke out words. "Tessa, water. Food."

Tessa came around and opened the door. She stood bathed in the parking lot lights, smoking.

"Why are you smoking?" he asked weakly. "Cigarettes aren't cool."

"I only smoke when I'm stressed," she answered. The she ranted. "And I think this qualifies as being stressed after everything that happened. Plus, you two might die. And I can't even get you to the room because you both are way naked. So, yeah, this whole thing is intense, and it stopped being fun when you threw me off the roof and that fucking guy with the RPG hit Aria twice, and then she breathed fire. Like, actual, fucking, fire."

He raised a finger. "Dragons, remember? It's what we do apparently."

She exhaled a cloud of blue-gray smoke then managed to find a little chuckle. "Yeah, apparently." She ashed her cigarette. "I tried looking at the book while you were out, but it's written in another language. It seems like a real thriller though, and there are plenty of pictures. For a high school dropout like me, that really helps."

"I didn't know you dropped out of school." Steven closed his eyes. "Can you get me something to eat? And some clothes. Then we can make it up to the room. Grab a blanket for Aria, and we can cover her and carry her up."

Tessa didn't move. "Maybe this is too much for me. Maybe I can't do this. Those guys … Shit, it was *Call of Duty: Spec Ops* all over again. But more dragon-y."

"I don't know what you should do, Tessa, but I do know if you could grab me a Hot Pocket, I'd be forever in your debt."

The barista laughed and rolled her eyes. "That I can do, I suppose."

Steven relaxed and fell asleep again.

The smell of the pepperoni-stuffed instant pastry roused him, and there was Tessa, an angel with a bottle of water and food. Food!

He bolted down the Hot Pocket and drained the bottle in a single go. Tessa had parked the Mercedes in a dark corner of the parking lot, away from the other cars. Good. He dressed in new jeans and a T-shirt, then helped get Aria out of the back of the car. In her human form, she was light enough for Steven to carry, though even with the blanket, it was clear she was naked. Nothing they could do about that, however.

While Steven grabbed Aria, Tessa grabbed the Drokharis Grimoire.

No way were they going to carry Aria up the staircase, so they went to the elevator. Steven prayed they wouldn't meet anyone inside, but they weren't that lucky.

A middle-aged man and wife walked into the elevator at the same time they did. When the normal couple saw Steven—sooty, pale, smelling like a campfire—they frowned. Scowled, really.

Steven, Aria, and Tessa were going to the top floor while the couple punched the fifth-floor button. The doors closed, and they started upward.

The situation was cringey and terrible.

Steven, holding Aria in his arms, finally had to say something. "Friday night in Firestone, Colorado. Amiright?"

The wife harrumphed. The man frowned deeper.

Tessa came to the rescue. "My friend, she had a little too much to drink. Don't worry, I'm here to take care of her."

Anger flashed through Steven. Who were these people to judge him? "Yeah, me, Tessa, Aria, we're a thing. It's a *ménage-à-trois* situation. Luckiest man alive, amiright?"

The couple didn't say a word, but the woman punched the third-floor button and they got off early.

"Uh, we'll take the stairs," the man grumbled, shuffling out.

When they were gone, Tessa laughed nervously. "You're bad."

"I guess I am," Steven said with a shrug. "But we gave them something to talk about at their next PTA meeting or whatever."

The elevator dinged, and they went down the hall to the suite at the end. Back in the comfort of the spacious room, Steven could relax.

Aria was breathing, she was healing, she just needed more time to come around. Or at least Steven hoped that was the case. Could he take her to the hospital? She wasn't human, and he didn't know what the protocols were.

She looked so small and hurt in the big king bed.

In the living room, Steven finally had a chance to look at the leather-bound tome, but if it was written in another language, how was that going to help him?

He opened the cover, his eyes widened, and his world changed once again.

FOURTEEN

T HE WORDS ON THE OPENING PAGE WERE TOTALLY unfamiliar, slashes and jagged characters that reminded him of Klingon. As a good dork, he knew what the Star Trek language looked like. But as he sat there, stomach growling, throat dry, the words straightened, and he could read them. It was like some hidden part of his brain had been unlocked.

Right at the top of the page were three sets of words that seemed to have been added later: *The Gift of a Book. The Magic of Ink. The Power of the Pen.*

Underneath that, the book began in earnest.

It was the spell book of the Drokharis family, compiled by Stefan Drokharis and augmented from other texts.

Tessa sat next to him, looking over his shoulder. "Can you read that?" she asked, brow scrunched.

"Yeah, seems like." His chest was tight. It was hard to breathe. If he didn't have a connection to this family and this book, how could he understand the strange language? *The Gift of a Book.* It was a present for him, he knew it.

He read onward for several long moments until Tessa asked, "What does it say?"

"This guy, Stefan Drokharis, put this grimoire together based on a bunch of other books and scrolls dating back to the Babylonian Dynasty. The *Clavis Salomonis*. The *Sefer Raziel Ha-Malakh Liber Razielis Archangeli*. *The Picatriz* and the *Liber Juatus*. Plus, one called *The Book of Abra-Melin the Mage*. Shit, looks like Hammurabi himself contributed, and that was back in the day of cuneiform."

"And I'm all out of clay tablets," the barista quipped.

Steven raised an eyebrow at her.

She shrugged. "Yes, dropped out of high school but I didn't stop learning. I dated an anthropology professor for a bit. She, uh, educated me in more ways than one."

A quiver of lust ran through Steven at the idea, but then he was drawn back into the book. "Even back then, there were Dragonsouls in the world, but fewer, and they were less powerful. Keeping the secret was harder. It mentions something about the Others, or Outsiders, or the Exiled."

"Which word is it?" Tessa asked.

Steven was surprised that he didn't find the barista's interruptions annoying. Normally, when he studied, he liked to be alone. This felt different. Tessa had a hunger to learn more about the strange world they'd discovered, and he found he wanted to feed her whatever tidbits he could.

"The translation is funky," he replied. "The word is *Zothoric*. But yeah, it seems the Zothoric were powerful demons that could kill Dragonsouls, but they haven't been seen on Earth since Hammurabi. So, that must've been like three thousand years ago. And then there's talk about multiple worlds, other realities. Looks like this Stefan character was trying to learn how to open portals to them. But it says over and over that it's forbidden magic."

"Maybe that's what killed Stefan Drokharis and wrecked his Aerie," Tessa murmured. "Maybe he did open the door and something really nasty got out. Or maybe something from the 'darkest timeline' broke through."

"Was that a *Community* reference?" Steven asked, grinning.

"Bingo." She shot him with a finger gun.

"Cool, cool, cool." Steven couldn't believe how great Tessa was. He smiled and read more. "Not sure, but it looks like this Drokharis family was one of the original Dragonsoul clans on Earth. And Stefan was apparently one helluva sorcerer. He could teleport and create doorways here on this planet, in this dimension, from one continent to another, but he was looking for something. Something called the *Scrolls of Shanos*. Shanos, the Traveler, was some kind of uber Magician. Not sure if Shanos is part of the Zothoric or not, but he seems like one bad dude. Or not. Hard to tell."

Steven leafed through pages while Tessa watched. Illustrations illuminated the text, sketches of dragons, swords, and people. One of them drew Steven's attention. It was the drawing of a woman with a name carefully scrawled underneath: Persephone. Unlike the goddess from Greek mythology, this one wore modern clothes—a skirt, a blazer, pumps. The pencil sketch drew out her beauty and accented her long dark hair—hair not so different from Steven's.

Was there a resemblance? Maybe.

Steven turned the page and his heart leapt to his throat. There, on a full-page spread, was the image of the gaming tree he'd been picturing, a perfect replica of the dragon-shaped skill tree. But this one had a more complete picture, the neck and the tail more filled out. Below that was a list of skills.

Transformatio **(Head of the Dragon)**
- Partial Transformation
- Homo Draconis
- True Form (Dragonsoul)

139

Pugna (Tail of the Dragon)
- DarkArmor

Exhalants (Left Wing of the Dragon)
- Inferno

Veneficium (Right Wing of the Dragon)
- *Magica Defensio*

Obviously, as he grew more adept at using the Animus, he could expand his skills. After taking such a thrashing at the hands of the spec-op guys, he was very excited to see what DarkArmor, under the *Pugna* category, did. *Pugna*, as in pugnacious. Those must be combat abilities.

The Exhalants were easy to understand—that was the ability to breathe various deadly things. He recalled his vision that first night after Aria's kiss; the man in the vision had told him about other things he would eventually exhale: lightning, acid, poison gas, ice. But those weren't on the skill tree for now.

As for *Veneficium*? The word quickly shimmered and morphed in his head: Sorcery.

Magica Defensio sounded like shielding magic, which would be super useful in time, but he couldn't even begin to fathom how he was supposed to cast spells.

Beneath the list of introductory skills, the book had instructions. It said that to harness more of his powers, he needed to understand the *Magic of Ink* and the *Power of the Pen*. Like what it had said at the beginning. He held the grimoire, which was the *Gift of a Book*. Maybe he needed to find a pen and ink? He turned the page. The minute the paper settled, the words on the page faded away. He was left staring at a blank page.

"What? Where did it go?" he stammered.

Tessa touched the blank paper. "I see it, too. No more words. Damn! And it was just getting good."

Steven stood up to pace. He needed a shower and to sleep, but he wanted to make sure Aria was okay first. The book had answered some of his questions, but it had raised a hundred more. "Okay, so I must be a part of this Drokharis clan. Right? Why else would I be drawn to the book and to the tower? Besides, the woman in there, Persephone, she looks like me, I think."

The barista sat on the couch with the book on her lap. She swept back pages until she found the sketch. "Yep. Definite family resemblance. Maybe she's your real mom?"

Speaking of which ... Steven grabbed his phone and hit redial to call his adopted mother. Nothing—just a continuous ringing until the voicemail kicked in. His mom remained MIA, and now he was more worried than ever. What if she was hurt? What if whoever was after him had her? But there was nothing he could do for her, not at the moment, so he shoved the worry to the backburner of his thoughts and continued pacing.

He found himself clutching the pendant.

The burning inside of him was back and hurting like always. He wasn't at full Animus, and yet he felt so full of power now that he had a little better understanding of how the mystical energy worked. But he had no real idea of what to do with the primal energy. Before, he'd been able to use instinct to change his shape, but this time it felt different. If only he had a teacher. "Okay, I have some Animus, but I'm not sure how to spend it on spells or exhalants. I could try True Form, though that feels kind of extreme. Not sure I can wrap my head around that yet."

"We should wait until Aria wakes up," Tessa said cautiously.

"Yeah. You're right. I'll shower ... and pizza, we should order pizza, and lots of something to drink. Gatorade, an ocean of it."

"I'll get right on it while you shower. But before you go, can you show me some of the words?" the barista asked, gesturing to the book. "I want to learn to speak Dragon or at least read it. Maybe even write it. The script is so beautiful and strange." Her fingers traced over the lines on the page. "Compelling."

Steven remembered she liked calligraphy and sketching. He nodded and took a minute to point out the basic alphabet that he could somehow read. Tessa wrote down the jagged letters on Marriott stationary. She held up the paper, inspecting her handiwork. "My first spell book. Kinda cool that it's so ghetto."

"Ha, nothing ghetto about a Courtyard Marriott," Steven replied with a small grin.

It was almost midnight, and Tessa somehow managed to find a pizza place that was willing to deliver. She ordered ten bottles of whatever sports drink they had, but it still didn't seem like enough, so Steven had her order five more.

While they waited, Steven showered. He cranked the hot water up to full tilt and it still felt cool on his skin. He recalled how Aria's fire hadn't burned him. It had felt good. Awash in steam, Steven thought boiling water would feel even better, but he had to make do. Clean, he left the bathroom and stared at himself in the mirror. Cuts and scrapes covered him, but he was healing them at an accelerated rate.

He thought about trying to channel Animus into his new DarkArmor ability, which seemed within reach, but what if he could cast a *Magica Defensio* spell instead? What even was that? He needed to ask Aria about where he should focus his Animus, and why the words on the pages had disappeared. Maybe it was a normal Dragonsoul thing.

But what had the book said? The power of the pen and the magic of ink? He had two more flames on the map to explore. Could one have a pen and the other ink? It seemed as likely as anything else.

He left the bathroom, which is when Aria called to him. "Steven, I need you. Please, help me."

Fear spiked through his belly. If anything happened to Aria, he'd be even more lost than he already was.

◇◇◇

Edgar Vale walked the smoke-blackened, corpse-littered rooftop of the ruined Drokharis Aerie. The St. Vrain River trickled behind him, and he could smell the wet stink of the bank. That and cinnamon, courtesy of that foreign bitch. There was also a lingering scent of orange blossoms from the Dragonling. He hated the smell more than anything. He kicked at a charbroiled hand and freed one of the magic swords. He'd come to collect them.

He'd known the weakling would come here, along with the pathetic Escort he was collecting. It was late Friday night. Rhaegen Mulk would arrive at midnight, Sunday, for his wedding, which meant Edgar

143

had about forty-eight hours to finish the job. He'd had high hopes the mercenaries could handle the kid. He'd given them swords touched by magic, but he probably should've come himself with the Slayer Blade. It rested on his back, sheathed, warm against his spine.

Edgar collected the three swords and wrapped them up in the crispy Kevlar vest of one of the dead assholes. He'd underestimated his enemy again and again, but next time, he would strike with everything at his disposal. He already had spies in place, checking out the possible locations of other Drokharis Aeries. If the Dragonling showed up there, he wouldn't escape. Not again.

The three doors set in marble animals seemed to vibrate.

While Edgar didn't know the entire story, he did know that Stefan Drokharis had been messing with shit he shouldn't. There were things in the universe that would love to devour all life on Earth; Rhaegen Mulk had mentioned them every now and again. He said sorcery was best left to the ancients. Modern Dragonsouls had the power of technology, well understood and controllable. While Mulk did cast the occasional spell, he focused his energy on his exhalants and his combat skills. He had Magicians to do the spell work, like enchanting swords.

But Stefan Drokharis and his entire family hadn't been slaughtered by otherworldly gods, and they hadn't been killed because of his studies into forbidden magic. No, Rhaegen Mulk had other reasons for wiping out the Ronin Dragonsoul clan.

Edgar counted the bodies, both on the rooftop as well as on the ground. Four were missing. He would find them. He would encourage them to tell the truth and admit their guilt. They had broken their vows to kill the Dragonling and his small Escort, and there was a price they would pay for such betrayal. When a human swore an oath of fealty to a Dragonsoul Prime, it was an ironclad agreement. For money. For power. For life.

They'd run, but Edgar would find them. And kill them. Slowly. Painfully.

First, though, the Dragonling.

Edgar drove away from the ruined Aerie and soon was on I-25, speeding south. On the way back to Mulk's Aerie at the top of the Wells Fargo building in Denver, Edgar knew what he had to do.

When he walked into the penthouse, Mouse was there, like always, drinking wine and dreading the return of her husband. The lights were off. Candlelight gleamed off every bit of polished wood and the slick metal of the furnishings. Denver's lights sparkled as an echo to the candlelight.

"I want you to help me finish the ritual," Edgar said flatly. "I can't wait anymore. I need all the power I can get. And I need it right now."

Mouse laughed. "Why yes, I'd love to help you kill yourself." She was wearing a black dress with no shoes, and her hair was mussed. Petite, blonde, and smiling, she was as gorgeous and sarcastic as ever.

"I won't die. But I will assume my True Form," he said.

More cutting laughter from the beautiful woman. "No, your True Form is you as you are right now—a rather tall primate. And a stinky one, no less. My True Form is that of a dragon. Please don't confuse the two."

"Semantics," he snapped. "The important part for you to understand is that I want the dragon form. I want to become a full Dragonskin, and I want to do it in the next few hours."

"Twenty-four," Mouse mused. "If we start the ritual now, it will take at least twenty-four hours if not more. And it's gonna hurt, you bastard. It's going to make you want to die." She smiled as though enjoying the thought immensely.

"Mulk will do worse to me if I don't kill this Steven Whipp," Edgar said.

"He will," Mouse agreed with a nod. "But that might be better. You don't know what you're asking. You don't know the agony."

Edgar smiled. "I wasn't born special, bitch. But if there's one thing I know, it's pain. I've learned about that all my life, and I've learned to like it. So, you're going to get the brazier, we're gonna go to the rooftop, and you're gonna make it hurt so good."

Mouse paled, closed her eyes, and drained her glass. "For that, I'm going to need a whole lot more wine."

FIFTEEN

A RIA COULDN'T WAKE UP, COULDN'T ESCAPE THE pain in her chest, where she'd taken not one but two rocket-propelled grenades. She wished she had spellcasting skills, but her father had said as the Escort of a Prime, she wouldn't need it. He'd tolerated her combat training but just barely. She'd insisted the world was a dangerous place, and that had struck a chord in him. He'd agreed.

Now, though, she longed for the healing spells she'd watched her father cast with ease, repairing himself, repairing the wounds of his vassals and the other Dragonsouls who served him.

Feverish, sweating, she called out, "Steven, I need you. Please, help me."

Both Steven and Tessa hurried into the bedroom. The barista brushed damp hair out of her face while Steven held her hand. "What is it, Aria? How can we help you?"

"Animus," she whispered. "I need Animus to heal. Kiss me. Both of you. Kiss me." She hated how weak and vulnerable she was. She should've avoided the grenades. She should've fought smarter, better, and she knew this was only the beginning. So far, Mulk had only sent his human vassals at them. It wouldn't be long before they were fighting forces that were far more skilled and powerful.

The thought evaporated as Tessa's kiss landed. The barista's lips were soft and warm on hers, her body equally soft and warm. Aria was mostly muscle, while Tessa had such nice womanly curves. The barista's eyes glowed, and Aria felt fresh energy enter her.

She turned, and Steven kissed her. His smell made her sigh, then moan. It was becoming so familiar to her, so comforting. They were coming together to form a powerful entity, one that might be able to save her. Steven had showered; his hair was still wet, and she brushed her fingers through it.

He was becoming excited again, which was good, as more of the sexual energy would heal her faster.

Aria parted her legs and guided his hands down to her center. She arched her back, her wounds and weakness momentarily forgotten. Instinctively, Steven knew what she needed. He kissed his way down her body until his mouth was on her. And while Tessa kissed her, Steven brought her quickly to a climax of heavenly pleasure.

Then Steven surrendered to his own need. Tessa was stripped in seconds, and the two made love while Aria kissed them both, drinking in the energy of their raw passion. When both cried out, Aria felt herself dragged back into bliss along with them. Animus filled the room and left them all satisfied, breathing hard, and sweating.

Aria had fallen back asleep when the knock came on the door. She heard Steven burst out about "Pizza!" and she found herself alone again on the bed. She curled up into a little ball, knees pulled up against her chest— the way she liked to sleep—but missed the warmth and heat of her friends.

While her body healed using the Animus, her mind began to churn.

She hated her father, Rhakshor Khat, the Dragonlord Prime of Maharashtra in India, as much as she hated Rhaegen Mulk. What they were doing was unfair.

At first, Aria had been thrilled to be in America, despite the predicament she found herself in. She'd had the idea that she would live normally until the very last moment, so she had enrolled as a normal college student at Denver Metropolitan University. She'd pretended to be human, and it had been fun even as her minutes of freedom ticked away. And then Steven had happened, at the very last minute.

But could this Dragonling really rise to be powerful enough to challenge Rhaegen Mulk? So far, this Skinling, Edgar Vale, hadn't thrown any serious forces against them. The mercenaries they'd fought at the St. Vrain Aerie had magic swords, but they'd been normal humans, not Warlings. Once Vale brought to bear the real power of Mulk, there was a good chance none of them would survive.

However, if Steven could prove himself competent, if he could destroy this Edgar Vale, that might make Mulk pause. He might not go at Steven directly.

149

The Dragonling had done well during the fighting. He'd handled the violence, and he'd killed in self-defense. But letting the last mercenary go? He had to get tougher, harder on the inside, if he were going to form a Primacy of his own.

Aria fell into a little fantasy of ruling a Primacy with Steven, together with Tessa, who had a surprising amount of Animus. And her glowing eyes ... something about her was special, without a doubt.

Yes, Steven would kill Edgar Vale, then Rhaegen Mulk, and he would rule the Great Plains Primacy with her at his side.

She thought about telling him everything about her life—her father, Mulk, and the whole tragic situation.

But no. Not yet. He might push her away or he might see her as weak and vulnerable. Aria hated what her father had done to her life. No one must know. Perhaps she could keep all of her secrets to herself. Steven and Tessa would never need to know.

◇◇◇

The next morning, Steven stood with Aria as they checked out of their hotel right before noon. Aria was showered and made-up, looking spectacular in a green dress and sandals with straps up to her knees. Tessa was outside, smoking, which neither he nor Aria liked.

"She says it calms her nerves," Steven said, "but nicotine is a stimulant. It doesn't make sense."

"Very little of what humans do make sense." Aria switched subjects. "You shouldn't have let that mercenary go last night. You should've killed him."

They walked out into the sunlight. It was a warm spring day, not a cloud in the very blue sky.

"I'm not going to be that guy," Steven said with a flippant shrug. "I don't like killing people, and besides, he'll spread the word. No one can mess with us without paying the price."

"You have to be that guy," Aria insisted. "Showing mercy will get you killed. In the world of Dragonsouls, only the strong survive. Any weakness is seen as a liability."

Steven took her arm and stopped them in the middle of the parking lot. Tessa was by the Mercedes, ready to get in.

"What are you getting out of this?" Steven asked. "Why are you helping me?"

Aria lowered her green eyes, fixing him in a steely gaze. She was so beautiful and yet so cold, she could've been an emerald sitting in a freezer. "I have my reasons. Just know, I've chosen you to support because I have no one else. If you die, I die, in a very real sense."

Steven met her glower and didn't look away. They stood there, staring at one another, until Steven had to grin. "You're not going to tell me shit, are you?"

"No," she said simply.

"But I can trust you?" he asked.

She nodded. "You can. I'm trusting you with my life. And you can trust me with yours."

Tessa called out to them, "Come on, guys, I'm dying for some Hostess Donettes and terrible gas-station coffee. It's road trip time!"

Steven had decided to hit the Colorado Springs fire marker on the map. They'd slept through the morning, mostly, though Tessa had wanted one more round of lovin', and it had done wonders for him and

Aria. Their wounds were slowly disappearing, and both had more energy.

They piled into the Mercedes. Despite his size, Steven took the backseat so Tessa could enjoy the comfort of the passenger seat. Aria buckled in and drove off, heading for the nearest gas station. They needed to fuel up before heading down I-25 toward Colorado Springs.

Steven was confused by Tessa. He leaned forward between the seats. "Let me get this straight … you like gas-station coffee and donuts? This from the barista who criticizes Starbucks coffee?"

Tessa sighed like she was having to explain two plus two is four to a graduate student studying mathematics. "First off, it's not donuts, it's *Donettes*, trademarked by the Hostess company, all rights reserved. I prefer the powdered-sugar ones, but I'll settle for chocolate so I don't trash Aria's car."

"Whatever you get is fine," Aria said absently. "I have a cleaning service."

"How rich are you?" Tessa asked.

"Very," Aria answered. "Or at least I will be until midnight on Sunday. So we better use my American Express while we can."

"But you aren't going to tell us much more than that, right?" Steven asked.

"Correct." Aria turned into a Conoco travel complex.

Steven frowned and then kept on trying to figure out Tessa. "So, Donettes, okay. That I can get behind, I guess. But what about wanting terrible coffee? You're a total coffee snob."

"I am," Tessa agreed. "It's like with the Donettes, sometimes you want something that is mass-produced goodness. For me, that's total comfort food. Before my dad died, he'd take me to the gas station close to our house and buy me convenience store junk food on Saturday mornings so my mom could sleep in. I got used to it. As for crappy gas-station coffee, it's made without love, and it's supposed to be bad. I can celebrate the bad. Like a B-movie. You know it's bad, but you can like it anyway. Big-time corporate coffee shops are supposed to be good. Sometimes they are, but not like the small mom-and-pop shops."

"Like the Coffee Clutch," Steven said, putting it all together.

"Yeah, and our baked goods are homemade awesomeness. No Donettes for us."

Aria pulled up to the pump next to a brand-new black Camaro full of young college guys, probably from CSU in Fort Collins.

When Aria got out, they started hooting and hollering at her. The normal douchebag dickhead behavior of assholes traveling in a pack.

It was a whole lotta "Hey, Baby" and "Hot car, but yer hotter" and "You've got the longest legs I've ever seen. They start at the ground and go all the way up to heaven."

Aria ignored them.

Tessa whispered, "What a bunch of jerks. Do they think that does anything other than make us feel uncomfortable?"

Steven felt like he normally did when faced with a bunch of guys who had more money, were better looking, and traveled in a herd. He felt awkward, uncomfortable, and scared.

But then something new trickled into his chest. *Anger*. He pushed the driver's seat forward and stepped out. "You're going to shut the fuck up right fucking now."

He knew what was coming. All four of the guys piled out of the Camaro. "What did you say to us, dickweed?"

"You're going to leave my friend alone," Steven said. His chest tightened as his heart hammered in his ears. It was hard to talk, but he was going to stand up to them.

They were a collection of muscles, trendy jeans, and sunglasses, and of course, one wasn't wearing a shirt. There was always the shirtless guy with the six-pack abs and biceps. Guys like that were never hairy and always blond.

The biggest guy stuck his face into Steven's. "This is America. We can tell a girl she's pretty if we want. And you can't stop us."

Tessa had gotten out of the car. Aria watched from the pump, not saying a word. Both watched him. Steven knew if he really put the hurt on these guys, it might draw the police, and something was going on with Aria. Midnight on Sunday was her deadline. They couldn't waste time in a police station answering questions and filling out reports.

And Steven also knew if he dragoned out in front of them, it might bring the wrong sort of attention. From the little he'd read from the Drokharis Grimoire, Dragonsouls were forbidden to reveal themselves to humans.

"Hey, Tessa," Steven said. "Can you throw me my coat?"

The shirtless guy sniggered, "What a collection. Hottie, Gothie, and dickless here, in a hundred-thousand-dollar car. One of these things doesn't belong."

Tessa tossed Steven the new coat he'd bought. It was warm outside, but he put it on anyway. He then pushed past the big guy and went to the Camaro. "It's a nice car. I can admire it, but I don't have to say shit. Like with my friend. She's gorgeous, but making her feel uncomfortable is fucked up. As fucked up as this is gonna be."

He transformed his left hand into a dragon claw and he changed his left arm into a scaled plate of armor. His coat concealed most of the change. Then he dug three talons into the paint of the front fender. His talons squealed on the metal as he walked down the car, ruining the pristine paint job.

All four guys were on him like stink on a monkey. Steven caught the first punch on his scaled arm, and he decked another. Whirling, he slammed his armored arm into the face of the shirtless guy. Blood poured down his chest.

The big guy, the fourth attacker, drove a fist into Steven's face, but it was nothing compared to being hacked up with a magic sword. Steven was able to catch other punches on his scaled arm. The knuckles and bones of any fist that hit him cracked, leaving the hands broken and useless.

"He has iron in his jacket!" one of the douchebags howled.

Another just screamed, "My hand! My hand!" over and over.

All four of them were on the ground, in pain. Steven walked back to the Mercedes. "So, a little lesson here, treat women with respect and don't go picking fights with people you don't know. Four of you? One of me? You're lucky you're not all dead."

Sirens wailed in the distance. Someone obviously had called the cops.

Back in the Mercedes, Aria was the essence of calm as she slowly maneuvered her car back onto the main street, headed for the I-25 on-ramp.

Tessa started up the chatter, hard-core. "Oh my God, you took them down so fast. And yeah, you're totally right. They outnumbered you, and if you hadn't been, you know, a dragon, they would've hurt you. But next time, I bet they'll think twice. Catcalls, such a waste of fucking breath and time."

"You handled yourself well," Aria said, faint approval shimmering beneath the words. "But pick your battles wisely next time. There was no need for the fight. You did hide your abilities, which is important. Any Dragonsoul who exposes our kind to the humans is immediately sentenced to death."

As they pulled onto the freeway, Steven idly wondered if that was what happened to the Drokharis clan.

Five exits down, Aria pulled off the freeway so Tessa could snag her Donettes and bad gas-station coffee. Steven went for a ton of beef jerky, a bag of ranch-flavored CornNuts, and a bag of Oreos for dessert—assuming you didn't count the Cherry-Coke Slurpee as dessert. Aria got a small coffee and a bag of trail mix that didn't have any M&Ms. It was only a variety of nuts and fruit.

"We know who's eating healthy here," Tessa said. "And I will for lunch … er, dinner, but now, I gots to have me my processed goodness."

Outside, they sat at a picnic table the employees used for cigarette breaks under the shade of a cottonwood. The continuous stream of traffic on I-25 was loud, but the sound quickly became background noise they could ignore.

They ate, and Steven was amazed at how huge his appetite was.

Aria picked up a CornNut. "What is this?"

"Travel food," Steven said. "I only ever get them on road trips. They're originally from South America. You take a corn kernel, soak it for three days, and then deep fry it. Salt it down, ranch it up, and there you have it, a CornNut."

She ate it and smiled. "Deep-fry anything and it's good. Growing up in Mumbai, I would sneak away from my father's Aerie and buy deep-fried peppers from the market. I'd get them in newspaper, and after I finished eating the peppers, I'd read about the strange things humans did."

"We are wacky," Tessa said. "And notice, I'm not smoking. I'm happy, being with you two on this adventure."

Steven realized how great his life had become almost overnight. He was on a road trip with two beautiful women, and he was growing into his powers. Even that short fight with the dickheads had given him a boost of Animus. Yes, killing gave him the biggest dose of the mystical energy, but any fighting helped fuel him.

He couldn't wait to learn more about his past. Again, he thought of what he had read.

The Magic of Ink. The Power of the Pen.

Which one would he find in Colorado Springs?

SIXTEEN

RIDING IN THE BACK SEAT, STEVEN CALLED HIS mom again at work, and like before, her supervisor answered sounding annoyed. She said she would relay the message. Then she hung up on him.

Steven saw a sign for I-70.

"Let's hit DIA really quick," he said to Aria, pointing at the flashing green sign. "I can ask my mom directly what she knows. Her memory is a little off, she's quirky, but it might help us."

"No," Aria said flatly. "We don't have time. What she knows isn't as important as what we might find at the next Drokharis Aerie. You have to grow into your powers, and quickly."

Anger flashed through Steven. "Because of Sunday night. Because of your big secret."

Aria didn't speak. The inside of the Mercedes grew tense. All of the energy had changed, and Steven felt it keenly. His ability to sense the shifts in Animus was growing.

Tessa was in the process of calling in sick to work. Again. She closed her phone case and then asked innocently, "What's happening Sunday night?"

Aria kept her eyes on the road. She sped around a slow-moving rig and then floored it, staying in the left lane. "I don't want to talk about it. Let's stay focused on the task at hand."

"Okkkaaay." Tessa said slowly. "But Steven is worried about his mom. I-70 is coming up. It would only take about forty-five minutes."

"No," Aria repeated. And didn't elaborate.

"Aria," Tessa said gently. "It's us. You can trust us with any secret you have. You don't have to be like this. If we're going to have a relationship together, we need to be honest and open."

"And, uh, this isn't a dictatorship," Steven added, trying to keep the anger out of his voice. "We should vote."

"You humans and your voting." Aria sighed. "I'm driving. I'm the Dragonsoul in control of her powers. And please, let's find the next Drokharis Aerie and not fight. I'm not ready to tell you about me yet. Please."

The exit to I-70 was coming up, and they were quickly approaching it, until a snarl of unexplained traffic slowed them to a crawl. Aria gripped the wheel with both hands, her jaws tight.

"I think we should go to the airport," Steven said. "It would make me feel better, it might throw off anyone following us, and it wouldn't take too long. That's my vote."

"That's my vote as well," Tessa said.

Aria grimaced. "Of course you are going to agree with Steven. Tessa, you can't think clearly around him, obviously. His power is pulling you to him."

"What do you mean?" the barista asked uncertainly.

"Before I kissed him and woke the Animus in him, what did you think of Steven?"

Steven did not like where this was going. And he didn't like Aria's fear, because that was the real problem. She was afraid, and she'd rather fight them than give in.

Tessa waited for a second and then answered. "I liked Steven. He was working hard to get ahead. He was focused."

"But romantically, he meant nothing to you. Is that correct?" A car swerved in front of her, some idiot trying to find a way through the traffic jam. Aria hit the horn and cursed him in a foreign language, probably Hindi or Marathi.

"I'm not sure I want to know," Steven said.

Tessa opened and closed her mouth. "Well, no, Steven was just a nice guy who came in and cleaned at the coffee shop. I didn't think he was interested in me. He never showed it."

"I was shy!" He tried to defend himself from the back seat. Even at their slow crawl, I-70 was coming up. The day had grown warm, and the inside of the car was stifling. Steven felt the fire in his chest and tried to swallow to relieve the tension.

"And then what changed?" Aria asked.

"He stood up to Bud," Tessa murmured. Her face grew pensive, then a little worried. "And he just …

161

changed. He walked right up to me, we talked, we kissed. Then did more. He got that glow."

"What glow?" Aria asked.

"That glow that people get when you like them," Tessa explained. "Sometimes it happens right away, and it's intense and hot, and sometimes you have to kind of grow into the glow. Believe me, I know about this stuff. I've dated a lot. I really like people and sex."

"That glow was the Dragonsoul in him, drawing his Escort. You are under his spell, Tessa. That is what Dragonsoul males do. They gather an Escort, acquire a Hoard, and build an Aerie. The Animus from their Escort gives them energy to prepare for battle with other Primes and to do the work necessary to grow wealthy and powerful."

When Aria finished, neither Steven nor Tessa said a word. Tessa sat scowling, while he found himself lost in thought. "What if I don't want my life to be endlessly fighting for money and Aeries? What if I want something else?"

Aria gunned the engine, swerved through the traffic, pissed off a world of people, and then pulled off to the edge of the freeway where there was a narrow strip of asphalt banked by a concrete wall. "Tell me now, then," she spat. "If you do not want to embrace your destiny, your legacy, tell me now. I've risked everything on you."

Tessa burst out of the car and marched down the highway.

In seconds, their adventure and their friendship had come unraveled. Steven had no idea what had happened, but he could pretty much put the blame on Aria. And yet, she was just acting out of fear. Of what?

He had no idea. He'd watched her fight. She could become a fucking dragon. What could scare her?

"Aria," Steven said, "in my vision, the Dragonsoul said that I should play the game, but my ultimate goal was revolution. I don't know what that means, but I do know that I'm not going to be the Dragonsoul Prime you expect. How can I be? I grew up human, and suddenly I'm facing this whole new reality I never knew existed. I'm different. And in the end, I think that's going to be in our favor."

Tessa continued to walk farther away.

Aria and Steven watched her go.

"I don't know if I can join your Escort if you can't be strong," Aria said quietly.

"Well, that's up to you," Steven said. "I think we should see what the other two Drokharis markers tell us, and then we can all decide. I'll agree to skip the airport. Since my mom is at work, she's probably fine. So we'll go right to Colorado Springs. Now, I'm going to go see about Tessa."

Steven pushed the passenger seat forward and climbed out of the car. He jogged down the freeway, aware of the eyes watching him. Well, if anyone was searching for them, they weren't being very inconspicuous.

"Tessa!" he called to her.

She turned. Tears streaked her cheeks. She had a cigarette in her fingers, but she wasn't smoking it. Then she continued her march forward.

Steven ran up to her. "Tessa, look, I had no idea I had any sort of power over you. I wouldn't have taken advantage of you like that. I've had a crush on you since

163

I met you. This is all a dream come true, but I would never manipulate you."

She whirled back to him. "How can I be sure? Aria was right. Before that night, even after you saved my life, I was all like, 'Steven is nice but not boyfriend material.' Then, suddenly, we're having sex, and I'm thinking about marriage and babies and forever. That's not just the glow. That's fucking voodoo for someone like me. Losing my dad, watching my mom take care of my brother, I take forever seriously. I know what it means." More tears streamed down her face.

What could Steven say to any of that? He considered joking about how he wasn't sure he could get her pregnant since she was human, and he was a Dragonsoul. But he instinctively knew that wouldn't fly, not right then.

The sun beat down on them, and the air was full of smog from the cars creeping along. In the distance were police officers, an ambulance, and a helicopter. There had been an accident, which explained the traffic jam.

The two stood on asphalt, surrounded by concrete, in the middle of a big city that apparently had more than just people, pets, and rodents in it. There were dragons as well.

The enormity of his situation hit him hard. "Tessa, I've been a Dragonsoul for three days. I don't know what forever means. I don't know if I age like a human, if I can get sick, or anything. You've seen me and how I am. You know even if I could cast some kind of love spell on you, I wouldn't know how to do it. I'm the worst Dragonsoul ever."

Tessa laughed a little. "Not the worst. You saved my life over and over. And that just makes it worse. It makes me feel even more for you. Suddenly, I can't trust myself or my instincts. That's scary, right?"

Steven nodded. "I can't imagine it. If you need to take some time away, Aria and I can drop you off at your apartment."

"No, you can't. I'm fridge material, remember?" Tessa crushed the cigarette in her hand and dribbled the paper and tobacco onto the freeway. "I'm in this. I want to be in this with you, with Aria, even though she's having trouble being open with us. It's just …"

"It's just what?" Steven asked.

An anxious expression lit Tessa's eyes. "I want this all to be real. As real as what I'm feeling for you. It's all been so outrageous that when Aria said I might be under a spell, that made so much sense. It explained everything. And then I thought maybe I'd gone crazy." She paused and chewed on her lower lip for a beat. "Am I crazy?" she asked tentatively.

"As crazy as I am," Steven replied softly. "And I can turn into a dragon."

Tessa sniffed through her tears and laughed.

Someone honked. Some asshole screamed, "Kiss her already!"

Steven lifted a hand. "Should we listen to them? If you can't trust some douchebag ordering you to do shit from his car, who can you trust?"

Tessa took his hand. "I'll kiss you because I want to. I have to believe that."

Steven smiled. "And I'm letting you kiss me because you want to. If I thought for a second you didn't have a choice, I'd stop this right away."

Their bodies met, their arms circled each other, and they kissed right there on I-25 in front of God, the Department of Transportation, and everyone.

When their lips finally left one another's, Tessa whispered, "It's going to take me a while to get used to this, you know?"

"Yeah, I know," Steven said. They walked back to the car.

Aria got out and motioned for Steven to take the wheel. "You can drive. I trust you. If you want to get to the airport and see your mother, we'll do it. I'm sorry … for everything."

Steven grinned at her. "I can't speak for Tessa, because she's her own person, but I will take you up on the offer to drive. Me, in a Mercedes, get out of here! It's about as outrageous as me having supernatural powers."

He got behind the wheel, Aria got in back, and Tessa rode shotgun. The barista reached around and the held the Indian woman's hand. "We can be patient, Aria. You'll tell us about yourself in time."

"I will," Aria murmured. "I promise."

Back on the road, they made it past the accident and were back up to seventy-five miles an hour as they rushed toward Colorado Springs. The car, though, really wanted to do ninety. No, make that a hundred. Steven kept having to pull off the pedal. This vehicle was made to go fast, without a doubt. The highways in Germany didn't have speed limits. His father—well, his adopted father—had told him that. Joe Whipp had been all around the world, running schemes, working scams, and throwing cards.

Steven sighed.

"No airport?" Tessa asked.

"No airport," Steven said firmly. "Aria is right. If my mom's safe at work, then I need to focus on figuring out my end of things before I talk to her. She works best if I can give her some cues that might trigger her memory."

They zoomed through Castle Rock, which always made Steven think of Stephen King. He'd read some of the famous author's books, but mostly, he knew about him because so many people always wanted to spell Steven's name with the "ph" and not the "v." Yeah, no.

Aria let out a long breath from the back seat. "I want a CornNut. Or something. I know you want to know the truth of your past, Steven, but I think I want it just as much."

Steven turned on the radio and flipped channels until Aria got frustrated with the constant switching. She jammed herself between the seats and hit the satellite radio option. They settled on the "road trip" channel, which had a good variety.

But Tessa *tsked* her. "Dude, first rule of the road? Driver gets to choose the music. Obviously, you're not American."

"Nor am I human," Aria insisted. "And I would've been fine if he chose a station, but the constant switching? Very annoying. I will add this to things I need to learn about American human life. So, the driver chooses the music and CornNuts are road trip food, and Donettes are a thing."

"A definite thing," Tessa said happily.

Steven enjoyed their banter and then said, "I thought the first rule of the road was no one rides for free. Gas, cash, or ass, which one is it going to be?"

"That's insulting,' Aria said wearily.

"And it's not your car," Tessa added. "Besides, we did pay Aria with ass, and it must've been good because she's still with us."

"Very insulting," Aria repeated.

As they got closer to Colorado Springs, Steven activated the pendant and the fireburst appeared downtown, at a big hotel called the Hotel Antlers.

He turned into the parking garage, frowning all the way. Not only did he not want to scratch the paint on the Mercedes, but he realized the problem they were facing.

"Okay, geniuses," he said, shaking his head. "How are we going to find the right room in a building full of rooms?"

"Ooh, a puzzle," Tessa said smiling. "This is all so *Da Vinci Code*. Could this get any better?" Despite her doubts about her attraction to him and Aria's secrets, by the excitement in her voice, it was clear she was having the time of her life.

SEVENTEEN

THEY PARKED, TESSA GRABBED THE DROKHARIS Grimoire, and they walked into the lobby. The hotel was super fancy, and Steven realized this was his life now. He'd stayed in a few motels, mostly budget places where you didn't want to look too closely at the floor or consider the last time the sheets had been washed. Those crappy rooms had lines of black mold in the bathroom tiles and surly night clerks. His dad had known most of the owners, and so they'd stayed for cheap. The few vacations Joe Whipp had taken his family on were mostly so he could play poker and not feel too guilty for abandoning his family.

A real peach, was Steven's dad.

Aria walked over to get some berry-flavored water in a tall, glass water dispenser. Every man in the place watched her walk, their eyes full of desire. A thrill buzzed through Steven. They wanted her, and he'd seen her naked, had been with her, intimately, though they hadn't had sex yet. Other men checked out Tessa, who

169

hugged the big leather-bound tome to her chest. And there Steven was, with both of them. Was this really his life now?

He couldn't turn on the pendant map, not in public. What were they going to do? Another puzzle.

Aria came back carrying three plastic cups full of the water. They sipped it, considering their next move.

"Any suggestions?" he asked Aria.

"If this was an Aerie, we should go to the penthouse suite. That would be where Drokharis would've set up his residence." She walked over, garnering more stares, to the desk clerk, who immediately got nervous because she was so pretty.

Steven threw Tessa a glance. "Do you know everyone is staring at you?"

The barista rolled her eyes. "No, they're drooling over Aria, clearly. I'm just the interesting sideshow girl." She changed her voice to mimic a dude's. "Look at her, Ms. Emo. Didn't I see her on SuicideGirls.com?"

"That's not true." Steven hooked an arm through hers and they went to the front desk. "You're superhot, Tessa. Like amazing. Believe me. And what's Suicide Girls?"

"I love you for not knowing." She kissed him on the cheek. "I'm okay with them looking, but compared to Aria? Not one in a thousand girls could compete with her."

"There's no competition. You both are equally amazing." He took her hand and squeezed it.

At the desk, the clerk was sputtering, "Ma'am, I assure you, we only have fourteen floors and seven executive suites. All of the suites are currently booked. I really want to help you, but I'm not certain I can."

Aria reached into her purse and withdrew a slender leather wallet. She withdrew five one hundred-dollar bills, wrapped them around her American Express card, and gave them to Jimmy, the desk clerk. "Have all the guests checked into every single one of the penthouse suites? If not, I would like to book one, or at the very least, I'd like to see it for my next trip. My father in India is very wealthy, and he is looking to create business in Colorado. You do take American Express, correct?"

"We do," Jimmy muttered, holding the credit card in one hand and the cash in the other.

"The cash is for you, because I know you really want to help me and my friends," Aria said evenly.

Steven felt stunned. He was watching a bribe happen, right there, in front of him. His dad had talked about greasing people's palms, but this was the first time Steven was seeing it with his own eyes.

Jimmy went from pale to the color of a royal flush. He blinked. "Well, ma'am, not all of our guests have checked in yet. If you were quick, with your, uh, friends, you could see the presidential suite on the fourteenth floor. But you'll come back in say, twenty minutes?"

"A half an hour," Aria said. "My lovers like to take their time. You'll need to change the sheets. And who knows, whoever has the suite booked might cancel."

Tessa pulled Steven close to her and gripped his butt as if to punctuate what Aria had said.

Jimmy blinked and gasped like a fish out of water. "I, uh, will let housekeeping know. And perhaps, I can … I will do … maybe … yes."

171

Aria patted the desk. "I'm not sure what that means, but can I have the key card please?"

Jimmy got them set up, and they were off into the elevator.

Steven's head was still whirling at what had just happened. Aria hadn't just stunned Jimmy the desk clerk, but him as well. And Tessa had played along, but she wasn't giggling or laughing. It was just like another day in the life of a Dragonsoul. On the fourteenth floor, the elevator car dinged, and Aria led the way out. She swiped a card, and the two big doors opened automatically, showing them a suite even bigger than the one they had stayed in the night before.

"So this is what money gets you, huh?" Steven asked, mystified.

"Just one of the perks of that whole 'acquire a Hoard' part being a Dragonsoul," Tessa said. The suite had two massive rooms on either wing of the central living area, which contained a view of the Rockies, a kitchen, and a sunken floor. The bathroom was large enough for a jacuzzi in the middle—burbling and hot.

"This is how the other one percent lives," Steven said. "Too bad we can't stay here tonight."

"Perhaps we can. But for now, we need to find the Drokharis Aerie." Aria stood in front of the bookcase searching for a hidden lever, but this place didn't have the same sconce in the wall.

They all scoured the room, searching for a way up, but there were other rooms on the fourteenth floor. What were the chances the suite they were in led to a secret loft? Not good.

Tessa pulled out her phone and started scrolling through screens. "I'll do a quick history check. Built in 1964, and yeah, fourteen floors. Officially."

Steven lifted the pendant out of his shirt. The topaz wasn't glowing nor was it warm. It was just a normal gem at that moment.

Aria went to the window and slid it open. There wasn't a screen. "We are very lucky," she said. "Normally, this would be sealed. But I have an idea. It was clear Jimmy had no idea about any kind of hidden floor or secret loft. So, I believe it remains hidden from human eyes. Luckily, I'm not human."

She kicked off her shoes, dropped her purse, and swept off her dress and underwear. Standing naked, she backed up and dove out the window. In midair, she whirled and changed. For the first time, Steven was watching her become her True Form, the next level of transformation. Her body shimmered, growing brighter as her skin became scaled. Wings erupted from her back, her arms and legs grew longer, and her fingernails and toenails became gleaming obsidian talons.

Steven and Tessa rushed to the window.

"Are you seeing this?" he asked, unable to contain the awe in his voice.

"I saw her jump out the window," she said. "But then she disappeared. Gone." She snapped her fingers. "*Poof*, just like that."

But Steven knew better. She might've vanished from the eyes of humanity, but like Aria, Steven was no human. The crimson dragon soared around the building, once, twice. Watching her slide through the air was beautiful. It was like watching a dancer completely in control of her movements. Then Aria whirled and flew back toward them. At the last moment, she went from dragon to human and nimbly soared through the open window. She rolled off her momentum and landed on her feet. The sweet scent of cinnamon hit them in a wave.

Aria smiled. "There are windows above us, hidden from undiscerning eyes, but I can see them. There is a room, and I think I saw a landing, but it might be closed to me. I think warding magic is in place here, which is why we are having trouble. If this Stefan Drokharis studied powerful portal magic, he might've known a spell to keep outsiders away. If you can open a door, you can close it as well, correct?"

"We should be careful," Tessa said. "Remember, there were those spec-ops guys outside the St. Vrain Aerie. They might be here as well."

Aria nodded. "Yes, that is possible. Steven, I will change into my True Form, and you can ride on my back. While we are connected, you should remain invisible to human eyes."

"That's right," Tessa said. "That's why I couldn't see you. Can all Dragonsouls hide themselves?"

"Yes, it's very important—otherwise there would be a million videos of dragons on YouTube. Are you ready, Steven?" Aria asked.

Steven gulped. He wasn't exactly scared of heights, but damn, they were fourteen floors up and there was nothing but thin air between him and the concrete hundreds of feet below.

Aria went back to the edge, hopped out nonchalantly, and then it was his turn. She was a long slender form with wide leathery wings under him. He steeled himself. Now wasn't the time for fear. It was time for bravery.

He stood on the windowsill in his new athletic shoes. And then, he jumped off. Aria swirled around herself, long head arcing, long tail whipping, wings sprouting, and then she was flying up to meet him. Wind whistled cold and insistent in his ears. The adrenaline of falling made every detail stand out, especially the strong spicy scent of the dragon wafting up.

He plummeted, she soared up. They met in midair. His left hand found her neck, and he used it to guide himself onto her back as Aria adjusted her flight. In seconds he was sitting on her back like he'd been born on Pern.

He was riding a dragon. Him, Steven Whipp, riding a dragon like he was a Targaryen in Essos. She circled the building, climbing steadily higher. Their speed and the general temperature of the air chilled him, and his fingers were numb in seconds.

He wished he could talk with her while they flew, but he didn't know it was possible until she growled in a voice that vibrated through his entire body. "Steven, there, do you see?" It was like Smaug from *The Hobbit* being voiced by Scarlett Johansson.

Steven had to yell over the wind. "Yes, I see it."

There was a fifteenth floor, but it was hidden in the architecture, an ingenious floor added at the very top of the hotel under the Hilton sign. And it was completely hidden from human eyes because Stefan Drokharis had loaded the place down with spells. Steven could see the shimmering of magic even at a distance.

The pendant flashed on his chest. From inside the hidden floor, a brilliant golden radiance burst through the windows. A rocky panel slid out from the front of the secret room, creating a landing ledge. Aria flew over to the platform and touched down light as a feather, letting Steven slide off her body. It was farther than he thought,

175

and he hit the stone floor with a thump, falling onto his butt. Aria shifted into her human form, still naked, and offered a hand to help him up.

He grinned. "In middle school, I had a friend who used to dip toothpicks in cinnamon oil. Every time I smell you, I think of Corwin Kristofferson."

Aria didn't pause. She was all business. "I'll go get Tessa." Then she was gone, turned back into a dragon, flying around to the other side of the building.

Steven walked across the landing platform. The floor had windows now, which had appeared on the outside, but he didn't see a clear way in. It was all just black stone. The pendant flashed, and a wall slid downward while candles flickered on inside the room.

Though long abandoned and completely covered in dust, it was a plush, comfortable parlor, not wrecked like the one in the St. Vrain Aerie. The place smelled like beeswax candles and the dusty ghost of ancient incense. Thick red couches sat on a plush Persian carpet covering a hardwood floor. Gilded hand-carved clocks decorated the room, but their pendulums had long ago stopped moving. Paintings, covered in a layer of gray, hung on the walls. Their frames were baroque wonders, treasures in and of themselves. Various tables were covered with expensive looking knickknacks: a large number of jeweled daggers, a silver mirror, a wooden box full of gold coins—all just lying right there out in the open.

"Acquire a Hoard," Steven whispered, greedy hunger blooming in his belly. Under a lamp sat what might have been a Faberge egg. It had the jewels for it. If that really was a Faberge egg, he could sell it for millions of dollars. Which made him immediately wonder what the paintings on the wall might've cost. He now regretted not taking a single art history class. Could one of the paintings be a lost masterpiece by Michelangelo, Donatello, or one of the other ninja turtles?

He chuckled at himself. He knew far more about popular culture than he did about real culture.

He walked deeper into the room. Tomes filled bookcases, but these hadn't been ruined like the ones in the other Aerie. The whole floor was a mixture of rooms, all connected. He wandered into the master bedroom, which was bigger than the entire Marriott suite where they had crashed the night before.

A massive king-size canopy bed, covered by thick comforters, seemed small compared to the size of the room. As he neared the bed, a roaring fire burst to life in the fireplace, painting the room in a warm glow. In the bathroom, the fixtures were from before he was born, but it wasn't like the place was from the sixties. No, it was like a penthouse from the nineteenth century. Back in the main room, he traced a finger through the dust on a grand piano. A fire erupted in this room as well, orange tongues licking at thick logs.

Did the magic know he was chilly?

It seemed so. And those candles, they had lit themselves.

Then Steven noticed what looked like a pirate's chest under a swath of velvet. He'd thought it was a coffee table, but no, it was definitely a big ironclad chest.

Tessa and Aria walked inside a moment later, one fully clothed, the other as naked as a jaybird. The minute Tessa, holding the spell book, drew near, the keyhole in the chest glowed. Steven tried to lift the lid, but it was locked, solidly shut.

She lifted the Drokharis Grimoire. "It's heating up. I can feel it. And wow, this place is like a French palace threw up on itself." She took a long look around, lips pursed. "Talk about old-school," she finished.

Steven nodded. "I didn't light the candles or the fire. They just turned on by themselves. There's a bed …"

He wasn't sure why he said it, but Tessa *tsked* him. "Not now, you horn dog. I'm guessing we have to figure out how to open the chest."

Aria removed the velvet covering and threw it behind her with the flick of a wrist. It wasn't just velvet, it was a flag, scarlet and golden. Steven remembered seeing a picture of a similar flag the Spanish flew hundreds of years ago when their ships had been destroyed by the British. The entire strange floor was full of such artifacts. Just how old were those sabers crossed on the wall? Who had used them?

Steven tried to open the chest again. Locked. It was clear, though, whatever they'd come for—either the *Power of the Pen* or the *Magic of Ink*—was inside that rusty, mysterious locked chest. The keyhole continued to glow.

"Okay," he said. "Where do you think the key is?"

EIGHTEEN

T RYING TO FIND A SINGLE KEY IN THE TREASURE trove of relics, artifacts, and antiques seemed like an overwhelming task. Magic would be involved, Steven had no doubt. Too bad they couldn't use a jeweled dagger to open the chest. There were a ton of those lying around. An arsenal of them.

A chill wind blew through the wide-open front of the building and flipped up a corner of the Persian carpet covering the hardwood floor. Most of the wood was polished maple planks, but under the rug, there was a design.

Steven left Tessa and Aria standing by the chest in front of the sofas. He grabbed the edge of the rug and pulled it back. A dark polished starburst was inset into the pale wood. Yanking back farther on the rug, another star was revealed. An idea formed in his head. It was a long shot, but it was worth trying.

"Help me move the couches and the rug," Steven said.

"Wow, an adventure that involves moving furniture," Tessa said, smiling. "This sounds like a union job. I need two fifteen-minute breaks, a half hour lunch, and if I hurt my back, you better have workman's comp."

Aria shrugged. "I don't know what any of that means. Stand back, Tessa." The woman transformed into her Homo Draconis form, a slender cinnamon-scarlet dragon humanoid.

Steven nodded, understanding what she was thinking. He undressed. Accessing his Animus, he focused on his own transformation, and soon his black-scaled body matched hers. They were so much stronger than humans, and they were easily able to lift the sofas and move them back. The chest was huge and full of something wickedly heavy, but their draconian muscles were able to do the job with utter ease.

Tessa helped by moving the small fragile items off the end tables: the box of coins, the jeweled daggers, the silver mirror, and everything else. Meanwhile, the pair of Dragonsouls carefully rolled up the fancy carpet and carted it off to the side. Tessa went back and forth, moving bundles of swords, old books, scrolls, and a wide collection of random antiquities—any one of which might've been worth a fortune.

Finally, the beautiful wooden floor was revealed in all its glory: starbursts of the Draco constellation, rendered in gorgeous dark cherry wood, stretched across the light wood floor. The long line of stars ended in the uneven sides of a square-like shape, which was the head.

Tessa cocked her head. "Well, if we ever needed money, we could start a moving company. We'd have to put in a nondisclosure agreement, though. People would need to swear they never saw big lizard people moving their piano. Which brings up a question. How come I can

see you now, Aria, and I couldn't see you when you were flying around?"

Aria shifted back into human form. "Dragonsouls have a variety of supernatural abilities to keep themselves hidden. Simple concealment spells to hide our shapes from humans as well as a Mind Wipe spell we can cast to make everyone forget what they saw. We have to remain hidden. I'm letting you see me. When I flew around the hotel, I had to block all human eyes from discerning me."

"Gotcha," Tessa said.

Steven, though, wondered why secrecy was so important. He figured it was for the normal reasons: avoid the law, avoid being studied by government agencies, avoid the paparazzi and notoriety that would bring. However, there were other reasons, he knew it. And it was pretty remarkable the Dragonsouls had remained hidden for centuries. He shifted back to being human, and he pulled on his underwear and pants.

Aria rolled her eyes.

"Why so modest?" Tessa asked. "It's not like we haven't seen you naked."

Steven felt his face heat up. "I don't want to try and figure out my past with my junk hanging out. Clothes make me feel better, okay?"

"You'll get over that," Aria said. "Now, we see the Draco constellation on the floor. How can that help us open the chest?"

"Not sure," Steven said, staring at the pattern in the floor, then glancing at the chest. "Hand me the grimoire, Tessa."

She placed it in his hands. He walked the line of inlaid starbursts, but nothing happened. At least, nothing happened until he got to the boxy head of the dragon. When he walked into the square, his pendant glowed, which didn't surprise him, but it also seemed to attract the dust motes floating in the air. Moving the furniture around and rolling up the carpet had beaten up a cloud of dust.

The motes blazed in the light, each one painted a golden color, and they were forming something.

A key shape.

Curious, Steven walked away from the squarish dragon head. The pendant quickly dimmed, and the dust mote key vanished in a blink. He grinned. "I get it. Help me with the chest."

He put the grimoire down, and they tried to lug the chest over as humans, but it was too heavy. From inside it, they felt something slosh around. What the hell? Finally, Steven had to drop his pants again and turn into a Homo Draconis. In his middle form, he and Aria were able to lug the chest over to the square engraved into the floor.

He adjusted the chest so that the lock lay above the square. Then they shifted back into humans. And yes, he pulled his pants on *again*.

"You're going to have to get over your modesty," Aria said with a slight look of disgust on her face.

"Yeah, I'm sure that will happen eventually, but not yet," Steven said, then cleared his throat. He lifted the pendant off his head, held the topaz over the square, and watched as the golden dust key coalesced right before his eyes. As he lowered the pendant, the key went with it, dripping dust from the movement in swirls. Would this really work? The key didn't seem so solid, but it did glow with unearthly power. Carefully, he guided the dust key into the lock and turned it.

The rollers in the lock clicked, and the latch sprang open.

"That is so cool!" Tessa burst out. "Steven, you're a genius!"

Steven blushed at her praise. He slipped the pendant back around his neck. Then he lifted the lid of the chest, and the rusted hinges squeaked in protest. Whatever was inside was dark and liquid, but how could that be? It wasn't like the wooden slats could be waterproof, and yet, it seemed the chest was full of ink.

Steven dipped a finger into the goopy black, and the result was immediate. The dark liquid shot up his hands, wound around his arm like a python, then hit his shoulder, only to spread down his chest and gush up his neck. He had jeans on but that was it. In seconds, the ink covered every bit of him, pants or not.

The pendant exploded in a supernova of light, which flung the ink away until it formed a cloud of black that swirled through the room, carried by some mystical wind.

The light bursting from the square of topaz abruptly turned into a prismatic spray of rainbow. The room seemed to explode with multicolored light, and all the while that cloud of ink continued to swirl and dance. Steven glanced down into the chest, but it was empty.

"Holy fuck me!" Tessa spat, her eyes wide. She'd fallen to her knees and stared in wonder at the twirling ink cloud. Her voice could hardly be heard in the screaming breeze.

Aria had inched her naked self to the landing platform, and it looked like she might bolt at any minute. Even she seemed mystified by what was happening, which probably wasn't good.

"Aria!" Steven called to her. "What's happening?"

"I don't know," she yelled in a frightened voice. "I've not seen this kind of magic. Like I said, with the rise of technology, Dragonsouls have used less and less sorcery. This is something … beyond me."

Like a shadowy demon, the mist of ink circled the room, exploring nooks and crannies, sweeping around Aria, checking out Tessa, and then returning to form a cyclone of darkness with Steven directly at its center. In moments he couldn't see anything except churning black, and all he could hear was the thunderous roar of the unnatural tornado.

Then a voice shouted, echoing and reverberating in his ears, "No, Persephone, run! I have it set up. I knew this would happen!"

A figure formed in the ink, made of black dots of the murky liquid, a strong, powerful man with a heavily bearded face. Steven recognized it as the red Dragonsoul from his vision. But who was he?

A woman's voice answered the first. "Stefan, they're coming in. The book, is it with the stars?" The ink coalesced into a woman—the same woman who had been sketched in the Drokharis Grimoire. That was Persephone Drokharis, and she was speaking to Stefan Drokharis.

"The Gift of the Book, Magic of Ink, and the Power of the Pen, yes!" Stefan said. He spun, and the ink slipped off him for a second before being sucked back into his form. "I've hidden them. He'll know about us.

On the eve of his third decade, our son will discover who he truly is."

Stefan Drokharis transformed into a dragon just as another dragon hit him. They slashed at each other with their talons, rising into the air. The scope of the ink tableau changed, grew smaller, as a tower rose from the floor, and cottonwood trees resolved into view. It was the St. Vrain Aerie—Steven recognized the four animal heads on the tower, the four doors. The two dragons continued to rise into the sky, tumbling, swooping, battling. A second and third dragon joined the first, desperate to kill Stefan.

Stefan tumbled from the air, slamming through cottonwood branches like a careening freight train of muscle and scale. Down, battered, though still alive. Inky flames exploded among the ink cottonwoods as more dragons appeared. There were five of the great beasts now, all attacking Stefan in concert. All breathed different things—acid, lightning, some kind of strange white fire—which struck the beleaguered Stefan Drokharis.

The woman, Persephone, hadn't shrunk, and remained as tall as Steven. Like him, she stood above the miniature view of the dragon battle as her husband was burned, electrocuted, struck by acid, and exposed to a cloud of poison gas.

The woman made of ink reached out to Steven. "My child, my nameless love, we had to hide you away and trust the gambler's luck would hold out. We sacrificed all for you, because Rhaegen Mulk would've killed you. Your way will be impossible, for you will think you are human, but you are so much more. My husband, your father, promised he could cross even the threshold of death to speak to you, but that this would be my only time to tell you how much I love you, how great you will be, how lucky I feel to have held you in my arms, if only for a brief time."

Tears of ink spilled from the eyes of the liquid woman.

Steven felt his own eyes fill. He reached out, and the ink woman's hands spilled over his.

Her voice broke through the crashing winds and the din of the dragon battle under them, however small. "My nameless child, on the eve of your third decade, your training will begin, and if we are all fortunate, Rhaegen Mulk will not have discovered you. For if he knows your true nature, he will come for you, kill you, lest you threaten his supremacy. If we are indeed lucky, he won't know about you. Less lucky? He will think you are the offspring of some Dragonsoul Ronin and not much of a threat. But if he guesses you are the last of the Drokharises, he will spare no expense in your destruction. Like so much of the lives of Dragonsouls, secrecy is key."

She glanced behind her, and Steven knew her time was growing short.

The five dragons—one of them surely Rhaegen Mulk—had pinned Stefan to the ground and were ripping into his charred, reptilian flesh with their long snouts.

"Even now, your father is being murdered by Rhaegen Mulk and his vassals. Know that he loved you. Know that I love you. We will both die, casualties in this war, but that does not diminish our love for you. You are now the last scion of the Drokharis family. While your fate will be difficult, your destiny is full of awe and wonder. You will change things for all time, my nameless child. You are the last of us. And you will be mighty."

Another frightened glance. "I must flee. I love you. I long for you to see this ... They are coming. Rhaegen Mulk has murdered everyone else, and now he is coming for me."

The ink tableau spilled away and shifted into another scene, this one of various murders. It was like a movie montage, as scene followed scene. It was all war and butchery.

Two women, both armed with swords, fought an endless stream of foes, some armed with medieval weapons, others with guns ...

Mixed in with humans were what appeared to be shape-shifters, werewolves, werebears, and weretigers. Even a wereboar or two. Wave after wave of foes died at the end of the flashing swords until a dragon appeared above. The two swordswomen were then engulfed in the flames of a dragon, roasted alive.

In another scene, a dragon swooped down and a man with a bow fired an arrow, radiating magic, into her chest. The shaft hit home in her heart, and the dragon fell to splash into a lake of ink ...

Another shift, and men with automatic weapons gunned down a dozen women fleeing. Were there children with the women? Steven didn't want to see that. He had to glance away.

The scene shifted to show two dragons fighting, back-to-back, unleashing their deadly breath, ripping off the heads of attacking humans, Homo Draconi, and Dragonsouls alike. The pair were holding their own until a man rushed forward with a familiar weapon. The

Slayer Blade. The man, flanked by soldiers with assault rifles, cut through the leg of one of the heroic dragons, dodged another blast, and slashed into the belly of the other.

Behind him, a woman raised her arms and inky missiles shot from her hands. The missiles flashed with a dark magic and levelled both of the dragons. They shifted back into women, dead women.

Steven's heart hurt from watching all the murders.

The scene changed again …

A couple, Stefan and Persephone, were on a dark street made of the dark fluid, with tall buildings rising around them. In her arms, the woman held a baby wrapped in a blanket. The family was approached by a man Steven knew instantly by his walk alone. No one walked like Joe Whipp, part slouch and part strut. He was wearing his long overcoat, which he loved, since he thought it made him look like a hard-boiled PI from a 1940's noire novel. Both mother and father kissed the bundle and then placed it reverently into Joe Whipp's arms.

Steven's adopted father's voice filled the room. "I'll keep the little guy safe, Stefan. You know me, I'm lucky, and I don't expect my luck to run out anytime soon."

Spoken like a true gambler.

Stefan Drokharis stood up straight, trying to be brave while he held his weeping wife, who had succumbed to her sorrow.

The tableau was wiped way and a final, tragic scene began to play. Persephone, alone and afraid, stood in the round living room of the St. Vrain tower that had been smashed apart. Now, Steven knew what had caused the damage. Five heavily armored men wielding swords blasted through the door and charged directly at her. The biggest one, a long-haired man with a scraggly moustache, drove his sword through her chest with brutal contempt.

Steven realized he was watching his mother die. Rhaegen Mulk had killed her, twenty years before, after slaughtering Stefan Drokharis' Escort and vassals.

The minute her heart was pierced, the ink was blasted apart. The black liquid roared around the room once more. The grimoire flipped open, and every bit of ink was sucked inside the pages. In seconds, the unnatural obsidian cloud was gone and so was the shrieking breeze.

The book slammed shut. Everything went silent.

Steven covered his face with his hands. He didn't cry. He was too full of fury, wonder, and loss.

NINETEEN

ARIA STOOD NEAR THE LANDING PLATFORM AT THE top of the Hilton Antlers hotel in Colorado Springs, which was possibly the main Aerie of the Drokharis clan now long dead. Rhaegen Mulk had slaughtered them all, with the help of his vassals: human mercenaries, Morphlings, Warlings, Magicians, and other Dragonsouls. He'd taken down Stefan Drokharis and had murdered his wife in the St. Vrain tower. It had been difficult to watch, but she wondered at Steven's reaction. He stood, hands over his face, clearly upset.

Again, doubt filled her. Could this Dragonling really hope to ever match the awesome might of Rhaegen Mulk and his brutal, bloodthirsty Primacy?

Tessa, sobbing, went and held Steven. But the Dragonling stepped away from her. "This is bullshit, total bullshit. That fucker killed them, killed them all, but why? Why?" He stormed around the room, and Aria watched as scales erupted across his skin. He was changing into his Homo Draconis form, then back into human, and she approved of his fury. He needed to vent, to *rage*, and he needed to use that primal fury to fulfill his destiny. It was the only way.

Steven approached her, and his eyes were the slits of an angry serpent. "Aria, you saw that, you saw what Rhaegen Mulk did. You should know why!"

Aria stepped up to him. "I know only a little. But I must confess, I'm as surprised as you are by the sheer savagery. Dragonsoul Primes must kill to protect their Primacy from threats. I would assume Mulk saw your father as a threat, and he had him eliminated. Your parents knew what was coming, and they gambled that having a human raise you for the first two decades of your life would keep you safe. Their gambit paid off. Otherwise, you would've been slaughtered along with the rest of the Drokharis clan."

"The eve of your third decade ..." Tessa said somberly. "Your twentieth birthday, starting your third decade alive. That was when the guy broke in and tried to kill you."

"Your father's luck held out," Aria whispered. "If Mulk knew about you, he would've come himself to kill you, and nothing would've stopped him. Your parents must've kept your birth a secret. Only your father's skill as a sorcerer could've accomplished that. You come from a powerful bloodline."

"A scion, me," Steven said. He was calming down, getting control over his shape. He went to the book and lifted it. He closed the chest and laid the tome on top. Leafing through the pages, he muttered, "There's more now. More about me, lessons for me, stuff on controlling my powers. I have all this Animus, but it's been leaking away because I don't know how to harness it. It's like gaming for hours, getting a buttload of experience points, but not knowing how to invest those points. Dammit, that sucks so hard."

"Like not saving when your PC crashes and having to redo stuff," Tessa agreed.

"And we don't have much time," Steven said. "But, Aria, how are you connected with this? The time for secrets is over."

Aria felt a cold sweat break across her skin. An anxious feeling boiled in her stomach. "Who I am doesn't matter. I'm not connected to what happened to your family, Steven, you have to believe me."

Steven approached her, as did Tessa, both of them staring intently at her.

Aria was naked and felt it—and not just in the flesh. She felt that her secrets were on the verge of being laid bare, and she chafed at the notion. She maneuvered around them, took the Spanish flag, and draped it around herself. "Sunday at midnight," she said over one shoulder. "That's when I'm supposed to marry Rhaegen Mulk. My father, in India, he is very traditional. Arranged marriages still happen there, even today, among humans and Dragonsouls alike. I've only met Mulk once ... He is arrogant, strong, cruel."

Aria squeezed her eyes shut, holding back a lifetime of unshed tears. Her wretched engagement made her look so weak. Would Steven even want her anymore as a part of his Escort now that he saw how vulnerable she was? How broken she was?

"Why at midnight?" Tessa asked.

Aria answered. "Dragonsouls marry in the dark of night, on a Sunday, when the world is hushed, and humans are sleeping. With their holy day finished, we have our own."

Steven's face seemed like a mask. "I still don't get this connection between Denver and India," he said. "I just don't understand."

Aria idly tucked a strand of hair behind an ear and tried to explain. "While most of the portals have been closed between continents, a few have survived, but their existence is a closely guarded secret. One portal links Mumbai and Denver, and so the Primes, Mulk and my father, have been scheming to trade resources and information, using spies to help one another. Both have grand aspirations of conquest on their respective continents. What better way to get what they want than through a secret alliance between cities that seemingly have nothing in common?"

She let the question hang in the air. When no one said anything, she continued with the hard truth. "But first, there had to be a show of faith. I was an offering to Mulk." She clutched the flag tighter around her. "Nothing more," she finished.

Tessa, being a clever woman, put together the pieces. "You went to Steven to help you, is that right? Somehow, you sensed what he truly was, and you thought he could help you fight Mulk so you wouldn't have to marry him."

Aria nodded. She opened her eyes and stepped away from them. "Yes, but I didn't know Steven was the last of the Drokharis clan. I didn't know anything, only that he was a Dragonsoul who didn't understand what he truly was. A truly strange thing in a world with so few true male Dragonsouls." She swallowed hard, trying to alleviate some of the fear she was feeling. "Now, it's only a matter of time before Mulk discovers who you are, Steven. Then, nothing will stop him."

"I don't know about that," he said. "He sent a Skinling to take me out. This Edgar Vale douchebag. I think my father's protection spells are keeping my true identity hidden. That gives us some time, but not much." He exhaled a shaky breath. "For now, let me read more. Up here, I think we're relatively safe, and if I can learn more about how to channel Animus, next time Edgar comes, we can put him down like a rabid dog."

He grinned. "At least I'm on my way to becoming a Dragonsoul. I have the start of a Hoard." He waved a hand around. "This is all my junk now, right?"

Aria nodded. "It is. You own this Aerie and everything in it."

Tessa picked up a fistful of gold coins. "Yes! Lunch is on Steven!"

"Yeah, but it's not like we can go to Subway and get sandwiches in return for gold coins. We're going to need to find buyers for all this stuff. Problem there, if suddenly pieces from the Drokharis Hoard show up on the open market, Mulk is probably smart enough to notice and put two and two together."

A thrill soothed some of Aria's fear. Steven was as clever as Tessa. "I will continue to finance us. Monday, however, when my father learns I did not marry Mulk, I will be penniless."

Steven walked over to her and took her hand in his. "You're not marrying that murderous dick. I'll die before I see that happen."

"You can't fight him, and neither can I." A tear slipped down her cheek, and she hated herself for it. She reached up with an angry fist and obliterated the traitorous tear.

"We'll see about that," Steven said. "But first, I need to become powerful enough to take care of Edgar Vale. Then I'll set my sights on Rhaegen Mulk. I'll read, you guys can rustle up some food, and then we'll drive to the last marker on our map. Okay?"

Aria stepped into the safety of Steven's arms. The flag fell away. The heat of his body and the touch of his skin sealed the deal. She would give herself to him and not look back. He was the last scion of the Drokharis clan. He could protect her when no one else could. She knew it, and she reveled in her decision.

She gave him a long, slow, sweet kiss.

Their passion made Aria dizzy, and she laughed at herself.

He broke the kiss. "I'm serious about the food," he said. "I'm starving. It's not like there's room service for the hidden suite of a Dragonsoul." He grinned. "At least, I don't think so. But there must be human access to the hotel, somewhere."

"Another secret passageway! Cool!" Tessa burst out.

Aria smiled widely and let herself love not only Steven but the clever barista who had secrets of her own, so deep even she didn't know what they were.

◊◊◊

While Tessa and Aria searched for a secret passageway down to the hotel proper, Steven settled down on a couch with the book. They'd put the room back together and he glanced around, somewhat in awe that all the treasures in this place were his now. He'd always wanted to own a real sword, and now he had bundles of them. He thought one of the pictures was a Rembrandt—his life was definitely about to change. No more college classes for him; instead, he'd have to learn about the world of high-end art auctions.

He thought about what he'd be doing on a normal Saturday afternoon. Generally, he'd be studying his ass off before going to his cleaning job. Weekends were for office complexes, lots of toilets, and lots of vacuuming.

His boss thought he was sick. Steven found himself rich instead, and reading a magic book written by his dead father. His real father. It made him grin. He didn't have any of Joe Whipp's blood in him, and that was worth any sort of violence and drama. He was the son of Stefan Drokharis, a Dragonsoul and a powerful Magician. Or maybe a sorcerer, he wasn't sure—not that it really mattered.

"Steven Drokharis." He smiled as he said his real name out loud. He closed his eyes. It felt right. He would change his name legally, once he faced down Rhaegen Mulk and put an end to that asshole's evil. But to do that, he had to study. His days as a college student were probably over, but if his time in school had taught him anything, it was how to study. He didn't skip to the new stuff. Instead, he reviewed what he had read before, skimming pages, noting sketches, and rereading the dragon-shaped skill tree.

He paused. More of the branches had been filled out, and he saw the first three abilities of each. As before, the skills were listed beneath the image:

Transformatio (Head of the Dragon)

- Partial Transformation
- Homo Draconis
- True Form (Dragonsoul)

Pugna (Tail of the Dragon)

- DarkArmor
- DragonStrength
- SerpentGrace

Exhalants (Left Wing of the Dragon)

- Inferno
- ElectroArc
- Toxicity

Veneficium (Right Wing of the Dragon)

- *Magica Defensio*

- *Magica Cura*
- *Magica Impetim*
-

He so wanted to try True Form and become a full dragon, but he wasn't sure he was ready for that yet. The combat skills were interesting. He'd managed to enhance his armor somehow, but if he could become stronger and faster, that would be useful. Checking out the wings of the skill tree, he recalled the ink tableaus and what they had shown him. The sorceress had used magic missiles to kill the two Dragonsouls who had been a part of the Drokharis clan. That had to be *Magica Impetim*—Attack Magic. And the Toxicity exhalant? That had helped kill his real father when the five other dragons had teamed up on him.

He thought about the shape-shifters that had been Rhaegen Mulk's army as well as the numerous warriors he'd seen, strong and fast, skilled in a variety of weapons. And the sorcerers hadn't seemed like Dragonsouls, so how did that work?

From another room, Tessa gave out a woot of triumph. "What has two thumbs and finds all of the secret passageways? This girl!"

Both of the women came out of a hallway covered in dust. "We found a way down to the fourteenth floor. What would you like to eat?" Aria was still naked.

Steven realized he was staring a bit too long and getting turned on. "I'll eat literally anything."

"No time for that, big boy," Tessa teased. "I have plans on what we can get. And yes, Aria should put on some clothes. I'm getting a bit distracted myself." She playfully smacked Aria on her bare butt.

Aria grabbed Tessa's hand and pulled her into a kiss. Lust and hunger played around in Steven's belly until hunger won out. "Guys, uh, stop that. I have to concentrate."

Tessa cupped one of Aria's little breasts. "Clearly, we're not guys. But we'll behave."

Aria jogged forward and said to Tessa, "I'll meet you in the fourteenth-floor suite. I'll gather my clothes." She hit the landing and transformed into her scarlet dragon form and flew off.

Tessa came and kissed Steven's cheek. "See you soon, Steven. Study hard!" She then disappeared down the hallway to whatever kind of secret passageway she'd found.

Steven returned to the book and found the pages that had been blank now were filled with writing. The ink from the chest had done its job.

There were instructions on how to focus his mind to channel the Animus into his various abilities. It wasn't just the words, it was the feel of the book in his hands, the smell of the dust in the pages, and the texture of the leather cover. The pain in his chest, that horrible heartburn, lessened, and he felt himself relax.

And that was the key: to relax the mind and to surrender to the thriving energy swirling inside him. He couldn't fight the hot pain in his chest, but he could *lean* into it and accept it as a part of him. As he did, it was almost as if his cells melted into the inferno of power. Yes, he could see how he could change his shape now. He'd subconsciously been able to access Partial Transformation, Homo Draconis, and DarkArmor through urgent need and instinct, but now he could unlock new abilities by choice.

Spells were still beyond him, as were the Exhalants, but his body? That he had control over.

Now, when he imagined the skill tree, it was in complete focus, and he could decide on where to channel the Animus he'd collected. In some ways it was very much like playing a video game, just as he'd imagined all along. He gained Animus from battle and sex, but he also gained some sort of intangible experience which allowed him to "level up." As he gained levels, the amount of Animus he could hold grew and grew, as did the raw force of his abilities.

True mastery over the energy, though, involved the application and focus of the power.

He decided to take his new abilities for a test drive, channeling his Animus into the DragonStrength ability. If he managed to unlock DragonStrength, it would permanently increase his strength in both human and dragon form. He put the book down, inhaled, closed his eyes, and focused his will. He was sitting on the couch, the outside doors to the landing platform were open, and a cool breeze blew in. He was glad he was alone in the Aerie, or Aria and Tessa might have distracted him. Yes, both of them were very distracting. Aria, with her long, lean body and small breasts and Tessa, with her curves and large chest.

He blinked. That wasn't helping. Something else was wrong, though.

He checked the book. A sketch showed a man, Stefan Drokharis, sitting cross-legged, spine straight, chin lifted, his hands folded in his lap. No, not folded. The fingers of his left hand rested on his right palm. The thumbs weren't touching, but they were only millimeters apart. The diagram was annotated, and it mentioned that his mouth should be slightly open, the jaws relaxed, and he should breathe in through his nose and out through his mouth.

Steven sat down on the floor, assuming the position, and immediately, the pain in his chest eased. It was like someone had reduced the heat on a gas barbeque. The flame flickered still, but it was far less intense. He envisioned his black dragon skill tree, fixing on the glowing orb labeled "DragonStrength." The effects were immediate. A wave of weariness swept through him, like he'd been up for days and working hard. At the same time, his muscles thickened. His pants split, as did his shirt. It had been awkward, sitting upright with his legs crossed, but with the added strength, it was easy.

Dizziness spun through Steven's head, and his stomach boiled with nausea. He slumped to the side, breathing hard, trying to get control of the vertigo. He reached out, and for a moment, he didn't recognize the flexing muscle. Holy shit, that was his bicep. Excitement flooded through him, wiping away the queasy, light-headed sensations. He stood, and his pants fell off him in tatters.

No wonder Dragonsouls had to acquire Hoards; they had to keep replenishing their wardrobes with every change.

His shirt fell from his back. Standing in his straining underwear, he looked down at the hard ridges of his body, his six-pack, the swell of his quadriceps. He put a foot out behind him and cranked his head to admire his calves. He was well below ten percent body fat. More like two percent. He picked up the couch easily, and with a grunt, he hefted it over his head. Was this really his body? Sure seemed like it. An angry grumble exploded from his stomach. *Yep, I'm your body and I need food,* that grumble seemed to say.

He set the couch down and leafed through the book.

The sections on the Spells and Exhalants were still blank.

That made sense. He'd found the *Gift of a Book* and the *Magic of Ink*, but he still needed the *Power of the Pen*.

With perfect timing, Tessa and Aria bustled in through the secret passageway, chatting amiably. Steven grinned. His transformation had diminished his Animus, but he knew exactly how to replenish it. First, he'd take care of his hunger, and then he'd deal with his lust and build his Animus back up.

Suddenly, having an Escort of women made perfect sense.

He turned—

On the breeze came the strong scent of leather mixed with citrus, like someone had poured lemon juice on their old leather jacket. It was unmistakable.

Steven didn't think anything of it, but it put a bad feeling in his stomach. He thought it was his stomach, howling with hunger.

It wasn't.

TWENTY

TESSA SHOWED STEVEN THE SECRET PASSAGEWAY while he gnawed on a rib. They'd gotten BBQ, heavy on any vegetable they could find: greens, corn, okra, and a variety of carbs like sweet potatoes, doughy potato rolls, corn bread, and French fries. There was easily a hundred dollars in BBQ of all kinds. Aria carried an enormous box, and now Steven knew how. She had the strength skill from the tree.

Tessa had one of the jeweled daggers that were sprinkled liberally around the suite. On the wall was a bright metal plate in the shape of a starburst with a slit in the middle. Inserting the dagger into the slot and turning it opened the wall. Small circular steps led down to another sliding panel at the bottom. Another gold plate was on the wall to open that door.

Back in the main living room, Aria used another dagger to close the sliding doors to the landing platform. The golden starbursts on the wall looked like the Drokharis markers on his pendant map. Cool that he could see the similarities. More and more he was feeling like a true Dragonsoul.

Another dagger plate opened the wall to the right to reveal a dining area. It was like Hogwarts, with how easily the walls moved. It seemed they could magically reconfigure the suite to whatever shape they wanted. Steven, Tessa, and Aria sat down at a rough-hewn wooden table that could seat twelve easily. They clustered at one end, surrounded by a ton of food.

"Something is different about him," Tessa said, eating cornbread slathered with butter and honey. "Is it his hair?"

Aria studied him, got up from her plate of ribs and vegetables, and felt his arm. She then caressed his face. "He's using his Animus to progress along the skill tree."

Steven nodded. "Yeah, Strength. The book is showing me how to harness the Animus. Once I get more, I want to see if I can achieve my True Form."

Aria sat back down. "I think that is an excellent idea."

Steven had lost count of the number of ribs he'd eaten. Several pigs' worth, at least. He followed Tessa's lead by combining cornbread and honey to make a delicious dessert. "So, Aria, where are you at in the skill tree?"

"I'm still learning," she admitted with a shrug. "For a Dragonsoul, I'm young, only a few years older than you. We are similar there, though I've been able to achieve True Form since I was a child. As for spells and Exhalants, I'm still practicing."

"How long do Dragonsouls live?" Tessa asked.

"No one knows," Aria answered somberly. "Most die in battle. If we stopped fighting one another, we might be immortal. There are stories of ancient dragons who were around during the time of Hammurabi that have withdrawn from the constant war. If such Dragonsouls exist, they will want to remain hidden."

Steven let that sink in. It was tragic, unnerving, but Aria had warned him days ago: if he accepted his life as a Dragonsoul it would mean endless warfare and struggle.

And yet, sitting there, feeling his strength, eating with two beautiful women, war seemed a small price to pay.

"Okay, next question," Steven said. "With the ink tableaus, I saw what looked like werewolves. Were those Dragonsouls?"

"Morphlings," Aria said. "Some humans have some Dragonsoul in them, half human, half dragon, and if they find a teacher, they can access some aspects of the Dragonsoul powers. For example, humans who can shape-shift we call Morphlings. Those that gain access to the combat skills are known as Warlings. We use the word Magician to describe humans who can cast spells."

Tessa listened closely, not eating and not saying a word.

Steven frowned. "So Rhaegen Mulk has Morphlings, Warlings, and Magicians on his side, as well as other Dragonsouls."

"Yes, he has many vassals in his command," Aria whispered. Fear filled her eyes as she looked off into the distance. "And Mulk will not stop until you are dead. Then the women in your Escort will be forced to marry him."

"That is so not happening," Tessa said abruptly, throwing down a half-eaten piece of cornbread. "We aren't just going to survive Mulk's attacks. We are going to bring him down for what he did to all those people. And I have to say, if Dragonsoul Primes can force women to marry them, that shit needs to stop. Like yesterday."

"Revolution," Steven said softly, thinking of what his real father had said to him in his vision.

"Right fucking on." Tessa stood and went to him. She kissed him hard, right on the mouth. Her mouth tasted like honey, and she smelled like a day of travel, and he loved every bit of it.

"I think it's time to make some Animus," she said.

He was strong enough to pick up Tessa, walker over, and lift Aria. He wasn't just human strong, he was dragon strong now. He carried the women to the master bedroom suite and the canopied bed there. He flung off the thick, dusty, embroidered bedspread, and it sank to the ground. The sheets looked brand new and clean, and he laid the women down on the soft mattress.

Their eyes twinkled up at him. Both were smiling. And then Aria grew serious. "I want you, Steven. I want to join your Escort and live my life with you. You are good, strong, and brave. And if I am to die, I want to die a free soul—and I know you will give me that freedom."

"No one is dying," Steven said with a lopsided, cocksure grin. "And you both will always be free to do what you want."

"I won't be once we make love," Aria murmured. Tears coursed down her face. "I'm afraid, but I want this." She faltered. "I want you."

Steven wasn't sure what Aria was talking about. After they had sex, things wouldn't change, but he figured he could talk with her afterwards. He stripped off his shirt.

"Damn, Hulk out much?" Tessa giggled. "Look at him, Aria. He's beautiful." She traced her nails over his abs. "Gorgeous."

Aria's face glowed. "It's the power of him, the Animus. He's chosen DragonStrength off the skill tree. And yes, he is gorgeous."

Steven felt himself blush a little. He'd never had anyone look at him twice, and now he had two women drinking him in with their eyes. It was intoxicating. He felt a little drunk as he helped Tessa out of her jeans. She in turn slipped Aria's dress over her head. They were all naked now, both of the women lying on their backs with their legs spread.

Steven went back and forth, kissing them, teasing them, tasting them, until first Tessa then Aria shuddered in ultimate bliss. Steven went to Tessa. He climbed onto the bed and between her legs, but Tessa stopped him.

"It should be Aria this time—it's her first time with you, after all," Tessa said. She kissed him softly and then turned to kiss Aria even more gently.

Steven moved over to Aria, admiring her long, slender brown body, her small breasts, and the little tuft of hair below her taut belly. He positioned himself to enter her, but before he did, he gazed into her bright green eyes. "Are you sure you want this?" he asked.

"Yes! More than anything!" the woman breathed.

And then Steven was inside her. The heat around him, the energy of her body, and the glow of the Animus passing between them almost pushed him over the edge. He scrambled to regain control. And then he was kissing her, moving slowly and steadily, enjoying the soft cries of her pleasure. Tessa caressed them both, kissed them both, until Steven lost control and let himself be consumed by the love and lust on that bed.

Afterwards, kissing Tessa brought new life to Steven's libido, and they made love while Aria watched. Again, Tessa's eyes radiated a bright brilliance as they shared Animus until both were sent spiraling into heaven.

"I want another turn," Aria said with a warm smile. "Can you manage it?"

To his surprise, Steven could. "I guess the DragonStrength skill comes with other benefits."

Hours passed, and the sun set. Eventually, the three found themselves sitting on the landing platform, wrapped in blankets, looking up at the stars above, the mountains in front of them, and the streaming glow of I-25 traffic below. The chill air felt good after their hours of sweat and heat. Again, Steven smelled the leather and citrus smell, but it soon faded into a damp scent of snow in the air. Spring in Colorado could be stupidly hot or wintery cold. You never knew.

"I bet it's going to snow tomorrow," Tessa remarked absently. "I love how the air smells. And I love snow. So win, win!"

Steven stood up and let the blanket drop. He was naked, but he was so comfortable with Tessa and Aria he didn't care. "I want to try True Form," he said. "After our, uh, marathon, I have a ton of Animus in me."

Aria and Tessa moved back, giving him room, which was smart since he wasn't sure how big he was going to get.

He envisioned the skill tree, focusing intently on True Form, and then felt the familiar itch of scales taking over his skin. He fingers became claws and a tail sprouted from his spine. He could easily achieve his Homo Draconis form, but now it was time to amp up the power and go full dragon. He concentrated. The burning in his chest exploded in new white-hot fury that felt like the birth of a star. He growled in pain but didn't let go or lose focus. He'd grown bigger.

He towered over the women now, and the cold felt nice on his scales compared to the agony within. His back felt raw, wounded, but he ignored the hurt as he tried to push wings out of his shoulder blades. He grew another foot, focused, and the Animus welled up inside him. Light emanated from his skin and even from his talons.

Doubt filled him. What if someone saw the light show on the landing platform at the top of the tall hotel? What if he hurt himself trying to achieve True Form too soon? One wing emerged from his back, but it wasn't formed well. The other remained tucked in the flesh of his back, refusing to come out.

He finally dropped to his hands and knees, reverting to his human form. He gasped. "Not yet. I couldn't get there, not yet."

Aria and Tessa came and knelt by him.

"It's okay, Steven, it happens to all guys at some point," Tessa joked.

Aria took up the joke. "Yes, performance issues aren't anything new. You'll get it up eventually."

Steven rolled over onto his back, still sucking wind. "Funny, guys. At least I could perform in the bedroom. I came close to True Form, but I got worried about being seen. I lost focus."

"Wise." Aria nodded. "We have to keep ourselves secret. That should always be your main concern."

Back in the bedroom, Steven found another starburst slot. With the twist of another jeweled dagger, the rock wall parted to reveal a balcony. He decided to keep the wall open, letting the cold air swirl around. He remembered how hot he'd gotten the night before.

He kept the fire going in the fireplace for Tessa, and all three climbed into the bed, under the sheets. Curled up in their arms, listening to the fire crack and pop, feeling the cool air and smelling the snow in the night, Steven found sleep easily. He'd never been so comfortable. Money would no longer be a problem. His mom could quit her job. He'd set her up in a nice neighborhood, maybe in Littleton, with a park close by.

And when Joe Whipp came sniffing around, which he would, Steven would let him know that he wouldn't get a single gold coin from the Drokharis Hoard. But the money didn't seem so important. No, keeping Tessa safe, making sure Aria didn't have to marry anyone she didn't want to, those things mattered more to him. If only he knew for certain that his mother was safe. He'd called again. No answer. He promised himself that after they went to the last Aerie in the mountains—the last fire marker on the pendant map—he would drive to the house.

She had Sundays off. She'd be home. If she was okay.

He prayed she was.

Tessa woke up before light and closed the wall. Steven cracked his eyes open, expecting to see snow, but there wasn't any. The fire continued to burn because yeah, it was magic, and it didn't need fresh wood. It was a perfect illusion, however. Tessa climbed into bed and kissed Steven, and he tried to go back to sleep, he really did, but being sandwiched by two beautiful women didn't help his usual morning situation any.

Aria woke to the bed gently rocking, and then it was her turn to be gently rocked.

When they all finished, they tried to go back to sleep, but the excitement of exploring another Drokharis Aerie was too much for them. After sealing up the hidden floor of the hotel, they took the secret staircase down to the fourteenth floor. They emerged from the wall, through a magical door that when shut, looked exactly like any hotel hallway. No wonder no one had ever disturbed the secret rooms above.

They stopped at Rosie's Diner in Monument, off I-25, and Steven embarrassed himself by eating three breakfasts. He'd polished off the entirety of the BBQ the night before, so they didn't have to worry about leftovers, and still he was hungry. And brimming with Animus.

"Can I drive now?" Tessa asked after Aria paid the bill.

Aria agreed, and they rocketed back toward Denver. The next Drokharis Aerie was located on Lookout Mountain. They buzzed through Denver, grabbed I-70, and headed west toward Golden. Clouds filled the sky and a light rain fell, but with the temperature dropping, there wasn't a doubt that the rain would turn to snow.

"So how am I going to be able to sell that stuff from the Colorado Springs Aerie?" Steven asked as they made the right turn up the long winding road that led to the top of Lookout Mountain. In better weather, the road would've been full of cyclists, but with the chill wind and slick pavement, they had the road to themselves. Not a single car or bike around.

"There is a Dragonsoul black market for such things," Aria answered. "My father knows ..."

The words died on her lips as a huge shape descended upon them, blocking out the light and plunging the interior of the car into shadows. The automatic headlights blinked on. Metal screeched as claws tore into the roof.

The sharp pungent stench of lemons and leather filled Steven's nose, the same odor he'd smelled before in the Aerie. A Dragonsoul in True Form. It was above them, ripping the vehicle to shreds.

And it seemed like they'd be next ...

TWENTY-ONE

E ARLY SUNDAY MORNING, EDGAR VALE WAS shrieking in pain. Mouse had said the Dragonskin ritual would take twenty-four hours, but he was going on hour thirty. Or thirty-one. It was hard to keep track. He and Mouse were on top of the Wells Fargo building in Denver, on a platform that was hidden from the eyes of the simple fuckers walking around the downtown below.

Edgar's hands and feet were tied to a metal rack with metal cables. The rack had a series of cranks and levers that would either tighten the cables, raise him, or spin him around so that the brazier of hot coals underneath could cook every inch of his skin. His blood and sweat smoked away in the fire, a constant plume of steam and smoke rising up. He could smell his hair burning away even as it grew back, over and over. That smelled better than the BBQ odor of his flesh crisping. He'd thought it would get better when night fell, but then he'd been in a strange situation, half of him roasting and half of him freezing.

Now, he lay facedown as the coals ate away his skin. Mouse was continually dosing him with morphine to keep him from going completely insane from the pain, but that did little to help. Though she hated him, she was doing her part, whispering the spells and adding the magic herbs—mugwort, yarrow, dragonpenny—to the coals. She downed glass after glass of wine. At first, she seemed to enjoy his screams, but now she was pale, clearly exhausted, and ready for the ordeal to be over.

Normally the Dragonskin rituals allowed weeks for the final burning, but he didn't have weeks. And he was strong, so strong—the pain would only make him stronger. When he'd gotten locked up for aggravated assault at the tender of age of eighteen, which in street terms was at least thirty, he'd met a hardened con named Dipstick who was in the pen for life. He had four counts of first-degree murder under his belt. Dipstick had taken Edgar under his wing, and he told him the secret to life. Life was pain. And the more you liked pain, the more you could like life, until it got to the point where you didn't want comfort, you wanted pain.

The special people on the planet had that shit figured out. You look at any Olympic athlete, any politician, any successful artist, and they didn't just want success and glory, they wanted pain and struggle. The real sick ones got off on it.

And Edgar wanted to be that sick.

So every minute, every second his skin was burning off him, that was good. Mouse would cast the spells to heal it back on, raise him up off the fire, only to bring him back down onto those coals.

He would scream, get hard, scream some more, and he'd remember he wasn't special, but he soon would be. And every bit of agony he was feeling now? Well, he would bring that same agony down on that fucker, Steven Whipp. Bring it down tenfold. It was his fault, his and his bitches, that Edgar had to cram weeks' worth of the rituals into a day and a half.

That shit, he'd never forget. Not ever.

Mouse pulled a lever, and he rose off the coals. She then touched him with a glowing vial, almost like a perfume bottle. She called it Elftears. Fuck elves. And fuck tears.

His roasted, blackened skin grew back, as did his hair, until he was just a naked guy in the cold. He got so he hated the chill air more than the mean lick of the flames.

"We have to stop." Mouse slurred her words. She was beyond drunk. "You're not changing. It's too soon."

"Fuck you, bitch," Edgar spat. "I'm not stopping."

"You'll die."

"I already died, at some point, last night. This is me, a fucking zombie, and I want more fire, bitch. Give me more fire!" He roared out the words.

"You're a sick fuck," Mouse muttered. Then she spun a crank, whipping him around, and lowered him back into the flames.

And like Dipstick promised, Edgar got off on it. He'd never been harder in his entire life even though his dick had almost been melted off any number of times in the last thirty hours.

Everything human inside of him burned away, and only the dragon in him was left.

He sniffed the air and tasted it, rotten pork on a BBQ, awful and delicious, and that was life. That was him. He had his Dragonskin smell, and it was terrible, but he liked it.

No, he loved it.

◇◇◇

Above Steven, the roof of the Mercedes gave way in a scream of metal and a flash of sparks. The dragon above flung the roof away, and it went banging and clattering across the wet asphalt behind them as chill air swept into the interior. The creature had mustard-colored scales edged in black and reeked of lemons and leather. Aria cursed, drew her pistol, and unloaded the clip into the chest of the dragon.

The dragon let out a thunderous roar. Its yellow beard waggled.

Tessa spun the car around a switchback and mashed her foot down hard, gunning the engine, leaving the dragon behind for a minute.

"Get to the Aerie!" Aria shouted, hair whipping in the pine-scented wind. She flung herself out of the speeding car. In midair, she transformed into a scarlet dragon, her scales steaming in the cold morning. She met the incoming dragon, and they clashed above the road, turning, twirling, summersaulting, as tails whipped, wings flapped, and claws raked at scaly flesh.

But the yellow dragon was almost double her size. She was fifteen feet long, and it was at least thirty and probably several tons heavier to boot. There was no way she could match its strength. Steven realized it was a male, and from what he understood about Dragonsouls, males were rare. *Is this Rhaegen Mulk?* he wondered.

Tessa slammed the brakes on, then spun the Mercedes around, tires smoking.

"What are you doing?" Steven asked, shocked.

"We are *NOT* leaving Aria behind," the barista said in her warrior voice. She slammed the gas pedal to the floor again, and the tires squealed in response as they rocketed forward.

Steven found himself pressed back into the seat. But only for a second. He pulled himself up and then went Homo Draconis. There was no roof to worry about, so he could expand outside. Using his enhanced strength, he got his feet under him and wedged his massive tail between the front seats to keep himself steady.

The two dragons, one massive and yellow, the other slender and scarlet, lashed out with fang-studded jaws, then went in with claws. The yellow worm threw Aria into the pines on the sloping side of the mountain. She bashed through the trunks, toppling dozens of trees and throwing up waves of black mountain dirt. While she was on the ground, the yellow beast unleashed a crackling blast of blue electricity.

ElectroArc. Steven was witnessing his first live display of the Exhalant.

The lightning sent Aria writhing and twisting in pain. Crimson scales spun away as that awful energy ate into her skin. The yellow worm didn't relent but kept up the onslaught.

"Faster!" Steven growled, his voice inhuman and brimming with anger. "Drive right by him. I'm going to use the speed to hit him hard."

Tessa was silent. They careened down the highway at a hundred miles an hour. Steven was about to see how good his armor really was. The wind screamed in his reptilian ears, and the cold froze his scales, but he didn't care.

"Faster!"

But the engine was already blaring, the tachometer buried into the red.

They entered a short straightaway, pulling in range, and Steven leapt from the car. He let out a roar right before he hit the enemy dragon. If it was Rhaegen Mulk, he was going to pay for murdering Steven's parents.

Like a bullet from a gun, Steven streaked through the air. He'd timed it perfectly. He slammed into the side of the dragon, and that lightning shit died like he'd hit an off switch. The mustard-colored worm struck the pavement, grinding away the asphalt and a good chunk of his scales. A wing snapped in the crash.

Steven gripped the belly of the worm with his talons, hands and feet. He wasn't about to let the bone-breaking collision stop him from exacting sweet revenge … dragon-claw style.

The yellow beast would pay for hurting Aria.

Steven clawed up the dragon, slashing him and causing as much damage as he could until the worm tossed him into a tree. He bounced off bark, tore through a few saplings, then rolled down the slope, his head aching, stars flashing in his eyes, his back protesting in agony. He tried to shake off the pain. But he'd been hurt. And not just a little.

But Steven couldn't leave Tessa and Aria with the enemy Dragonsoul. He refused. He would die first. He gained his feet through an effort of sheer will and sped up the slope as fast as he could manage. He crested the slight rise just in time to watch as Tessa swerved, guiding the Mercedes toward the yellow-scaled dragon. Amazingly, she was driving in *reverse*, going in to demolition-derby that asshat. Trunk first, she crashed into the dragon's head. Then, before it could get to her, she threw it into drive and floored the car.

She raced away, putting distance between the car and the downed monster.

Aria was still down. The yellow dragon was slow getting to its giant feet. It wobbled, weaving, obviously dazed.

Steven bounded onto the road. The yellow worm opened its mouth and breathed out a blast of orange flame. The fire melted through the asphalt, turning it into a quagmire of burbling black goop. Steven threw himself to the side and rolled away, dodging the inferno blast.

In seconds, he was back upright.

After all the marathon sex with his Escort, he had Animus to spare, and though he'd failed before, he accessed the skill tree, found the True Form orb, and focused on it. The yellow dragon was three times bigger than he was, and Steven didn't think he could take it down as a Homo Draconis. He needed his full dragon body.

Steven grew bigger, a lot bigger, and managed to flick his wings out from under the skin on his back. The pendant flashed brightly, slicing through the gloom. He raised his claws, now the size of car tires. He was doing it. He was achieving his True Form.

The yellow worm growled. "Vale said you were a Dragonling, but no, you're more than that. Fuck this."

Instead of attacking, the enemy dragon whirled and straightened his broken wing with a *crack*. He then swirled a claw in the air and boomed out two words, "*Magica Cura!*" The wing healed, as did some of the dragon's wounds, but he was still missing scales, leathery flesh peeking through from beneath. Even after healing, he looked like he'd found himself under Thor's hammer, and the beating hadn't been kind.

Aria lay in her human form among the destroyed trees. Her skin smoked from the lightning blast.

Steven took a step toward her, but keeping his True Form was too much for him. He knew he couldn't achieve it fully, not yet.

The yellow worm took to the air and swooped down onto Aria. He caught her up in one talon-tipped hand and then—with a deep belly laugh—the dragon wheeled and flew off, huge wings beating furiously at the air. "At least I won't be leaving empty-handed," he called back over his shoulder.

Steven bellowed, "No!" He felt himself changing back, first into Homo Draconis and then into his human form. Naked, standing in the cold on the ruined highway, he watched as the yellow dragon escaped with Aria dangling lifelessly beneath him.

Steven dropped to his knees, feeling every wound, from hitting the dragon at a hundred miles per hour to careening into fully grown pine trees.

Tessa pulled up, got out of the car, and went to him. "Steven, are you okay?"

"Aria," he gasped. "We have to go after her."

But only storm clouds were in the sky. There was no sign of Aria or the dragon who had taken her.

Steven and Tessa were alone.

TWENTY-TWO

TESSA HELPED STEVEN INTO THE MERCEDES, which mercifully still worked. It didn't have a roof, the trunk was a snarl of twisted metal, and the engine ticked loudly. Bits of metal tumbled away behind them as they drove away from the battlefield. Still, Tessa had done a great job in using it as a weapon without doing much damage to the engine.

"So what now?" Steven asked quietly.

"We have to find Aria," Tessa said. "We can't just let this Rhaegen Mulk dick take her."

"That wasn't Mulk," Steven said. "He mentioned Edgar Vale, and working for him. I think it was another of Mulk's vassals, or it could've been a Ronin."

"Shit, dragons for hire," Tessa breathed. "What a world we live in. Well, whoever that was, that was one big-ass beast. So that's a male dragon …"

"I'll get there." Steven closed his eyes. He was so cold, but inside, he felt colder despite the burning in his chest.

"When you went True Form, you were impressive." Tessa sighed. "So where do you think Aria is? I don't suppose you can use the pendant to find her."

"I can't." Steven lifted the chunk of mystic topaz and accessed the map. The fire marker was still above them, a few more turns on the road away. "But I can find the next Aerie."

The barista let a sob escape her. "We can't … not without Aria. We can't." She shook her head, tears streaming down her cheeks.

"We have to," he said softly. "Once we find the Power of the Pen, I might have access to spells. Not that I'll know how to use them."

They curved around another switchback and drew nearer to an outcropping of rock jutting out of the side of the mountain like an enormous broken thumb. The crag, rising high, split the forest. They were near the top of Lookout Mountain but not quite at the summit.

"Hold up," Steven said, squinting as he examined the rugged cliff.

She slowed the car.

He raised the pendant. It flashed a brilliant gold. The rocky side of the cliff edging the roadway opened, revealing a curving roadway into the mountainside. Holy crap.

"Wow, total Batcave action right there," Tessa said, awe in her words. "If only Aria was here to see it. I can't really enjoy it now that I know she's in trouble."

He put a hand on her forearm and squeezed reassuringly. "I understand. But at this stage, we have to find my father's pen. The last of the artifacts might be able to give us the power we need to get her back. To stop Rhaegen Mulk and his henchmen."

Tessa brushed tears from her face, then motored into the passageway, flicking the headlights on. Only one headlight worked, but it cut a wide swath into the darkness. Once they were inside all the way, the cave entrance magicked closed behind them and a series of torches on the walls flickered on. Tessa killed the headlights and puttered farther in.

They cruised past the rough-hewn rocky walls, wet with moisture, and headed around a final bend, which let out in an underground parking garage. A parking lot with more than a few vehicles: a handful of Harley Davidson motorcycles, a cherry-red Corvette Stingray from the 1960s, a yellow Dodge Charger from the '70s, a big orange Ford Bronco II from the '80s, and a BMW roadster from the '90s. Tools hung over a workbench flanked by two big, red, expensive tool chests. More of his Hoard, now that he was the last of the Drokharis clan.

Steven wanted to get excited by the wealth, but he couldn't find it in him. Not even when he saw the rack of keys that would match the vehicles. They had lost Aria. Nothing would ever be the same. Compared to that, it was hard to celebrate something as inconsequential as a couple of classic cars.

Tessa parked in an open space, and they got out. A sliding glass door had been cut into the rock wall in front of them.

Steven had to turn into his partial form to wrench open the crushed trunk to get to their luggage. Once that was done, he changed back, slipped into a pair of jeans, and drew on a sweatshirt. He didn't bother with shoes—

this changing clothes every fifteen minutes business was annoying as hell.

Tessa walked to the glass doors and stopped. "Look, this is horrible. But you're right. Once we find the pen, I bet we can magic up a solution. And Aria is tough, you know she is. I don't think that Ronin is going to kill her, not right away. I don't know how that whole Escort thing works, but I bet there are rules."

"I hope there are." He drew the barista into an embrace. Holding her, feeling her heat, smelling her hair, made him feel better. They'd only been together a short time, but already, hugging her felt like going home.

Holding hands, they entered the Aerie through the doors. Unlike the Colorado Springs secret floor, this Aerie had a modern feel to it. Sleek metal furniture with cream-colored cushions sat on a black slate floor, which was warm under his feet. It made sense to have heated floors in a cave. The walls were rock, but the entire front of the living room was a window, showing a dazzling view of Denver and the entire Front Range. At night, the light show would be spectacular.

The place smelled musty but only for a minute. As they entered, a fan whooshed to life, bringing in the perfume of the pines covering the mountainside. The sounds of water splashing filled the air. Were there fountains somewhere in the Aerie? It seemed so, though he didn't see them. Some more exploring was definitely in order.

A huge kitchen sat off to his right with marble countertops and the latest appliances—well, they'd been the latest appliances on the market in the 1990s. To his left was a hallway that likely led to the bedrooms and the bathrooms. In the left corner was a fireplace, which ignited, giving them warmth. In the right corner, a staircase spiraled up into the ceiling. That intrigued him. The sounds of splashing water came from there, above them.

"Up?" he asked, cocking an eyebrow.

"Up," the barista agreed.

Steven went first. He climbed the tight metal stairs, which were as sleek and chrome as everything else in the luxury Aerie hidden away on Lookout Mountain.

The staircase ended in a room that was something out of a fantasy novel. Unlike the room below, this upper room was mostly cave, but it too had windows facing eastward, which must've been hidden away by spells. Otherwise, Steven would've heard about such a palace outside of Golden.

The ceiling was tall, about twenty feet high and rough stone. Torches on sconces in the rock walls gave out a warm light. A waterfall of steaming water trickled down the western wall, filling a series of pools, fourteen of them, which could be accessed through steps carved into the stone floor. The placed looked like some kind of spa. The pools themselves were all different sizes, some only big enough for a single person, while the largest was rectangular and could fit fifteen people comfortably. The water in the pools glowed with a warm blue light, which was almost supernatural in appearance.

A grand fireplace hewed into the rock face itself sat along the northern wall, far bigger than the one on the entry level. Again, flames leapt to life. Running between the big rectangular pool and the eastern-facing window was a thick red carpet covered with furniture: club chairs, sofas, chaises, coffee tables, even a small bar well stocked with liquor. The views of the sunrise would be spectacular.

The cave was warm, wet, and comfortable. A light mist hung in the air, carrying the smell of sulfurous minerals.

Tessa went to one of the smaller pools and dipped a hand inside. "It must be fed by natural hot springs," she murmured.

"You should get in," Steven said.

Tessa sighed. "I couldn't. We have to find the pen. *The Power of the Pen.*"

"Maybe one of us has to be in the pools for it to work. Just go in."

She looked troubled for a moment, but then without another word, she undressed, dropping her clothes onto the Drokharis Grimoire she'd been lugging around.

Steven moved down toward the large pool and the fireplace. The pendant glowed and felt warm in his hand.

The pattern of the pools was familiar. It took him a second, but then he recognized the Draco constellation. The St. Vrain Aerie had mosaics of the stars, and the Colorado Springs Aerie had the constellation on the floor, and so it seemed appropriate that the Lookout Mountain palace would have the pools in that same shape.

Steven walked to the head of the constellation, which was also the largest pool. He gazed down into the blue-tinged water. In the bottom of the pool lights glowed. Radiant sapphires were scattered across the bottom. He put his junk cell phone on the stone and then walked down steps into the water.

"Aren't you going to take off your clothes?" Tessa asked from her tub.

"I'm so sick of changing," Steven said absently, gaze fixed unwaveringly on the gems.

The water was hot at first, uncomfortably so, but then Steven wished it were hotter. His tolerance for heat had increased exponentially. Now, he would've relished sleeping in a bed surrounded by the body heat of his Escort.

His Escort. Down by one. But not for long. He would get Aria back. Somehow. But first, the pen. He continued to walk until he was forced to swim. The bottom dropped away, and while he thought the sapphires were on the bottom, they were actually just floating there.

How deep was the pool? It seemed bottomless. For some reason, he thought of the three strange doors at the St. Vrain Aerie.

The sapphires moved to form a circle around him. They then began to spin, slowly at first, but faster by the second.

Tessa saw the strange swirling gems under him. "Steven, are you okay?"

He didn't know. But he didn't respond. He was soon caught in a whirlpool, treading water in the center as the water frothed around him, driven into a frenzy by the gems. The water gathered around him, pushing in against his body as it lifted him up, up, up, away from the pool below. The water and jewels spun around him like a tornado, and he was at the heart of it, hanging suspended in dripping clothes. The noise was incredible, making it hard to think.

227

The swirling waters continued to pick up in speed, tugging and pulling at his pendant until it was ripped from his neck with a sudden sharp jerk. Instead of flying off into the vortex, however, it rose, levitating above him. The steel chain melted away, as did the housing, and all that was left was the hunk of topaz. And then, in a flash, the topaz lengthened and shimmered, becoming pen-shaped. Morphing, finally, into a quill. A couple of the sapphires rose out of the whirlpool and connected themselves to the topaz quill. They became a single crystal feather poking up from the tail end of the pen.

The voice of Stefan Drokharis boomed through the cave. "MY SON. GATHER YOUR ESCORT. ACQUIRE YOUR HOARD. BUILD YOUR AERIES. FINISH MY WORK. AND BRING REVOLUTION TO THIS WEARY WORLD. IT IS YOUR DESTINY. LET NOTHING STOP YOU!"

Tessa screamed, "Steven, what's happening!" Her voice seemed distant and quiet in the maelstrom of noise and power.

The hurricane around him parted, and he saw that all of the water, from every pool, was swirling in the air—and Tessa had been caught up in it as well. She floated in midair, just like him, and her eyes were twin suns in her face. She cried out, writhing.

Steven didn't know how he could help her, but it was obvious she was in pain.

Acting on instinct, he reached out and touched the pen. The minute he did the heat in his chest exploded, and his body was enveloped in a roaring blaze. His clothes turned to ash in the conflagration. Orange flames licked up and down his body, and his hair turned to smoke. His skin fried, crisped, sloughed away. He was being cooked alive in the inferno, every nerve howling in agony. A scream tore its way from his mouth but died quickly as magic fire poured in, filling his throat, his lungs, his belly.

Some part of him knew this was necessary. That in order to unlock his final transformation he would need such suffering. Aria wasn't around to ask, but this excruciating agony would be worth the price if it gave him the power to save her, so he steeled himself. He endured, soaking up the pain like a sponge.

Right when he thought his sanity would snap, the fire vanished, replaced by soothing blue waters once more. The world seemed to shift around him, and he dropped, splashing down into the pool as the cool waters caressed his mangled, charbroiled body. The same force that had held him aloft now drew him down, down, down, through the depths of the pool, which was far deeper than he could ever have imagined. Below was a doorway. But to where?

Steven found himself gasping, thrashing his arms madly as he suffocated. He needed to breathe. His skin had mostly flaked away, to reveal muscle, and he yelled out in shock and fear.

He regretted that. Water flooded into his mouth and filled his lungs, just as the fire had done moments before. As intolerably painful as the fire had been, the water was almost worse, and he was suddenly sure he was going to drown. He must've done something wrong. This wasn't right …

Only it was. He pressed his eyes closed.

When he opened them again—almost against his own will—he found himself floating in a universe of stars and nebulas. A comet streaked by him. All of reality was there for him to see, and the power there, the throbbing power of life itself, felt so close. That celestial power enveloped him, wrapped around him like a second skin.

His heart stopped. He felt it stop. He was dead, floating in the middle of creation, and he knew there wasn't just one set of worlds in the universe, but an infinite number of realities.

He took a deep, shuddering breath, and it felt like the first breath he'd ever taken. An impossible memory filled him, of being held by his mother. His father was smiling even as tears streamed down his cheeks to fill his beard.

His heart thumped to life. First one beat, then another, then another. He was reborn. And his destiny wasn't just to conquer his own Primacy on one little bit of rock floating through space. Fate had chosen him to do so much more … but the extent of it seemed fuzzy. Hazy. He reached out an arm, fingers straining as though he could grasp his destiny in his hand. But no, it was too far away, and getting farther by the moment.

"Steven!" Tessa called to him from an impossible distance. "Where are you? Don't leave me, dammit. Don't leave me alone!"

He swam up through the empty space until he found himself swimming through water. Those gems, he realized in a flash of inspiration, weren't sapphires. No, they were stars. But then, they too were gone and he was back in the pool, kicking upward, arms pumping, until he burst from the water. He had skin again. That was good, and the pain was blissfully absent. He paddled to the side and clutched the stone, heart thudding like mad inside his chest.

Tessa ran and dove into the water. She clutched him. Her skin felt so good on his. He found rock under his feet. He stood and held her.

"I thought you were gone forever," she sobbed in his arms. "I can't lose you. I can't. You've become a part of me. I felt that. Before. When the water … Steven … what happened?" She cupped his head. "Where's your hair?"

He touched his bald scalp. "Uh, burned away I guess."

But he didn't care about that. He'd never been more turned on in his life. He parted her legs and found himself inside Tessa. She kissed him, savagely. Both gasped at the sudden heat. He gently but firmly pushed her to the side of the pool and slammed his sex into hers, harder and harder. She came, whining in his ear. He'd never heard her make those sounds before.

His own bliss was one stroke away, and he gave himself to the pleasure. The Animus between them could've powered New York City for a year.

Spent, they climbed from the pool to lie by the fire. They held each other. Steven knew everything had changed. Between them. And inside their souls.

The sacred pools of the Drokharis clan had given them powers even they did not fully understand. Not yet.

TWENTY-THREE

ARIA WOKE LYING IN A BED SURROUNDED BY statues. Some were ancient, obviously Greek in origin, while others were from some modern artist, who had used a mixture of stone and paint. There were even some female figures welded out of metal.

The noon sun was muted by the thick curtains as well as the clouds outside. A few fat flakes of snow fell against the pane, but since this was Colorado, that could mean anything. It could snow four feet, or in fifteen minutes, the storm could blow out to the Kansas prairie. The temperature could skyrocket thirty degrees in an hour.

Where was she? The last thing she remembered was being scooped up by the yellow dragon after he had hit her with his ElectroArc Exhalant. Where was Steven? Was Tessa okay?

Aria's bare feet hit the hardwood floor. She was dressed in a red silk gown. Where had that come from?

She heard classical music being played on a piano. She wasn't sure what was going on, but following the music seemed like the next logical course of action.

She left the bizarre room full of statues and entered a hallway where every inch of wall space was filled with paintings. She recognized the work of a few artists. A Jackson Pollock, a Picasso, a van Gogh, their work was undeniable. She paused. There were a few other cubist paintings she was unfamiliar with.

But the surroundings—the bed, the statues, the paintings—told her she was in a mansion, somewhere. There were any number of rooms off the hallway, and each was full of artwork, from other statues to huge murals which sat on the floor in large baroque frames. The place smelled like lemons and leather, the signature odor of the yellow dragon. It was his Aerie, obviously, and his Hoard was art, which wasn't exactly strange for a Dragonsoul, but it certainly wasn't normal. She didn't see any signs of gold or other precious metals and gems.

She stopped at the top of a sweeping staircase. Below, in a room crowded with more art and musical instruments, a big blond man sat at a grand piano, playing it with the skill of a world-class concert pianist. The man had a long, golden beard and his chest hair was that same gold tangle. He was shirtless. His bottom half was covered in jeans and cowboy boots.

He stopped playing. "So, you're awake."

"Where are my friends?" Aria asked. She'd healed some after her long sleep, but she still felt weak and bruised. The memory of being electrocuted made her shudder.

"I don't know where your friends are," the blond man said with a slight shrug. "You are here for one simple reason. When Rhaegen Mulk or his pet Edgar Vale come for me, to punish me for my failure, I will

233

give you over to them. So we don't need to talk any. Go back to your room. You won't be able to leave. While spells have fallen out of fashion among our kind, I have kept up the practice." He faltered, eyes flashing. "For obvious reasons."

"Which are?" Aria asked. She was intrigued in spite of herself.

"As a Ronin Dragonsoul, my life is in danger most days. Every little edge I can find, I will use." He then returned to the keys, playing a piece by Rachmaninoff, *Six Moments Musicaux* Opus 16 No. 4.

Aria descended the stairs and stood next to the piano. "Where am I?"

"My Cherry Creek Aerie," the man said, obviously annoyed.

"And what's your name?" Aria asked.

He sighed and lifted his hands from the keyboard. "Does it matter? You don't care. I don't care. So let's go with Liam Strider. It will work as well as any. But what's in a name?"

"A rose by any other name would smell as sweet," Aria murmured.

"I have one of the original texts of the play," Liam replied. "As you can see, I find the finer things in life worth the sorrow of our heartbeats."

He sat quietly, not looking at her. She stood by the polished piano, awkward. Most men would've been staring at her dressed in the skimpy scarlet silk. This Ronin truly was a mystery.

The mansion was silent. "Where is your Escort?" she asked. "Or your vassals?"

"I played that game for a bit," the mystery dragon muttered. "But I found such things tiresome after a while. This is much easier."

"If you like being alone, why did you agree to help Mulk and Vale?" Aria asked.

"Another edge," he offered. "I do the local Prime a favor, and he leaves me be. But Vale didn't tell me the whole story. He didn't mention you, nor did he say that the target was a Dragonsoul with remarkable power. This new Dragonsoul will disrupt this once peaceful Primacy. I have already been in contact with movers." He next grin was wistful. "And I had such high hopes for Denver. But few will survive the coming fury, that I am quite sure of."

The doorbell chimed.

Liam raised two fingers and mouthed two words, "*Magica Divino*." He stood. He was close to seven feet tall, lean, and striking. He moved like a panther, all power and deadly grace. "And that is Edgar Vale now. Alone. Strange. But with you gone, I can return to my quiet life. Not that moving is quiet." He sighed.

Aria thought about making a run for it, but she could feel the power of the yellow dragon's spells. Steven had shaken the strange Ronin, and that made Aria smile. She had been right about how powerful her mate was.

When Liam opened the door, the stench of rancid meat swept in. Edgar Vale, gripping the Slayer Blade, drove the sword into the Ronin's chest. The yellow dragon stumbled back, shock evident on his face, but already he was turning into his Homo Draconis form.

Edgar's face was as gray as a dead man's. The pink around his eyes was diseased. He shrieked crazily, "Screwed the pooch, Liam. Fucked up royally. I didn't want the bitch, I wanted the bastard!" He shoved the yellow back. Edgar sprouted scales, a terrible mottled green color to cover his gray skin. He took the Slayer Blade and stabbed himself through his side. He didn't want to put it down. He stuck it into his own body to hold onto it.

Aria stepped back. This Edgar beast was insane.

He strode through the doorway and continued to grow. The sword hung from his damaged body but was soon eclipsed by the sheer size of the dragon he was becoming. Somehow, impossibly, the Skinling had become a full Dragonskin, but either he'd rushed the process, or something had gone terribly wrong. His long, spiked tail smashed through a statue and swept paintings off the walls of the room. He unfurled his wings and took out a chandelier, then ripped through sheetrock. Bits of drywall rained down.

Liam Strider reeled unsteadily. Blood dripped down his chest to speckle the hardwood floor. He made a circle with the fingers on his left hand and held up his right palm. He shouted, *"Magica Impetim!"* Sizzling red missiles made of magical energy struck the Dragonskin. The smell of rotting meat grew sharper. Edgar raised a giant dragon foot and stomped down on the piano. He flung his head back and smashed through the ceiling. A bathroom set came plunging down, a toilet, a sink, a shower. All that porcelain hit the floor and exploded in a burst of white shrapnel.

Aria accessed her own True Form and felt her body transform into a scarlet dragon, half as big as the moldy green Dragonskin. Again, Liam called out, *"Magica Impetim,"* and more red energy bolts hit Edgar, but the villain brushed them aside with contemptuous ease.

Aria leapt onto Edgar. Though his stench repulsed her, she had to hurt him so she could escape. Perhaps Liam would let her leave now that all deals with Mulk's vassal seemed to be off.

Liam sped forward and leapt, lengthening into the yellow dragon Aria had seen before. He sank his massive fangs into Edgar's throat, tearing away scales and covering both Aria and himself in blood.

The three dragons thrashing around in the living room brought the rest of the ceiling down in a torrent of destruction. The staircase crumbled. Priceless works of art were crushed underfoot and smashed with whipping tails—the cost of the lost art was incalculable. The mansion had become an arena for battle.

Edgar swept his wings back and brought them forward, unleashing a massive gust of air that blasted Aria into the far wall. She hit with the force of a car crash, plaster cracking, studs snapping, drywall cratering around her. Only the sorcery reinforcing the building prevented her from punching all the way through.

Meanwhile, the yellow dragon lunged in, sinking his teeth in the villain's throat. Edgar flailed, but largely ignored the male dragon, instead focusing his gaze on Aria. Edgar twisted his head, opened his mouth impossibly wide, and unleashed an inferno of fire into Aria. Though she could withstand most heat, the dark fire erupting from the Dragonskin blistered her, and she found herself roaring in agony.

Liam pulled back, jerking his neck left then right, teeth ripping into Edgar, trying to stop the deadly flame attack. Blood sprayed from the wound in Edgar's neck, but Liam hadn't been able to rip out the green dragon's throat. Edgar moved like a snake, quickly melting back into his Homo Draconis shape to slip out from between Liam's crushing jaws. The second Edgar was free, he plucked the Slayer Blade from his side and struck like lightning, cutting a gaping wound into Liam's belly.

He rammed a clawed foot into the yellow dragon's guts. Edgar laughed with delight at the screams of pain from Liam. "And I thought you were tough, being a Ronin, living alone. But nope, you ain't nothing to write home about." He stuck the Slayer Blade back into his side, almost as if he liked it there, and returned to his dragon form. Wounds littered Edgar's body, but he hardly seemed to notice as he marched forward and bathed the yellow dragon in a sheet of fire.

The remains of the piano burst into flames, as did other musical instruments around them. The curtains caught, and in seconds, the three were trapped in a conflagration.

Hurt, barely conscious, Aria flung herself toward the door, scrambling on her hands and feet. There was a chance, a slim one, that Liam's spells had failed from the power of Edgar's attack. Aria forced her body back to being human as she crawled, hoping she could escape.

But a claw grabbed her foot and mashed her into the floor, forcing the air from her lungs. Edgar, towering over her in his partial form, pressed the Slayer Blade to her throat. "Bitch. You ain't leaving without me." His serpentine eyes traveled up and down her naked body. "We both know I can't rape you, but shit, I wouldn't want to fuck bait anyway. And that's what you are, sweet tits. You're bait." His fanged mouth opened in a leer.

Liam ran through the flames and out the door, escaping, leaving Aria alone with the Dragonskin and his rotten stink.

In the distance she heard the whoop of sirens. The humans had sent their fire department to take care of the burning mansion, but they would arrive too late to save her.

Edgar would take her to one of Mulk's Aeries, but how would Steven and Tessa ever find her? And even if they did manage to locate the Aerie, how could they fight the insane power of this mad Dragonskin who stank of rot and ruin?

◇◇◇

Steven watched as Tessa rose from beside the fire in the cave of the sacred pools and went to retrieve the Drokharis Grimoire from where she'd dropped it along with her clothes. Watching her walk, he was amazed at how sexy she was. Was there anything better than watching a naked woman walk? He'd caught a glimpse of the beauty and power at the heart of the universe, and yet that seemed to pale in comparison.

Returning with the tome, she smiled uncertainly at him. "Why are you looking at me like that?"

"You're so gorgeous," he replied with a wide grin. "Just admiring the view."

She blushed. "I bet you say that to all the girls." She lay down, opened the book, and then burst into tears.

"What's wrong?" Steven asked, shocked and worried.

"I can read it." She wiped the tears from her face. "The words, I can read them perfectly. Something happened to me … in the waters … something …"

He reached out and stroked her back. "What?"

Her first words came out hesitant, but as she talked, she became more confident. "When the water rose out of the pools, when I was suspended in midair, it was like I had a closed door inside me, locked tight. And then suddenly, this energy acted like a key, and that door burst wide open. I can feel the Animus. I think," she faltered, hesitating. "I think I can use it."

Steven nodded. "Remember how Aria talked about Morphlings, Warlings, and Magicians? They're humans who can use Animus to change their shape, fight, and cast spells. That must be what you are, though I wonder which one." His hands went to his chest, searching for the pendant. Then he remembered that his necklace was gone, but where was the pen?

For a second, he thought he might've dropped it during his trip to the heart of the universe, but then he found it next to the fire. He must've brought it with him after he and Tessa had made love at the side of the pool.

He raised it, a long piece of mystic, quill-shaped topaz capped by a feather crafted of sapphires. It was amazing to look at. To his surprise, the pen wriggled in his hand with a life of its own and leapt from his hand. It went to the book, flipped through pages until it found a blank space, then began to write furiously. Tessa and Steven watched in wonder.

The pen flipped back to the Dragon Skill Tree and filled in the last of the blanks.

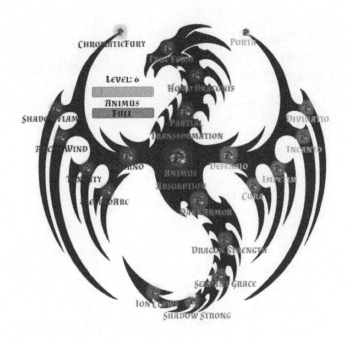

Transformatio (Head of the Dragon)
- Partial Transformation
- Homo Draconis
- True Form (Dragonsoul)

Pugna (Tail of the Dragon)
- DarkArmor
- DragonStrength
- SerpentGrace
- ShadowStrength
- IonClaw

Exhalants (Left Wing of the Dragon)
- Inferno
- ElectroArc

- Toxicity
- ArcticWind
- ShadowFlame
- ChromaticFury

Veneficium (Right Wing of the Dragon)

- *Magica Defensio*
- *Magica Cura*
- *Magica Impetim*
- *Magica Incanto*
- *Magica Divinatio*
- *Magica Porta*

Then it returned to scrawling out the rest of the book, page after page, like an automatic printer. When it was finished, the pen shuddered and lay still.

Tessa touched the pen reverently and caressed the book. "I don't know about that whole werewolf thing, and straight-up battle doesn't really appeal to me. But spells? Yeah, I think maybe that would be up my alley. It feels right, you know?"

Steven nodded and rose to his feet.

He was full of Animus from the sex and from his battle with the yellow dragon. He knew, without a doubt, he could achieve True Form. He stood, stretching his back, flexing his arms, and transformed into his Homo Draconis form with almost no effort at all. It felt as natural and effortless as being in his human form. And from there, it was only a bit more to expand out to his full dragon shape. His body expanded and grew, until he was thirty feet long. Thankfully the cavernous pool room was big enough to accommodate his bulk, even with his wings expanded. It felt good to stretch them out.

He examined himself in the crystalline blue waters. He was the color of midnight. His scales, his claws, his wings, everything was an inky black color, the same hue as a raven's feathers. He'd always liked his dark hair, but he liked his black scales even more. He also noticed for the first time that the burning in his chest was gone. Vanished. Apparently, he'd crossed a major threshold and had survived.

Tessa sat staring at him, hugging her knees to her chest. "Steven. You're…you're beautiful!"

"I bet you say that to all the boys," he growled. His voice was deep, inhuman—like a force of nature.

She laughed. "No, but then, you're the first boy I've ever dated that could turn into a dragon."

Steven closed his eyes, feeling out his huge, powerful new body. Idly, he wondered if he could fly yet. He flexed his wings. Probably, yes. He was a dragon with wings, and he knew with a little practice, he would soon be soaring through the air. That realization was delicious.

Tessa held the grimoire, reading it. "It's not just the skill tree that updated. There are spells in here, Steven. Pages and pages of them. The first set of spells are *Magica Defensio*. They include Shielding, Hide, and something called Mind Wipe. I think that's to stop humans from remembering they saw anything supernatural."

"Like in that movie, *Men in Black*," Steven rumbled.

"Bingo. But there are also blank spell slots, which makes me think maybe there are more spells out there to learn and unlock." Tessa shook her head and gently—reverently—set the book on the floor in front of her. She sat, cross-legged, back straight, with her hands resting on her lap, palms up. Her left hand rested on her right hand, and her thumbs were only an eighth of an inch apart. If she didn't keep her concentration, they would touch.

Clearly, she had read and understood the section on meditation. He knew she would be breathing in through her nose and out through her mouth.

He shifted from his True Form back into his human shape and joined her. Sitting there, he focused on his breathing and on keeping his thumbs from touching. He could picture the skill tree perfectly, and the *Magica Defensio* on the right wing called to him, throbbing with a dull golden light. Yes, he could feel how to manifest the Animus into a physical form.

"*Magica Defensio*," Tessa whispered. Then, "Steven. Look."

The air around her shimmered a light pink color. Then a semitranslucent sphere formed above them, drifting gently down until it touched his head. It felt like someone tapping on him. It was there, her magic, in the form of an orb.

"*Magica Defensio*," Steven said, following her lead. Animus flowed from his body to create a semitranslucent onyx orb. His sphere swayed, bumping gently into hers with a slight clicking sound.

"I can't believe mine is pink," Tessa murmured, rolling   her   eyes.   "So   sexist."

She morphed her sphere, *willing* it bigger and opening a hole in the bottom. She lowered the orb until it settled around her.

Steven lengthened his sphere until it was arrow shaped, then *willed* it forward, slamming the tip into her shield. The swirling pink around her flashed, and his arrow disappeared into a puff of smoke.

He stood, turned Homo Draconis, and tried to touch her with a claw. Again, the air around her flashed a more vibrant pink. Try as he might, he couldn't pierce the shield she'd created around her.

Tessa gasped. "You … me … am I doing that?"

"I think so," Steven said. "Welcome to the wonderful world of magic."

The pink shield faded, and Steven's claw came down to settle gently on the new Magician. He backed up, turned into his True Form, and carefully picked her up in his enormous hand. She seemed so fragile and soft compared to the hard edges of his scales. He raised her up until he was gazing on her.

She smiled at him. Her eyes were full of such love. "It's official, Steven, you've swept me off my feet."

He laughed in a thunderous growl and set her back down. Then he returned to his human form and pulled her into a tight hug. "The feeling is mutual, Tessa. All of this dragon stuff wouldn't mean much if I didn't have you to share it with."

She sighed. And cried one more tear as she reached up and ran a hand over his head. "Shifting must've given you your hair back. I'm glad. I really like it."

Steven was glad for that.

They reluctantly broke the embrace. "Let's get something to eat," he said. "And then we have to find Aria. I think we're ready."

"Hell yeah we are!" Tessa agreed.

Steven picked up his cell phone, then on a whim, tried his mom at home. He didn't have high hopes. He thought it would ring and ring. It didn't. She picked up. "Hello?"

Steven let out a sigh of relief. But then realized he had no idea what to ask her. How did you discuss your secret dragon heritage with your adopted mother?

TWENTY-FOUR

I N THE CAVE OF THE SACRED POOLS, TESSA DRESSED
while Steven stood near the fireplace, his phone
pressed against his ear.

"Mom!" Steven said in exasperation. "Where
have you been? I've been trying to call you for like three
days. I left messages at work. You missed my birthday."

His mother wailed, "Oh, Steven, your birthday?
I'm so sorry. How can you ever forgive me? And this
was a big one. I had things I wanted to tell you. No, not
this one. Next year. You're nineteen, now, right?"

"No, Mom," Steven sighed. "I'm twenty. Two
decades."

His mom's voice grew distant. "On the eve of his
third decade, he will know, he will know…"

Steven shivered. It was what Stefan Drokharis
had said.

Florence Whipp was quiet for a long time, and
then she said, "I can't talk about this on the phone. Can

247

you stop by? I forgot, or maybe I wanted to forget. We have to talk, though, and it might be difficult for you to understand."

Steven felt tears in his eyes. "I know, Mom. I know I'm adopted. I know most of what happened twenty years ago."

"I looked for that topaz pendant in the junk drawer, but I couldn't find it. Joe said it would be important." Again, his mom sounded strange. "Can you stop by?"

"Are you okay?" Steven asked.

This time the quiet on the other end of the phone felt ominous. Were there people with her? Was Edgar Vale there?

"Mom, are you okay?" Steven asked again, fear freezing his belly.

"Yes, Steven, come by. I'll be home all day. I won't leave."

"I'll be right there," he said. "And I love you, Mom. Nothing is going to change that. But are you okay?"

"Yes, I love you too. Just come quickly." His mom hung up the phone.

That definitely felt wrong.

Tessa gazed on him with worry in her eyes. "Everything alright?"

Steven shrugged, lips pursed into a thin line. "I don't know. I don't think so. We'd better hurry."

They headed down the spiral staircase and into the entry room. Steven threw on yet another set of clothes, which again, felt like the whole purpose of having a Hoard. From there, they beelined for the garage. Steven so wanted to take the Corvette or the Charger, but with the wet pavement and snow in the air, he reluctantly decided on the Bronco.

His eyes flashed over the damaged Mercedes and seeing it made him both mad and scared. Aria … they had to find her before midnight; otherwise, she'd be forced to marry Rhaegen Mulk.

Steven found the keys and slipped in the driver's seat. Tessa hit the passenger seat with the grimoire sitting on her lap. There was a loop of leather on the spine where the topaz pen fit perfectly. The barista turned Magician found the registration in the glove compartment. "Okay, no getting pulled over. The registration expired in 1997."

That made sense. A year before he was born.

"If there's trouble," he said, "you protect my mom. I'll do the fighting."

Tessa nodded. "Yes, with my new magic spells, which I can cast, since I'm the Magician. Me. Fuck yeah!"

He grinned at her as he backed up the Bronco. He threw it into drive and they went screeching through the cave toward the exit. The magical entrance opened automatically, and he was back on the highway. They heard sirens below as well as the chatter of radios. Lights flashed in the cloudy day. That would be the police and a road crew to investigate the remnants of their battle with the yellow dragon. Getting past them would be difficult, so he spun the Bronco around.

They would have to take the long way.

Tessa's phone had GPS and a map app, so she guided him over Lookout Mountain. They finally found I-70, and he roared west toward his mother's house in Thornton. Tessa read the grimoire the entire way.

Twenty minutes later, he pulled up to the house in the lower-middle-class neighborhood where he'd grown up. A quaint yellow-brick ranch style, it had an attached one-car garage and a front lawn that had seen better days. The street was wide, quiet, and shaded by tall trees, which lined the walkways on both sides. Like his mom's place, the other houses were mostly ranches—older, but well cared for. For the most part, at least. They both got out of the car. On such a wet, cloudy spring day, no one ventured out and the streets were empty.

A little mist rained from the sky with a snowflake or two thrown in to make things interesting.

Steven shivered at the chill, missing the warmth of the fires and the pools. Tessa nodded toward the house. "You go in first. I'll be backup."

"Sounds like a plan." Steven walked up to his house, used his key, and opened the door. "Hey, Mom. You okay?" he called out, scanning the living room. The living room had been the same for twenty years: a couch and an easy chair, with afghans covering them just like doilies covered the neo-colonial end tables. The coffee table was also doily central, with a SCENIC COLORADO book of photography on it. Everything was in place, just like it should be. No sign of a struggle.

The delicious whiff of his mom's cooking filled the house—waffles, breakfast sausage, eggs. Florence Whipp came out of the kitchen a moment later with batter on her nose. She was a thick middle-aged woman with wild hair, crow's feet poking out from the corner of her eyes, and a face that liked to smile. Her hands were bright red with thick knuckles. They were the hands of a woman who had worked her entire life to make sure her son always had food and shelter, if not other opportunities.

"Steven!" She hurried over and hugged him. "I'm so sorry I missed your birthday. And I can't find that necklace. He said it would be important, and I kept it around, but now I can't find it. I feel so stupid."

"You're not stupid, Mom." He hugged her tighter. Persephone might've been a great woman/dragon, but she hadn't been there every second of his life.

Steven broke the embrace and went to the door. "All clear, Tessa. We're fine." He turned. "Mom, what happened? How come you never picked up the phone?"

"I got tired of those scam people calling me. All the time with them. I tried to turn off the phone, but I couldn't figure it out, and if I left the receiver off the hook, it would make that awful sound. So I put all my phones in the basement. Then I forgot about them."

He chuckled. Such a mom thing to do. "What about your manager at work? I left a bunch of messages with her."

"She never told me." Mrs. Whipp frowned, forehead creasing. "That woman has it in for me, I swear!"

Tessa approached the door. For a second, Steven wasn't sure his mom would approve of her with her partially shaved head, tattoos, and piercings. But Tess was all class. "Hi, Mrs. Whipp. I'm Tessa. I'm Steven's friend."

"Girlfriend!" Mrs. Whipp shouted. "A girl, Steven! A real girl. You found a girl. Kathy Roberson thought you were gay, but I didn't." She shook her head.

251

"I know. Though if you were, that would be just fine. I just didn't want you to be alone in this cold, cruel world."

His mom bustled over and hugged Tessa with every ounce of her strength.

Steven about died of embarrassment.

Tessa, though, took it all good-naturedly. "I'm a real girl. And Steven isn't gay. I can assure you."

His mom blinked, then laughed and motioned them into the kitchen. "Come on in, and we can eat and catch up. I'll keep looking for the pendant. It was important. And I owe you a birthday. I made waffles, your favorite, with the bacon grease in the batter. I know it's too late to even call it brunch, but I also know you like breakfast food."

"Sounds awesome," Steven said and meant it. He was famished. Positively ravenous.

They all sat down at the round kitchen table. The tablecloth was as lacy as the doilies. The kitchen was big, green, and so 1970s. It hadn't been updated in the half-century since it had been built. The electric stove was the original and only half the burners worked. Steven, though, only had eyes for the spread laid out before him: syrup, waffles, sausage, bacon, and eggs, with grapefruit halves in the good bowls.

They talked while they ate.

"Mom," Steven said as he dug into his fifth waffle. "Tell me about Stefan and Persephone Drokharis. I know most of the story already, and I'm fine with it."

His mom frowned and cried a little, but laughed more. She was armed with her instant decaf coffee doctored up with non-dairy creamer and lots of artificial sugar. "You're just glad Joe Whipp wasn't your real father, amiright?"

Steven paused eating and then had to laugh. "Uh, kind of. But you'll always be my real mother."

"If you want me to excuse myself, I can," Tessa said. "If you want to talk in private, I'll understand."

"Please, stay," Mrs. Whipp insisted. "I can tell by how you two are, that you're close and bound to get closer. It's what happens with people your age."

Tessa nodded happily and stayed, but she remained quiet. A lot of history was about to come out.

"Joe was a scoundrel," Mrs. Whipp said. "He was exciting and adventurous, and I was just me. Being with him was part amusement park funhouse and part funeral … oh the sadness he could bring. But mostly he left me alone, which at times, was a kindness. I liked my independence." She paused, staring into her mug. "He didn't want you to know the truth. Not until you turned twenty. He said that you'd be safer if you didn't know you were adopted."

"Smart," Steven said. "Did you ever meet Stefan Drokharis?"

His mom didn't answer the question. She stirred her coffee, lost in the past. "You came to us, and you were a little baby, a cute little baby, brought home in a storm. It was cold that spring, so cold and snowy. I swore I'd love you like my own. Joe came and went, but it was always you and me against the world. To tell you the truth, I forgot you weren't mine. It was a poker game that started it all, though. That's how we ended up with you. Or, at least, how he ended up meeting Stefan."

"A poker game?" Steven asked, confused.

Mrs. Whipp nodded. "At the new Wells Fargo skyscraper in downtown Denver. Did you know that the building has its own zip code? 80274. I remember when they were building it. I didn't like how it looked at first, but now it really adds something to the skyline. I drive by it every day. It makes me think of Joe. It's supposed to be a cash register, up top, but I don't know that it looks like one."

Steven and Tessa exchanged glances. This felt important, though Steven didn't know how it all fit together. "A poker game at the Wells Fargo building?"

"Yes, you know, your father—well, adopted father—he liked to gamble. No, not like, it was his thing. He had a gambling addiction, but in the end, it brought you to me." Mrs. Whipp sipped her coffee and stopped talking, an empty look filling her face.

"Tell me about the poker game," Steven prodded gently.

"Joe said they were big rollers there, real dragons, he said. But Joe got strange. He said some of the people he met weren't human, but other things. I blamed it on his drinking. But he said that's where he met Stefan Drokharis the first time. But, he also said the whole thing was run by Ronald Reagan, which should tell you what his state of mind was. A president, gambling? With my Joe? No." She laughed a little and shook her head ruefully.

"Are you sure it was Ronald Reagan and not Rhaegen Mulk?" Tessa asked.

"I suppose that does sound a bit familiar," Mrs. Whipp admitted with a shrug. "But it was so long ago, it's hard to remember. In any case, Joe said they were all rich, and they didn't mind losing. They thought he was cute. I know women were there. That bothered me, some. But the only pretty faces that could truly capture Joe's attention were queens on cards. His ladies, he called them, when we played gin rummy."

"And you're saying those poker games were held at the Wells Fargo building?" Steven asked.

"That's right. At the top, in a secret suite, or so Joe said." Mrs. Whipp got up and went to the drawers in the kitchen. "But really, that pendant, Joe said it would tell you everything, but how can a pendant talk? I don't know. It's all very strange."

"Sit down, Mom," Steven said. "I have the pendant. And yeah, it told me everything." He wasn't sure if he should tell his mother about the secret world of Dragonsouls, not right then.

Tessa put it together in a whisper. "Another Aerie. Maybe Rhaegen Mulk's Aerie, in the Wells Fargo building. If that's the case, I bet that's where Aria is."

Mrs. Whipp sat down at the table again. Steven's phone twittered in his pocket. He took it out and saw that it was Aria calling.

He launched to his feet, spilling his mom's coffee. "Hold on, Mom," he said, thrusting a *wait a minute* finger into the air. "I have to take this."

He went out the back door and stood on the back porch. Thick snowflakes tumbled out of the sky now. Some of the flakes caught on the overgrown weeds and tangles of bushes in his backyard. He kicked himself for not taking better care of his mother's lawn. Well, once he sold a Rembrandt or two, he'd hire a service to take care of everything before he found a better place for her to live.

He pressed the answer button. "Hello?"

"Steven! Run!" Aria's voice was as desperate as it was afraid. Then static and rustling filled the speaker.

A new voice took over, deep and despicable. "Where you at, boy? You and I have one more dance before my Prime comes back for his wedding. I'm gonna give Mulk your head as a weddin' present."

"Edgar, if you hurt Aria, I'm going to eat your heart while you watch," Steven growled.

"Now that's a big threat. You don't even know where I am."

Steven grinned. But he did. "How about you and I meet at my old apartment? You know where that is? I want to kick your ass in the same place where Aria fried your ass."

"Sun sets at five. How about you and me dance there at six? You and me, whelp. Just the two of us. I'm gonna love watching you die."

Click. The phone went dead.

Steven walked back inside the house. "Mom, Tessa and I have to go. But things are going to change. I came into some money, and it's a long story, but now is not the time."

Tessa took her dishes to the sink while Mrs. Whipp went to him. "Steven, what's going on? You seem so different, older. What's changed?"

"Everything, Mom. Everything. I'll tell you all about it, I promise, but not now."

"Are you okay, Steven?" she asked, concern filling her words as she searched his face.

"Never better. But we need to go." He leaned in and kissed her on the forehead, then shrugged free of her arms.

After they all said their goodbyes, Steven was back in the Bronco with Tessa beside him.

Steven was quiet until he got on the I-25 on-ramp. "Okay, Edgar thinks I'm going to meet him at my old apartment to fight at six. We wait until he leaves the Wells Fargo building, and then we go into Mulk's Aerie and rescue Aria."

"What if your mom has the details wrong?" Tessa asked.

"She doesn't," Steven said, "not this time."

A plan formed in his head. He turned to Tessa. "I wasn't the only one crushing on you at the coffee shop. Bud had a thing for you as well, didn't he?"

The barista grimaced. "Yeah, I guess. But what does that douchebag have to do with any of this?"

Steven grinned. "Call him."

He told her his plan.

TWENTY-FIVE

I T NEVER REALLY GOT SERIOUS ABOUT SNOWING, BUT it did get colder as twilight took over the sky. Tessa paid to park the Bronco at a downtown lot, and it was wicked expensive. Steven missed Aria's magic American Express. But soon, soon he would be a millionaire, once they started selling off pieces from the Drokharis Hoard.

He and Tessa walked through the deserted downtown. Sunday evening, nothing was going on, and there were few cars and even fewer people. They posted up across the street from the Wells Fargo building, with a clear view of the front entryway.

A handful of uneventful minutes passed by before Bud showed up, walking down the sidewalk with a wide shit-eating grin on his face. It was the grin of a man who expected to get laid. He was dressed in jeans and a sleek North Face ski jacket, his hands shoved into his pockets. He had a scarf wrapped around his neck and a trendy stocking cap. His breath came out in clouds. He walked right into the Wells Fargo Building, just as Tessa had instructed him.

The phone in Tessa's pocket buzzed, and she picked it up after a few rings. Bud's voice came over the phone, indistinct. "Thanks so much for coming downtown for me," she said after a second. "The party is on the top floor—penthouse level. There's a security guard, right? Just tell them you're there to see Rhaegen Mulk."

More chatter from Bud. Tessa frowned. "Yeah, I know, Bud. I've always thought you were hot too."

A pause as Bud replied.

Tessa shook her head, her frown deepening. "If there's any problem, come back to the lobby. I'll have to walk you in. Sometimes the security at these parties are total assholes. See you soon." She hung up and turned on Steven. "You know, this wouldn't have worked at the Antlers in Colorado Springs."

"Yeah," Steven agreed, "but that wasn't an active Aerie. I'm betting he goes up there, everyone flips out, and he comes right back down."

Tessa's concern was evident on her face. "You're betting his life on that. What if they just kill him?"

"I don't think they will," Steven said. "Dragonsouls have to hide themselves, and civilian murders must be a big deal. Sure, it's possible that Rhaegen Mulk might have the entire DPD in his pocket, but that still won't stop the media reporting on some rando kid disappearing downtown."

Tessa reached into her purse, where the grimoire and topaz pen were stuffed, and came out with her cigarettes. "Just a half of one," she said. "This plan is all kinds of fucked. I know he's a bully, and I know he's kind of an asshat, but he's still a person."

"Him? I don't think so. He's a lower creature. Like all you humans," Steven said. He meant it as a joke.

Not only did Tessa not laugh, she glared at him.

He backtracked right away. "Totally kidding. But Tessa, we needed someone to help us, and we needed someone clueless. Once he gets kicked out of the building, then we can snag him and get info on what we're facing. You and I can't run recon. They're searching for us."

She didn't answer. Instead, she clicked open her lighter, lit a cigarette, and exhaled. "This is a side of you I haven't seen."

"What do you mean?" he asked.

She flicked the ashes from her cigarette. "Actually, there are a couple of sides, and they're dark. I have to say, they're darker than I would've thought."

Steven nodded. "I can be brutal when I need something. Like working eight jobs and not sleeping. And I can go scorched-earth when it comes to strategy. Maybe if Stefan Drokharis had more of that, he wouldn't have been killed. I don't know."

"I can respect all that," Tessa said. "But what gets me is your grudge against Bud. You stood up to him. You slapped him. It's over. If you use your new powers to go back to your old life to get revenge, this is never going to work."

He let her words sink in. Part of him did like the idea of sticking it to everyone who had ever wronged him. He had the power and he had the money. Todd Butch would pay for pantsing him in the seventh grade. Yes, Steven's revenge would be swift and brutal. But then he went back to what he felt for both Tessa and Aria. And his rage at what Rhaegen Mulk did to his parents and their vassals.

"You're right," he said finally. "I have a new life. My number one priority is keeping you and Aria safe. No refrigerator for either of you. And my second priority? To take down Rhaegen Mulk. He murdered my parents and he would've killed me, as a baby. We both know that."

"And if you kill Mulk, I'm assuming you'll get his Primacy. Which is kind of the whole point of Dragonsouls, right?"

"I don't know." The thought did seem appealing to him, in some strange way. If he was at the top of the pile, there would be less danger of anyone hurting his Escort. That word came so easily to him now.

Tessa went quiet, her face troubled.

Steven tried to make her feel better. "Look, when I realized that we needed intel on Mulk's Aerie, I had no other plan. Bud seemed like the perfect guy for the job."

Speaking of which, Tessa's phone buzzed.

Bud immediately started screaming at her. Steven couldn't hear every word, but he did hear "bitch" and not just once.

Tessa took it in stride. "Okay, okay, okay, calm down. I'll come and grab you out of the lobby. Better yet, come outside—I'll explain everything in a minute."

When she hung up, she rubbed her cigarette out on the building and then put it in a pocket on the purse. "Yeah, maybe I was wrong. Bud is total asshole. But he's alive. So that's something."

They made their way across the street and pressed their backs up against the side of the building, just out of view of the entryway. A few minutes later, Bud came storming out of the building, and damn did he look worse for the wear: one eye puffy, face red, hair mussed, bottom lip split.

"Over here, Bud," Tessa called out, waving at him with one hand.

Immediately, his eyes locked on Steven. "Oh, I get it. Hey, Steven, still trying to get back at me? This hurts, Tessa. This hurts a lot."

Tessa sighed. "Look, I'm sorry. You wouldn't have come if I didn't play it like I did, and we needed your help, Bud. Seriously we did. And this is life or death we're talking. You saw the guns, didn't you?"

"Yeah, like machine guns," Bud huffed, crossing his arms.

"Exactly," Tessa said.

Bud glanced at Steven again. "You've been working out. Damn, I'm sorry. I never would've dicked with you if I would've known you'd try and get me killed."

Steven shrugged. "Let's call it even. So, tell us what you saw. Our friend is most likely up in that penthouse, and we have to rescue her."

"You do know Aria, right?" Tessa asked.

Bud blinked in shock. "The foreign exchange student from India? Her?"

"Yeah," Steven said. "She's in trouble. We think she's being held hostage up there. Did you see any sign of her?"

"No, not her." Bud stood there for a minute, collecting himself. "So, the security guard in the lobby got all funny when I mentioned that name, Rhaegen Mulk. It was like a magic ticket. He walked me to the elevator, used a special key, and opened a hidden panel. Now, I was thinking this was all really cool, if a little strange. He hits a button, and I go straight up …"

Bud went on to describe a short hallway that led to a set of huge wooden double doors. He didn't need to knock. Three goons in black Kevlar flooded out, grabbed him, and socked him in the stomach and the face. They screamed questions at him—who was he, what was he doing there, how had he heard of Rhaegen Mulk. He kept telling them that Tessa was there, and he was there for the party. They laughed at that. Of course. Bunch of assholes.

Still, he managed to get a glance inside the penthouse, and it was swanky, expensive, but yeah, of course it was, with a view of the skyline and all. A whole panel of windows showing Denver's lights. There was a woman in there, small, petite, and blonde. She simply smirked at him as if the whole world were some big, sick joke. She wore a slinky black dress. Hot—like *knockout* hot. Around her were men with assault rifles. And some guy in a purple silk suit.

At that point in the story, Bud grinned. "Yeah, seeing the woman and the guy surrounded by mercenaries felt off. Like those two were tougher than all those men with big guns. Something about them was just ... off. Weird, you know what I mean?" He paused, squinting. "Kinda the way you're off, actually."

Steven knew why Bud thought that. Two Dragonsouls, most likely—vassals to Mulk. Doubt gripped Steven. Could he take on other fully grown Dragonsouls? He felt powerful, but with dragons in the mix, as well as Edgar Vale, it felt daunting.

Tessa sighed. "But no sign of Aria."

Bud shook his head. "Is she really up there?"

"We think so," Steven answered.

263

Bud turned pensive. "We have to get her away from those people. We should call the police."

"We think this Mulk guy owns the police," Tessa said. "We're going to have to rescue her ourselves, but this lot is on the lookout for us, which is why we recruited you."

That made Bud laugh. "You two? No offense, but that is not going to happen. What have you been smoking, and can I have some?"

"Thanks for the intel, Bud," Steven said. There was no way he was going to reveal his true self to this dipwad. "And we're sorry for messing with you. It won't happen again."

Bud went and gripped Steven's arm. "Look, whatever is between us, we can call it water under the bridge, okay. But please man, don't do it. Don't mess with those guys. They have guns, and they look like they know how to use them." His voice dropped low. "Between you and me, they only let me go because I started to cry. Otherwise, I think they might've killed me. If you go in there to rescue Aria, they'll definitely shoot you five ways from Sunday."

"We can't leave Aria. She's with us now, like, we're together. We love her, and she loves us," Tessa said.

Bud quirked an eyebrow. "Like, love, like together, together?" His voice rose in a lilt.

Steven nodded and shook off Bud's hand.

"Steven Whipp, damn, you've come a long way. I can't believe it. Except I also can. You've changed, bro. You've changed like no one ever has."

That was the understatement of the year.

Then Bud said the impossible. "If Aria is in trouble, I want to help more. Maybe I can be a distraction."

"Really?" Both Tessa and Steven asked in complete surprise.

Bud turned pale and sweaty, but there was courage burning in his eyes. "Yeah, I've come this far. I have an idea. I go get pizza and take it up, like as an apology. No one is going to kill a dude bringing pizza."

"That better be some tasty fucking pizza," Tessa breathed.

While he listened to the exchange, Steven couldn't help but wonder if this was how Dragonsoul Primes got vassals. Were people just drawn to him now? It made sense.

"No, I want to help," Bud said, resolute. "I know an all-night place not too far away from here. Give me a few minutes." He got out his phone and called an Uber. "I'll be right back." A few minutes later a Prius showed up, Bud got in, and the car drove off.

"We should talk him out of it," Tessa said, watching the car zip around a corner.

Steven wasn't so sure. If Bud could get the attention of the goons up in the penthouse, that might be the edge they needed. It was 5:20 p.m. They didn't have much time. At least Edgar wouldn't be there at 6. Or so they hoped.

But what if they got into the penthouse and Aria was gone?

Well, at least Steven would get more Animus from the battle. And it would draw Edgar back to his boss's Aerie. Worst-case scenario? Mulk was there, and

Steven would find himself fighting the Dragonsoul Prime himself.

Despite the wet chill, Steven shed his clothes. He then went Homo Draconis. He growled out the plan. "Bud keeps them busy by the door. And we go in through the window. But I'll have to fly up there. Time to practice."

Lucky the streets were empty. Steven easily transformed into his True Form. In a heartbeat, a thirty-foot dragon stood on Seventeenth Avenue in downtown Denver. He ran down the middle of the street, loping along like a wolf on the prowl. He raised his black wings and pumped them, acclimating to the new muscles in his shoulders, and then launched himself into the air. Lifting off was more effort than he'd imagined, but then he was off. Flying!

Then a wing dipped, and he came tumbling down onto the pavement, ass over teakettle. He thwapped his head on the road painfully.

Tessa's laughter echoed off the surrounding buildings.

He got to his feet and turned to her, lips pulled back to show his formidable fangs, which were like chunks of black diamond. "Laugh it up, magic girl. But I better get this right since you're going to be riding me."

"Been there, done that," Tessa quipped.

That made Steven chuckle. A car's light flashed in the distance. Steven turned back into a very naked human and dashed to the side. The car drove past. Marijuana smoke fogged up the interior.

"Colorado." Steven grinned. "Amiright?"

"Right you are," Tessa agreed. "Now try it again, dragon boy."

He shifted back into a dragon and went sprinting down the street once more. This time, he managed liftoff much quicker, but when he tried to climb he went careening to the right and hit a building—morphing into a Homo Draconis at the last minute so he'd cause less damage. To the building. Not to himself.

He landed on the ground, human butt first. "Any suggestions?" he asked, shaking his head.

Tessa made a face. "Uh, I've never flown before. But maybe it's too hard to both take off and fly. Maybe if you jumped off something tall?"

"Damn. Are you trying to kill me?" Steven hated the idea. It would make the crash even more painful. However, it was difficult to get enough lift while trying to maneuver in the relatively narrow streets. "I'll try it. But … ouch," he muttered, gaining his feet.

"You'll be fine." Tessa whipped out her phone. "Let me text Bud that we'll be at the parking garage on Sherman Street. We can try it off the top of that. It's only like five stories. You'll be fine."

"Says you." Steven threw his clothes back on. Another quick change. How did Superman and Peter Parker do it?

Then they were running down the street to the parking garage. They found steps and started up.

A thought hit Steven. "If Bud sees me as a dragon, he'll know my secret."

"There are spells we can use. I've been studying." Tessa gasped from the physical exertion of sprinting up the concrete stairwell. "No more talking. I'm so out of shape."

At the top, they jogged to the edge of the parking structure. The street looked small from so far up. It felt like ten stories, even though Steven knew intellectually that Tessa was right, and it was only five.

Steven once again shed his clothes. "I'm gonna get those snap-away clothes for quick changes—the ones those male strippers use—'cause this sucks. Hard. I'm getting chafed."

Tessa was bent over, hands on her knees, trying to catch her breath. "That's the least of your worries," she panted. "I'd be more worried about going splat at this stage."

Steven climbed up onto the concrete guard and stood there, swaying just a little. This was it. If he messed this up, he'd break a bone, or all his bones—assuming he didn't just die outright—and then their plans wouldn't mean squat. He threw his arms around himself, teeth chattering. It was so fucking cold! Still, he could feel himself sweating. This was crazy. He was trying to teach himself to fly. Still, there was no other way, and nothing ventured, nothing gained.

Before he could talk himself out of jumping, Steven dropped off the side. Stupid, there was no place for his wings. He was too close to the edge.

He assumed his partial form and kicked off the building, then turned into a dragon as he plummeted, the ground rushing toward him. His wings loved the feel of the whistling wind under him. He craned his neck, arched his back, and stretched out his wings, which allowed him to bank up—gliding more than flying. Damn! That was so much easier! He pumped his leathery wings a handful of times, gaining altitude, then wheeled around a corner and saw the pot-smokers in their car again. Good thing they were stoned, or they might've been surprised to see a dragon.

But his scales were midnight black, providing him natural camouflage in the night. He beat his wings again, harder this time, and rose higher. He was doing it! He was flying!

It was like a dream, where he could control every aspect of his flight. His wings now felt like an integral part of him, and he knew it was partly because of his heritage. The Drokharis weren't normal Dragonsouls, he knew that. They were special, which meant he was too.

He soared up higher and higher, until he was coasting above the skyscrapers. Clouds swirled overhead, but there was little wind, and the snow had completely stopped. He wasn't cold now, not a bit. He saw Tessa standing on the parking structure, next to his bundle of clothes.

Uh, he'd forgotten one little detail.

Landing.

He drifted down.

This was gonna hurt.

That was when Steven saw Bud holding the pizza boxes on the street. The guy's mouth hung open in shock.

Well, there went the big secret thousands of Dragonsouls had kept for thousands of years.

Leave it to a butthole like Bud to blow the whistle.

TWENTY-SIX

S TEVEN COULDN'T WORRY ABOUT BUD LEARNING the truth. He had to focus. He didn't like the idea of going directly from the sky and hitting the top of the parking garage at full speed. And he didn't think he could poof his wings out like a parachute.

Then an idea hit him.

But it would give Bud an eye full.

Steven glided down the empty street, next to the parking garage, careful not to hit either side of the steel-and-glass canyon. He beat his wings once, which gave him enough lift to get to the top of the parking structure. He banked right.

He nearly took off Tessa's head. She ducked as he came down onto the roof. It was only a six-foot drop, but he was going way too fast. His front feet hit, then his back, but then the weight of his tail flipped him over, and suddenly he was several tons of dragon rolling out of control across the top of the tower. The world became a blur. He ended up on his back, as a human, staring up at Tessa, who had her phone to her ear.

"No, Bud, I didn't see a dragon. You feeling okay?" Tessa asked.

Steven stayed on the ground and wrapped his arms around himself. He hurt from the terrible landing, but he was still alive, and he hadn't broken a bone. He had a handful of bruises and scrapes, but nothing that would keep him down for long. Besides, he hardly even noticed them because he was absolutely elated with the fact that he'd flown! Yes, he had everything to learn, taking off, landing, all that. But that first flight, beneath the clouds, above the city, the wind on his face and the breeze under his wings, holding him up, it had been magical.

He grinned.

Tessa frowned. "Bud, you shouldn't go up there. It's crazy. They might kill you." A long pause. Then Tessa sighed. "And he hung up on me. Bud's on his way up. He said he'd text me from the elevator. He totally saw you."

"Yeah, that's a problem." Steven sat up with a wince.

"Well, that might not matter. If things go off the rails with the pizza, we might've seen the last of Bud."

"I flew, Tessa," Steven said softly. "My landing was terrible, but I think it might've been momentum and the weight. I'm going to try changing into Homo Draconis next time, and maybe try to bank it better so my speed is less."

"Hopefully, we'll have Aria with us and she can help you with all that madness," Tessa said. "Otherwise, Bud's sacrifice will be for nothing."

Steven got to his feet and jogged over to the edge of the building again. "I think it will work better if you're right on my back when we dive off. And we are going to have to dive. I was too close to the parking structure last time."

Tessa let out a long breath, hands balled into fists, eyes pressed tightly closed. "I don't know if I can do it. I'm not a fan of heights. And I hate flying on airplanes." She opened her eyes, lips pressed into a thin cut. "Maybe you should go on without me."

Steven didn't say a word for a long time. He'd been so caught up in his plan, he never realized how crazy it was. And that there was a very real chance Tessa might get hurt. Or even die.

"You're right," he said. "I can't ask you to go. And especially since I'm not a very good flier yet. I completely understand if you want to stay here."

Tessa was quiet for a long beat, her face surging through a range of emotions—fear, worry, anxiety, disgust—before finally landing on determination. She slung her purse so it crisscrossed her chest. Then she rushed over to him and shoved him. "Never, Steven. I'm in this with you to the end. I'm going with you. You fight. I'll find Aria. If we can get her into the action, they won't stand a chance. And if shit goes sideways, I'm going to fucking cast a spell and fix it. Because I'm a Magician. Remember in the coffee shop, when we talked? We both knew we were special. Well, this is my chance to prove it. And I'm going to. Case closed."

Steven drew her in and kissed her. And then he hopped up onto the edge. He put out a hand and drew Tessa up onto the concrete wall.

"I'm keeping my eyes on you, Steven," Tessa said. "I'm not looking down."

"Okay, we're going to run to the end and we're going to jump. I'll turn into the dragon, and you'll grab hold of me. Okay?"

"You have a cute butt," Tessa teased in a breathless voice.

Steven rolled his eyes and grinned. "Let's get through this and then you can look at it all you want. Now let's do this thing." Steven jogged with Tessa behind him, and then he launched himself off the top of the parking garage. He immediately started falling, but at the same time, he transformed into a dragon and spread his wings wide; he tried to give Tessa the biggest target possible.

The minute his wings caught the air, he rose, and Tessa slammed down onto his back with a *whoof*. She rode on his right side, gripping one of the spines on his back. Her legs were near his right wing. She scrambled, pulling herself up, until her legs straddled him, her hands clasped around the spikes jutting up near his neck. Steven had never been more focused in his life. He couldn't mess this up. He wouldn't. He loved how Tessa felt on his back, her warm body, and he loved her trust in him. She was afraid of heights, and yet, here she was, riding on a dragon through the air.

"I can't believe I'm doing this!" she screamed out. It was part terror and part happiness. Steven raised and lowered his wings and got a good bit of speed going.

He felt Tessa kiss his back. "And I love the way you smell!"

The wet stink of the city was eclipsed by his smoky orange blossom odor. Steven turned slightly, carefully, so Tessa wouldn't be thrown off. He spiraled

273

around the Wells Fargo building, rising higher and higher. The night would hide him, and yet he knew that the first order of business needed to be the hiding magic, which was part of the *Magica Defensio* spell family.

His ears twitched when her phone twittered. That would be Bud, in the elevator, hell's own pizza delivery service. He circled one more time, gaining elevation. He leveled off and streaked toward the windows. He hoped he'd timed it right or Bud might find himself on the wrong end of a bullet enema.

Steven accessed the skill tree in his mind and focused his Animus on the DarkArmor ability. He thickened the scales on his tail until they were stronger than steel.

"Hold tight!" he roared to Tessa.

She dropped low, pressing her body into him, wrapping her arms around his neck as he banked his wings. He bashed his extra thick, extra heavy tail into the windows, shattering them. It was like the Incredible Hulk had come with an iron whip to break through the windows. Glass and metal rained down to the streets below.

Steven flapped away, spun, and then stormed in through the gash in the side of the building. His landing was going to be as terrible as it had been on the parking deck, but fuck it. He and Tessa couldn't fight if they weren't inside the penthouse.

She continued to grip him as he turned into his partial form. Then they were both rolling across the floor. He bounced through a glass coffee table, and it shattered into a million pieces. He was up in seconds.

Half a dozen mercenaries in Kevlar were in the room, and half a dozen were in the hallway, eating pizza. Bud, unbelievably, must've brought tasty fucking pizza indeed. All the mercs, both inside and outside the room, were armed with M4 assault rifles. They opened fire. Like before on top of the St. Vrain Aerie, Steven spun and took the bullets to his scaly back. Tessa stood up, covered in cuts and bleeding. She huddled into his arms, and he kept her safe during the initial onslaught.

The second the barrage of bullets tapered off— they were reloading from the sound of things—Tessa darted away, taking cover behind an upturned couch and quickly conjuring her pink, protective dome. Knowing she was safe, Steven whirled and leapt across the room. He landed, spun again, and lashed out with his tail, taking out two soldiers near the door. He then lurched forward and slammed the doors closed and engaged the lock. Eventually, the guards in the front hall would get back in, but this would buy him a little breathing room.

He turned and threw himself at a mercenary on his right, who was pulling out a sleek, matte-black Glock. With one swipe of his claws, he tore through the soldier's face and neck. The man went down, screaming and clutching at where his nose and eyes had been. One hand migrated down to his ruined throat, blood burbling out. The minute his soul left his body, fresh Animus flooded into Steven, filling him with life. With power.

With energy to spare, Steven went True Form, filling the room with his gigantic shape. A glass table exploded harmlessly against his scales. Furniture crunched into kindling. A flick of his tail smashed through a bar and the adjoining barstools. The doors, both to the hall and to the bedrooms, opened inward and he felt them all knock into his legs and arms. No more of the soldiers could get in. If Bud was smart, he'd be running for his life right about now.

Steven opened his fanged mouth and struck like a cobra, chewing a mercenary in half. Warm blood filled his mouth, and he spat it out. A little flame came with it, but only a little. Reaching out, he wrapped his talon-capped hand around another merc, crushing the man like he would crush a Coke can. Both of the destroyed soldiers filled him with more Animus.

Two pistol shots exploded in the tight room, ringing Steven's ears. He felt one bullet whizz by his head while the other round struck him in the hip like a nail into a board. Somehow, that shit got through his scales. Which meant it wasn't a normal gun, not by any stretch of the imagination.

He shifted into his Homo Draconis shape and whirled, facing the attackers. The two mercenaries he'd whipped with his tail were back on their feet. They had old-fashioned pistols, six-shooters, long and thick. Those were Colt Peacekeepers from the nineteenth century. But acid-etched runes, blazing with wicked green light, covered their barrels. Magic if he'd ever seen it. The front door rattled, the handle shaking, the wood bowing in its frame. Thinking fast, Steven seized a destroyed sofa with his tail and hurled it against the entry—jamming the door, hoping to buy a little longer.

But there were still the gunmen with the magic pistols to deal with. With a thought, he accessed his skill tree and located the *Magica Defensio* sub-option on the *Veneficium* side of the tree. With an effort of will, he poured his recently gathered Animus into it.

The revolvers barked again, but the rounds smacked harmlessly into his shield, which was a dusky black color, so unlike Tessa's pink magic. Golden sparks flashed as the bullets ricocheted away—one slamming into a leather club chair, another two smashing into a nearby wall. With a roar he shot forward, and more bullets bounced off his magic. He swept the shield spell to his left side so he could lash out with a claw to rip out the throat of the gunman on the right.

As for the pistolero on the left, Steven kept charging forward until the magic barrier crushed the guy against the wall. He screamed as his bones gave way, and still Steven pressed in. After a few seconds, the guy's eyes glazed over, and Animus rushed in like life-giving air.

Their magic pistols thudded to the floor, as did their bodies.

Steven dropped his shield as he turned, scanning the penthouse. He'd lost track of Tessa in the madness. She wasn't by the sofa. His taking True Form had destroyed so much of the room. It was a wasteland of ruined luxury: scattered debris, crushed furniture, drywall dust, and fragmented glass.

A cold wind blew from the windows he'd whipped out with his armored tail.

The mercs in the hallway were still struggling to get the doors open—they were probably heavily reinforced—so it seemed Steven had the place to himself … at least, he did until a man in a purple suit sauntered in from the connecting master suite, holding the Slayer Blade lightly in one hand. The way he moved, it was like watching a panther stalking a deer. He had a close-cropped beard and stubble on his head. His eyes were a piercing blue. Of course, when he talked, he had an accent. Possibly French.

"So, the Dragonling has become a Dragonsoul," he said with a short nod. "Good. When I kill you, your Animus will be mine."

"Stay back," Steven warned.

"Or what?" The man in the purple suit darted forward, blurring with speed. He cut into Steven's side, then spun the blade around and cut into Steven's arm.

Steven reached for him, but he was too fast. The swordsman wasn't shapeshifting, and he didn't smell like a Dragonsoul. No, he was human, but the way he moved, the way he fought, he obviously had enhanced abilities.

"You're a Warling." Steven gasped in pain, grabbing at his blood-soaked side.

"And you are a Dragonsoul who can cast spells. A lost art, from what I've heard," the man replied. "Rhaegen Mulk severely underestimated you by sending Edgar Vale to do what is obviously a difficult job. Mulk will be very pleased with me when I accomplish the task. I'm Kai Charon. And you? You are a dead man."

The Warling advanced again, coming at Steven like a dancer—lithe, fast, graceful. He feinted, lunged, then twirled the blade and slashed at Steven's chest. With one eye on the door and the men spilling in, he backpedaled, narrowly avoiding the deadly cuts. The sword crackled with power, blackening the air in front of Steven. The Warling darted left, then shot straight in, but this time Steven was ready. He ripped a metal light fixture from the ceiling and smashed it into the side of the Warling's face.

But the Frenchman was good—far better than Steven in a fight. Even as the Warling stumbled to the side, he lashed out, driving the glowing Slayer Blade into Steven's side. Blood flowed freely. Steven reacted on instinct, pulling back, then driving a knee into the Warling's chest, knocking him back and onto his ass.

A small win. The front door groaned and shuddered a second later, wood splintering at last as it gave way. The mercenaries from the hall vaulted over the couch, their weapons held high. Some had M4s, but other wielded magic swords that looked very familiar. They were same weapons the mercs had used at the St. Vrain Aerie.

Those weapons could kill Steven.

Shit, shit, shit.

And there was even more bad news …

A tiny blonde woman appeared in the room. She wore a slinky black dress and strode across the broken glass on bare feet. She changed as she walked, first growing golden brown scales and then claws as a tail elongated out behind her. The smell of almonds washed into the room. Her Homo Draconis form was long, slender, and lethal.

Steven gulped and wondered if this was the end of his adventures. He'd bitten off far more than he could chew, no matter how big his mouth could get.

The last Drokharis was in real trouble.

TWENTY-SEVEN

ARIA SHIVERED IN THE BATHTUB. SHE LAY THERE, naked, chained by enchanted metal. The handcuffs were linked to ankle cuffs by a silver chain engraved with runes of ancient power. The steel on her skin was as cold as the porcelain. The men outside were laughing about some guy they had beaten up, some loser who had wandered up to the top floor looking for a party. Cleary, he'd been a simple, luckless human. And yet, Mulk's vassals had talked about murdering him as casually as talking about a bad poker hand or an unfortunate football play. Their precious Denver Broncos … Men could prattle on about them incessantly.

There was a Warling about, Kai Charon. Mouse, the strange Dragonsoul, spoke the name and teased him relentlessly. This Mouse person was an obvious drunk. And she was mean. Yet, she smelled so good, like roasted almonds. No, candied roasted almonds. There was a definite sweet scent about her. Yes, sweet, even though she hated everything and everyone around her. Aria had never met such a caustic person. It was that very same Dragonsoul who had put her in the tub.

"Be nice," Mouse had hissed, hate glimmering in her gaze. "Or I'll turn on the water. I'll make it nice and warm at first. But then it will grow colder and colder and colder, until you are a frozen little bitch. Still, that would be better than Mulk. You can get used to the cold water. You'll never get used to his touch. Not really, no matter how much you try and convince yourself you love him."

Then the Dragonsoul had simply left.

Shivering, cold, Aria wondered if water wouldn't be better.

She was glad that Edgar Vale, however damaged he was, however rotten inside and out, understood the rules of Dragonsoul mating rituals. While sex, even bad sex, enhanced Animus, outright rape destroyed Animus and could kill the rapist as well as the victim. In the long history of Dragonsouls, sexual violence was rare. Aria was grateful for that. And besides, most Primes didn't need to resort to that. No, they burned with charisma, drawing others to them. Men wanted to be them, to bow before them, and women … Well, few women could resist their natural charms and swagger.

Still, she wanted to be saved. She didn't want to lose her new Prime, her Steven and his other Escort, Tessa. She was surprised to think of Steven in those terms, as a Prime, and yet he was. She knew it. He would eventually kill Rhaegen Mulk and take over the Great Plains Primacy.

She wished she had been honest with Steven and Tessa from the very start. Now, it might be too late. Yet, she felt an odd sense of pride. She hadn't gone quietly into an awful marriage with Mulk. And while she hated him now, once she spent time around him, she would feel herself drawn to him. Eventually, she would want to have sex with him. She might never love him like she loved Steven, but she would learn to want him.

She recalled what Mouse had said about Mulk's touch. It was infuriating and frightening to be so ensorcelled and seduced.

Aria had to find a way to escape. It was Sunday evening, the sun had set, and it was time to flee. Before Rhaegen Mulk came. Aria had heard talk that he would arrive around 11 p.m., an hour before his midnight wedding.

That was how little Mulk thought of the occasion.

Aria was wrestling against the chains when the doorbell rang out in the main room. "Pizza? Would you believe this fucking guy?" one of the mercenaries shouted in disbelief.

Another of Mulk's vassals piped in, "He just don't learn. It's the same guy as a before."

"He must like getting his ass kicked," added a third.

The voices outside dipped and rose, there was a scuffle, and Aria knew the luckless guy wouldn't survive the night.

And then the grand windows in the penthouse were destroyed in a teeth-rattling thunder of destruction. Automatic weapon fire followed. Aria prayed they didn't have any magic rounds in them. Steven's armor was thick, but it wouldn't protect him against sorcery. Not yet.

Pistol shots rang out, and even in the tub she could hear the deep thrum of magic. Damn. Enchanted rounds. Those would be a real problem. And Kai, he had the Slayer Blade. Edgar had made a big show of leaving it with the Warling when he left to duel Steven alone.

But Aria had the idea Steven had not shown up for the fight. Instead, he had come to rescue her.

All thought of the battle fled as Tessa scurried in, her clothes torn and bloodstained. She knelt and yanked on the chains. "Aria, we have to get you out of here. Now!"

Aria felt Tessa's desperation keenly. "You can't break them. I certainly can't. They are magic."

Tessa's face darkened in thought. Then she brightened. "DragonStrength, the second sphere on the Pugna tree."

"I've tried that, but I don't have the Animus," Aria murmured. "Maybe you should go. You're hurt. Steven can't stand against the Warling and Mouse."

"The blonde chick." Tessa nodded. "There was a time where I'd have killed to look like her—small, blonde, petite, super cute. I was able to dodge her. I'm not sure anyone else knows I'm here. We have a minute."

Tessa leaned over and kissed Aria. "I can give you Animus. I have a ton. Let's try."

Aria had never felt less sexual in her entire life. And yet, when she smelled Tessa's familiar scent and felt the soft lips on hers, she felt Animus pass between them. And not just a little. Something had changed at the core of the barista. Once upon a time, Aria had taken a lover, another Dragonsoul woman in India, who had that same amount of supernatural energy flowing in her. But it was rare. Incredibly so. She couldn't help but wonder what in the world had happened in her absence.

She leaned into Tessa, breathing in her immense power. The woman was like a supernatural battery, or maybe a well with no bottom in sight. Aria flexed her wrists, stretching the chain linking the handcuffs to the ankle cuffs. The runes on the silver links radiated a blinding white shine, fighting against her. But they couldn't withstand her strength.

"Keep your hands on me," Aria growled. She needed Tessa's touch to keep her Animus levels up. Aria sat up and pulled apart the metal linking her ankle cuffs. She still had the handcuffs on, but now, she could run. And she could do other things.

Aria rose from the bathtub and caught Tessa before she collapsed. "Are you okay?" she asked.

Tessa nodded. "It's just a lot. And I'm bleeding, but I don't want to stop and look at the wounds. I'll be okay. I can cast spells, Aria. Maybe just one at this point, but I'm going to make that motherfucker count."

"What happened to you?"

Tessa grinned wearily. "Best hot tub experience ever. Make that two. Now, let's go save Steven."

They ran from the bathroom into the master suite, where Aria looked ruefully at the bed. She'd avoid Mulk's touch by any means necessary.

"Open the doors for me," Aria ordered.

Tessa grabbed them and flung them open.

Steven was in the middle of the room, tossing mercenaries into Mouse, who was in her partial form—a slender dragon woman the color of roasted almonds, with long claws and a lashing tail. The hurled bodies kept the Dragonsoul busy, but the Warling was there, hacking away at Steven. Steven whirled and whipped Kai Charon with his tail, but the Warling's skin went dark and shiny. He was using DarkArmor to keep Steven's tail from flaying the skin off his bones. The Warling then used SerpentGrace to speed around. He was on the brink of stabbing Steven in the back when Aria opened her mouth.

Unfortunately, she couldn't shift her shape—the magic of the handcuffs was keeping her trapped in her current form—but she still had a few tricks up her sleeves. As a human, she exhaled a gout of flames that swept over both Steven and the Warling. Aria had caught the Warling unaware. The purple suit caught fire, and he dropped to the floor, rolling to get the flames out even as he used his DarkArmor ability to keep his skin intact. Being a Dragonsoul—and a powerful one to boot—Steven seemed unfazed by the abrupt blaze.

Tessa raced into the room and pulled an M4 from a dead man's hand. She shouldered the rifle and aimed the barrel at Mouse. The bullets wouldn't kill the female Dragonsoul, but they would slow her down.

Aria's throat and face burned from the fire she'd breathed. But she couldn't stop to feel the pain. She hurled herself across the room and seized the Slayer Blade before the Warling could get it.

A terrible smell swept into the wreckage of the penthouse. A familiar smell. Rotting meat.

Aria could almost smell the maggots. Edgar Vale had returned.

◇◇◇

Steven growled when he saw the naked man stride in through the window and walk across the debris on the floor. He didn't have preternatural tough feet of the female Dragonsoul Steven was fighting. Mouse. Her name was Mouse.

Edgar Vale left bloody footprints, and it was clear he didn't give a shit. His beard was wet and tangled. His hairless scalp was a patchwork of shiny pink skin and flaking scabs. His eyes were a diseased red color.

Steven booted the Warling into the wall. Kai Charon hit the wood paneling with a spine-shattering crunch. His purple suit smoldered, and a good portion of his skin was blackened from Aria's Exhalant attack. He might have enough Animus to get to his feet, but that Warling was in bad shape. Aria's attack couldn't have come at a better time.

Mouse broke off her attack, scales pocked from Tessa's bullets.

All turned to face the newcomer to the battle.

Edgar grinned. "And here I thought I might miss the fun. Good trick, Dragonling. And I thought you were too human and stupid to break your word."

Steven was hurt—bleeding from a series of bullet wounds and deep lacerations—and the Animus surging through him from the combat was the only thing keeping him on his feet. He was in no shape to take on his first and worst enemy. But this was the guy who had first attacked him. The assbasket who would've shot Tessa without caring, and he was working for the Dragonsoul who had murdered Steven's birth parents. Edgar Vale had to be put down like the rabid dog he was.

"Not a Dragonling," Steven growled, still in his Homo Draconis form. "I'm a Dragonsoul, like my father before me."

"Well, whoopy fucking do," Edgar snarled. "I'm a full Dragonskin. You think you're so fucking special. Well, you aren't. Being born into royalty isn't as badass as grabbing the crown off the king's head with your own fucking hands. I was born in the gutter, but I'm going to live like a fucking dragon!"

The man transformed into his Homo Draconis form and kept right on going, surging up and out, his bulky gray-green body quickly filling the penthouse. He lunged forward, huge maw snapping closed around Steven's thigh, wicked teeth sinking down. With a jerk of his massive head, Edgar pulled Steven from his feet, dragging him from the posh apartment and flinging him through the shattered window and into the frigid Denver air.

The sickly Dragonskin launched himself from the penthouse, wings outstretched, eyes locked on Steven as he fell.

The wind whistled in Steven's ears and slapped at his face as he tumbled down, down, down. He used his waning Animus to change into his True Form—though the pain of his ruined leg made it damned hard to focus. Still, that pain was nothing compared to what he would feel if he hit the asphalt far below. He got one wing up. But then Edgar was all over him like stink on shit, claws slashing, teeth biting; it was like the rotting Dragonskin didn't care if they plunged to their death. Then again, Edgar wasn't wounded. He might survive. Steven wouldn't.

Steven got his hind talons up, and he raked them down Edgar's chest, leaving deep gashes in scale and flesh. He used the leverage to launch himself away from the Dragonskin. Steven's back slammed into a building, but his bony spines caught steel, stone, and concrete, slowing his fall. With a grunt and a growl, he hurled himself away from the skyscraper, extending his wings as much as he could. They caught a draft and lifted him up.

He soared away, rising, pumping his wings for greater lift.

Edgar wasn't done yet, however. The Dragonskin snaked through the air, hot on Steven's heels. Both leveled off in front of the penthouse window. Until Edgar smacked into him. Again, Steven felt the bite of the Dragonskin's fangs. Right on his neck. Those teeth pierced his scales, and fresh blood oozed down.

Steven beat his wings, furiously trying to stay aloft and get away. Again and again, he slashed into Edgar with his claws, but the villain wouldn't relent.

A gunshot echoed through Denver's manmade canyons. Edgar roared in pain. He released Steven from the death grip and whirled. Tessa stood on the wrecked remains of the windows. She held enchanted Colt Peacekeepers in both hands. She thumbed back the triggers and shot him again.

Aria, still human, armed with the Slayer Blade, fought the female Dragonsoul across the penthouse. The pair danced, back and forth, Aria slashing with the magic sword, and the female Homo Draconis attacking with her claws and tail. Mouse lashed the sword out of Aria's hand, and it went swinging to the edge of the penthouse. The Slayer Blade came to rest near Tessa.

Edgar flew toward the barista, snarling, spitting, and growling.

Steven wheeled around and leapt onto his scaly back. He circled an arm around Edgar's serpentine throat, clutching the writhing, rotting body to his chest before chomping down on Edgar's neck. A foul taste filled his mouth, but he didn't relent.

Edgar laughed. "Oh, this is so much fun! This is so badass! I'm fighting a fucking dragon as a dragon! And all above those stupid humans. They don't know about us. But they will. They will!"

Steven couldn't let that happen. He had to end Edgar, but he felt his strength waning. He was close to losing consciousness. And even if he kept his wits, he couldn't keep up his True Form for much longer. His very cells were screaming in violent protest. *This is too much! Please stop!* But he wouldn't stop, not until Edgar was dead and he was victorious.

Through the gaping holes where the windows had been, he saw Aria backhand the female Dragonsoul across the face, stunning her, then drive a foot into the slender Homo Draconis's belly, throwing her back like a ragdoll. Pretty damned impressive considering Aria weighed a buck ten at most in her human form. Mouse shifted back to human as she sailed through the wrecked penthouse, landing, unconscious, in a heap of limbs.

Still, Steven wondered why Aria wasn't transforming into a tougher body, either Homo Draconis or her True Form. He didn't know, but he was fairly sure she couldn't help him with the insane Dragonskin.

Edgar, screaming, swept toward the penthouse. He was reaching out his thick green claws to rip Tessa to shreds. The Peacekeepers' hammers clicked down on spent shells. Tessa was out of bullets.

Steven had one arm around Edgar's throat. With the other, he shredded the wing under him. Edgar broke off his lunge, then worked his one remaining wing, sending them smashing into the side of the building, taking out another collection of windows. Glass

289

shattered and rained down toward the street below. In the same instant, Steven felt his scales change to skin, his arms shrinking, his legs returning to normal. He started to slip from the Dragonskin's back, but managed to grab a spine at the last second.

But he was weak. Tired. His body filled with agony.

Unencumbered, Edgar got his wings working, despite the damage Steven had dished out. The crazed Dragonskin careened crazily toward the penthouse—a kamikaze pilot on his final run. Going that fast, filled with such rage, if he hit the building, he might kill everyone inside.

He had to be stopped before he reached the Aerie.

And that's when Tessa raised the Slayer Blade. She'd picked it up now that her pistols were empty. She stepped back, scrunched her face up in iron determination, and took a running jump out of the penthouse, a war cry crashing from her mouth. She hung in the air for a full two seconds, before smacking into Edgar's side and driving the sword deep into his chest—though she missed his heart by a solid foot.

Edgar roared in fury and pain. The stink of his rotten flesh intensified, coming off him in a palpable wave. Steven scrambled up his spines to get to the Dragonskin's shoulder. His wings were still beating, keeping the monster airborne. Steven glanced down to see Tessa clutching the sword, which was buried to the hilt in Edgar's scaly abdomen. It wasn't going to be enough to slay the beast, and Steven knew if he didn't do something right then, both he and Tessa would die.

End of story.

He had to regain his True Form. He had to push himself to the very edge of his capabilities.

Steven closed his eyes, pictured the skill tree, and remembered the ink tableau of Stefan Drokharis and his wife giving Joe Whipp a baby bundled away in blankets. More memories flooded in: Diving in front of the bullet to save Tessa. Aria's first kiss. Tessa, on the road, eating a Donette. Aria giving Steven sidelong looks, as if evaluating him. Finding himself in the middle of the universe, floating between galaxies, at the heart of all existence.

Reaching for that power, he triggered his True Form.

And this time, no matter how hard the transformation, he was going to force himself to change. And change he did. He felt his soul lurch. Stagger. Tear. Too much. The effort would kill him. But not before he killed Edgar Vale.

The minute Steven felt his wings spread, the minute he had fangs, he ripped into Edgar's throat like a starved bear. Noxious blood filled his mouth and splattered his chest. Animus flowed into Steven, filling him, keeping him from careening over the edge of death, healing his damaged body a bit, but not much. No, in order to *really* heal, Vale needed to die. And by Steven's hand. The gray-green dragon thrashed and flailed, wriggling to free himself from Steven's jaws, but it was a useless endeavor.

He held fast, leeching off Animus and strength.

Edgar's thrashing slowed, his wings beating spastically. Finally, he howled, and that mighty call went from a dragon's thunder to a human's shrieking. Steven felt the body beneath him shudder and shrink, but instead of easing up, he bit down deeper, tearing Edgar's head from his shoulders, then flicking it away in disgust. The man tasted of spoiled meat. The head flipped, once, twice, and Steven caught sight of Edgar's face: eyes glazed, shock etched into his skin. *No, it's not supposed to happen this way,* that look said. *I'm the underdog, the king.*

And then the head flipped again.

Steven still held Edgar's body, his wings now keeping them aloft, and good thing since Tessa was clinging to Edgar's wrist, her feet dangling over the street far below. But Steven was so tired, so weak. He beat his wings, struggling to stay in the air, knowing that it was only a matter of seconds before his strength failed for good and he reverted to human form. They'd never make it back to the penthouse. Tessa gritted her teeth and pulled herself up to Steven, climbing onto his arm.

He promptly dropped Edgar and angled toward the busted window. He failed. Ten feet away, his Animus reserve faltered, and he felt himself changing back into a frail, wingless human. In a flash, they plummeted through the frigid night toward their deaths.

Face to face, he gazed into Tessa's eyes. "I can't … I can't …"

"I can," Tessa said. "I got this." She closed her eyes in concentration. She let go of him and brought her arms up between them. She circled her fingers and thumb.

They hurled down toward the unforgiving pavement below.

And then she called out, "*Magica Defensio!*"

A pink shimmering sphere appeared around them like a giant soap bubble. Steven had little faith. Sure, the bubble might stop a sword blade or even a bullet, but with how fast they were going? The orb of energy around them would strike the street, and they'd be crushed inside.

Tessa shot him a knowing wink as though she could read his thoughts, and waved her hands down. And the pink shield elongated into a long, smooth slide. Suddenly, Steven found himself cruising down at a steep angle, Tessa curled up against his side.

The ride was breakneck fast at first, but the slide leveled out the closer to the street they got, until it eventually ran parallel to the ground. Steven and Tessa shot off the end of the pink energy field and went rolling across the pavement, bouncing, ripping off layers of skin, until they came to a stop twenty feet away.

Steven opened his eyes. Every inch of him was in pain. But he was alive. And nothing seemed broken. He crawled over to Tessa, who was gasping. Her clothes looked like they'd gone through a paper shredder, and she had gash on her forehead, oozing blood. In the corner of his eye, he caught sight of what remained of Edgar: a pulpy pile of red meat. The Slayer Blade lay next to him. Considering *that* was the alternative, Steven thought they'd done okay after all.

He pulled himself up next to Tessa and collapsed onto his side. She lay on her back. When he touched her, she turned to him. "Shit went sideways," she offered with a tired grin. "I fixed it."

Steven laughed. "Yeah, you did."

Her eyes went back to the penthouse above. "It looks normal, I don't see any damage. But I know it's not. Aria must be using hiding magic." Regardless of the concealment spells in place, police sirens erupted, sending lights and noise through the downtown area. It was clear that someone had reported something, probably the bloody splotch surrounding Edgar Vale's jellied body on Seventeenth Avenue.

Tessa helped Steven stand and retrieved the Slayer Blade. Together, they limped toward the lobby, bruised, bloody, and battered but alive. Victorious.

"Where are we going?" Steven asked. His head was fuzzy from the pain and exertion.

Tessa smiled. "I have to get my purse. I left it up in the penthouse."

TWENTY-EIGHT

STEVEN AND TESSA WALKED INTO THE LOBBY OF the Wells Fargo building to find the security guard sitting at his desk, his eyes glazed over. Another guard stood-stock still near the polished metal desk. Both seemed to be in some kind of trance. More concealment magic at work, no doubt. But was it from Aria or Mouse? Which one was still alive?

Steven was having trouble keeping his eyes open. That last transformation had taken everything out of him. Only the Animus from killing Edgar had kept him alive.

Tessa propped Steven up against the wall, went to the guard sitting behind the desk, and pulled off his uniform trousers. Then she fished keys out of his pocket. Returning to Steven, she helped him slip into the polyester pants.

In the elevator, they found a slot in the shape of an X. Finding that key was easy, and like Bud had said, a secret panel popped open. A button in the shape of a dragon was there. Resting the Slayer Blade against a wall, Tessa thumbed the button and the elevator shot upward.

Steven collapsed to the floor. Tessa knelt. "Steven, it's okay. We'll get Aria, and then we'll get you to a hospital."

That made sense. He'd taken two bullets, and he wasn't sure if those magic rounds were still in him. "Tessa, you can't do shit like you did," he mumbled in a daze. "You can't jump out of buildings."

She *tsked* him. "I can. I did. I wasn't completely sure I could manipulate my shields like that, but I watched this derpy cartoon growing up. *Spider-Man and His Amazing Friends*. Iceman was always using his cold powers to break his fall."

"Not derpy," Steven replied. "It saved our life."

Tessa laughed. "And my mom said that all the TV would rot my brain."

"You're amazing," he said.

"Right back at you."

When the elevator dinged open, they found Bud lying against the wall. He looked dead ... totally dead. He was lying in a pile of pizza slices and cast-off boxes. The mercenaries had beaten him into a pulp. But in the end, they'd met their end. Steven felt a flare of remorse, but then Bud twitched—just an arm, but enough to proclaim that he was alive. He twitched again, this time his leg, then pushed himself up with a groan.

"Did you get 'em?" Bud asked, glancing at Steven through swollen eyes.

Steven nodded. "Yeah. But you look like I feel."

"Even beat to shit, I look awesome," Bud said, smiling. Yeah, he was missing a fair number of teeth. "So you must feel awesome. You don't look it, though."

"And I might still have to fight," Steven said. "We'll be right back."

Bud sighed and flopped back down. "Sounds good, I'll just be right here, trying not to die. Probably won't ever be able to eat pizza again, so there's that."

As they walked away, Bud called after them, "You look killer with that sword, Tessa. For real."

"I know," she said simply, cocking an eyebrow.

Through the big doors, they found Aria standing over the female Dragonsoul, who was human again and bleeding freely. Both were dressed in ripped gowns. Aria, still in handcuffs, scratched the female's throat with one of the magic swords. Tessa and Steven crunched over the debris on the floor, but Aria didn't take her eyes off their enemy. "Did you take care of Edgar?"

"We both did," Tessa said. "I stabbed him, and Steven bit his head off."

"Good," Aria said, the word cold as the heart of winter.

An awkward silence fell across the room. Kai Charon was nowhere to be seen. Steven had the idea the Warling had fled the battle, obviously having lost the fight.

"So, what now?" Steven asked.

"Take me with you!" Mouse said, stealing a frightful look at him. "Take me into your Escort. Please. Mulk will punish me. Please."

"Quiet, Mouse," Aria warned, pressing in just a little harder with the sword tip.

Steven approached the two women. A smashed clock on the floor showed it was 6:45 p.m.

"Is Mouse your real name?" Steven asked.

She gave him a weary look. "What do you think, genius?" Then her eyes flashed in fear realizing what she'd said and how she'd said it. "No, my lord, it's not. I was born Melissa Craygore, daughter of the Rocky Mountains Prime, but that was before the new Dragonsoul Prime took over."

"So how did you get the name Mouse?" Steven reached out a hand, batting the sword aside then helping her to her feet.

Aria stepped back. "Steven, we can't—"

Mouse interrupted her. "I was always really small, and the rest is the result of a lack of imagination. On everyone's part, I guess. I could've stopped it. But I was never very necessary. Mulk married me when I was important to his Primacy, and then when my father was killed, I stopped being anyone or anything. Mouse is probably a good name for me."

It hurt to hear her talk about herself that way. Her eyes were clear, and yet Steven felt like she wanted to cry but couldn't. Those soft parts of her had hardened into a shell. And he smelled alcohol oozing out of her pores along with her almond Dragonsoul scent.

Aria stepped forward and gripped Steven's arm. "We can't take her with us. She is part of Mulk's Escort. It would be the ultimate insult. He would come for you with every single one of his vassals. We wouldn't stand a chance." Aria winced when she swallowed. Clearly, her throat was bothering her.

"Please," Mouse pleaded. "Mulk is awful to me. I can't help but love him, but I also hate him. I hate him so much."

Steven listened to her, hearing her pain, but he kept his eyes on Aria.

She was trembling, hurt, and slightly scorched from the battle and from the Exhalant attack she'd unleashed while in human form. The handcuffs must've had magic to keep her from changing.

Steven couldn't help himself. He took her in his arms, felt her slim, muscled body against his, and kissed her long and hard. Holding Aria felt so right. She had started him on his journey and he was so glad they'd saved her.

Aria still had her eyes closed when Steven pulled back.

"I can kiss you like that," Mouse said, her words slurring slightly.

"No, not yet," Steven said. "I think you need to sober up, and then we'll see. But yes, we will take you with us."

Aria's eyes flashed open, full of fury. "Steven, no, you don't know what you are doing."

"He killed my parents," Steven said. "I want to hurt him. And if he comes for me, I'll kill him. It's pretty clear he's done a number on Mouse." He turned to her. "Why haven't you left on your own?"

She dropped her eyes to a ring on her left hand. "I can't." She glanced at Aria. "She knows why." Mouse retreated to a smashed desk drawer, took out a small key chain, and unlocked the handcuffs. They fell from Aria's wrists.

Aria nodded. "When you join a Dragonsoul's Escort, it's for life. Only another Dragonsoul male can free you. There is powerful magic involved. In the end, you might not be able to free her."

Mouse lifted her hand. "Take the ring off. Free me. And I'll be yours. I swear it."

"I don't own people," Steven said, shaking his head. He wasn't liking this, not any of it. "What you're talking about sounds like slavery."

"Yeah, this is fifty kinds of fucked up." Tessa spoke for the first time. "We have to free her, Aria. We have to."

Steven gripped the simple gold band on Mouse's left ring finger. He tried to simply remove it, but it wouldn't budge.

Instinctively, he knew what to do. He reached out a hand. Tessa took it, and the touch of her skin on his fed him a bit more Animus.

Aria sighed. "This will call down the wrath of hell upon us. But I suppose if you two could break into an Aerie to rescue me, we might be able to defeat Mulk." She walked around Steven and held him, pressing her face against his back. She cupped the muscles of his chest with her hands.

More Animus flowed into him.

He focused his mind on removing the ring. He slid it off in a flash of light. The gold ring promptly disintegrated into dust. Mouse burst into tears and threw herself into Steven's arms. Tessa held them all, and they stood there for a minute, all four embracing.

A voice boomed through the room. "WHAT DO YOU THINK YOU ARE DOING, WHELP? I DON'T KNOW WHO YOU ARE, BUT I WILL COME FOR YOU. AND YOU WILL KNOW PAIN BEFORE I TEAR YOUR HEART FROM YOUR CHEST." A great presence, Rhaegen Mulk, without a doubt, filled the room for a moment, and then both the voice and the entity were gone.

"Bring it," Steven whispered. "I'm not afraid of you."

Unexpectedly, Aria burst into laughter. "He still doesn't know who you truly are, Steven! That might give us the edge we need."

"Please," Mouse said. "I want to leave this fucking penthouse. I'm so sick of looking at these walls. The wine was good, but freedom tastes so much better."

"Amen to that," Tessa agreed. She went over and collected her purse and then found the two Colt Peacekeepers and shoved both into her purse, already near to bursting from holding the Drokharis Grimoire.

Steven quirked an eyebrow at her.

"Yeah, Steven," Tessa said. "I have spells, but I also want guns. This is just the beginning."

It was.

They left the penthouse, all four of them together.

Bud hadn't moved. His eyes widened when he saw Steven with the three beautiful women around him in a semicircle. "Not bad, Cool Whipp. Not bad at all." The guy then paled. "Sorry, I know you hate it when I call you that."

Aria went over to him and touched his face. Animus flashed from her eyes. Bud's own eyes muddied. And then he looked up at them. "Uh, what the fuck happened?"

Tessa knew exactly what to say. "Quite a party, wasn't it, Bud? You hit that Jägermeister hard. But you shouldn't have mouthed off to those three huge guys."

Still a bit confused, Bud grinned. "Yeah, you might not know it, but I can be kind of an asshole sometimes. You know it's a party when you can't remember a thing."

Steven nodded. And just like that, Bud wouldn't remember seeing a dragon or the battle he'd witnessed with all the strangeness. The Dragonsoul secret was safe once again.

Mouse left Steven's side and stood over Bud. She made a sign over him with her fingers and whispered, "*Magica Cura.*"

The worst of Bud's wounds healed, and he was strong enough to stand. Tessa helped him limp to the elevators.

Mouse visited Steven next, tracing his various wounds with one extended finger. "*Magica Cura,*" she whispered, finger still gliding along his skin, sending chills racing along his arms and legs as her almond scent filled his nose. He watched as the magic bullets fell from his wounds and clattered on the floor. The shallow cuts disappeared next, and the deeper gashes scabbed over at once. Neat trick.

Already, his new vassal was earning her keep. She'd saved him an awkward trip to the ER.

In the lobby, the security guards were still frozen.

"Is this your work?" Steven asked Mouse.

She shook her head. "Mulk. He had special Mind Wipe spells ready to take care of the humans in the building. They went off automatically once the supernatural shit started. Don't worry, no one in a mile radius will remember a thing. They'll snap out of it in an hour or two."

Outside, emergency vehicles clustered around the remains of Edgar Vale. It felt satisfying, watching them try and get the shattered-bone sack—still reeking of rotting meat—into a body bag.

He'd like to think it was a case of one down, one to go, but Steven knew the truth. Even if he somehow managed to take down Rhaegen Mulk, there would always be another Dragonsoul coming for him, to take away his Escort, his Hoard, and his Aeries.

Aria had warned him. To be a Dragonsoul was to court constant battle.

He grinned anyway. That first kiss had still been worth it.

TШENTУ-NINE

STEVEN WOKE TO THE SMELL OF SOMETHING wonderful cooking in the kitchen of the Lookout Mountain Aerie.

He was in the bed of the master suite in his new home. He'd called his various employers the night before and left messages for all his jobs, telling them he was quitting, and apologizing for not giving them two weeks. Bottom line, he couldn't dick around with human life anymore. He had to prepare for Mulk's inevitable counterattack. The Dragonsoul Prime was back in Denver. He'd come for a wedding, but instead, he'd be holding a funeral for Edgar Vale. Worse, Mulk he had lost one of his wives to the very guy he had sent the Dragonskin to kill.

Steven smiled, recalling all the sex from the night before. Tessa and Aria had upped their game, and though they'd all been exhausted, the sex gave them Animus and that helped them heal.

Tessa cuddled up closer to him. She liked to sleep right next to him, and he loved the feel of her touch. He was sore, every inch of him, but he felt himself get hard. Yeah, but there was also his belly to consider. He was hungry in every way.

Seriously, what smelled so good! Aria had to be the one doing the cooking, since she wasn't in bed with them.

Mouse had spent the night in another bedroom, sleeping alone. She had been so excited, so relieved, to be in a new place with people she didn't loathe. Yet she also found the wine cellar, fully stocked, and that also made her happy. Girlfriend had a drinking problem.

He couldn't blame her. Being married to someone you both loved and hated would drive anyone to drink. He swore he wouldn't pressure her to join his Escort, but he had the feeling that the strange power he had over people would draw her to him. And she was so pretty.

Steven eased himself out of the bed so he wouldn't wake Tessa. He stood next to the fireplace, which was sparking and snapping like a real fire. But it was better than a real fire because he didn't have to keep adding logs. He sauntered over to the enormous wall of windows and gazed down at the highway below, edged by a forest of snow-kissed pines. The clouds had finally unloaded the white powder onto the Colorado mountains. It was gorgeous, silent, and peaceful. Snow continued to flutter down.

The hideaway felt so cozy and warm compared to the storm outside.

He'd found soft pajama bottoms the night before. Partially dressed, he padded out of the master suite and into the great room. Like he thought, Aria was in the kitchen, busy cooking breakfast. Full King Soopers bags covered every inch of space. Aria herself was in jeans and an All India Football Federation 2018 T-shirt. No bra. Which was a plus.

When she saw him, she smiled. "I went out early to get groceries. Believe it or not, my American Express card still works. My father though ..." She sighed, lips pressing into a thin line of worry. "He'll cut me off. He has to in order to save face."

"We'll get money," Steven said, thinking of the opulent Colorado Springs Aerie. He went through cupboards until he found a coffee cup. Then he went to the coffee maker and poured himself a drink. He sipped it. A bitter, terrible taste filled his mouth. He didn't want to be rude, so he swallowed the muck. He so wanted to spit it into the sink.

"Yes, I know, terrible," Aria said. "The barista needed to sleep. Here, try this." She moved from a deep-fat fryer to the stove, where a pot burbled. She grabbed another cup and filled it with steaming liquid from the pot. She gave the cup to him, hugged him briefly, and went back to the fryer.

Steven took another sip, dreading the taste, but then the chai tea mixture filled his mouth. "Oh, that is so good!"

"The British and their empire aside, we Indians know how to make a cup of tea," she said with a smile.

He drifted over to watch her work. Using tongs, she eased a big ball of fried dough out of the fryer. It was puffy, the size of a softball. On the big marble island were a number of small bowls filled with dipping sauces.

"And now, you will sample a traditional Tamil Nadu breakfast. That's called poori." She took a tray of the fried spheres and offered him one. He took it, still warm, and dipped part of the ball into a green sauce. When the taste hit his tongue, his eyes lit up. "Damn, Aria, that's so good!"

Tessa came out in the soft pajama top that matched Steven's bottoms. She had sleep-filled eyes, sleep-mussed hair, and the Slayer Blade in her fist. "What is it? Are we under attack?"

"No, we're fine. Just a little heaven on earth this Monday morning." Steven crossed the room and gave her his mug.

Tessa sipped it and closed her eyes. "Oh, now that's good stuff. I can see why you woke me up."

"The chai is good, but dude, try the poori," Steven said.

"Food!" Tessa dropped the Slayer Blade on a couch and hotfooted it over to snatch a doughy ball off the plate. She dipped it in a bright red sauce, and then she just had to kiss Aria. "Girlfriend, you can cook too? Is there anything you can't do?"

"I couldn't save myself," Aria said, turning serious. "Thank you, Tessa."

Mouse shuffled, half-asleep, out of a side bedroom. She had a bathrobe on, kind of. It had slipped halfway off her body. Her eyes were still closed, and her blonde hair stood up straight on one side of her head. Wordless, she took Steven's coffee cup, threw the contents in the sink, and then poured herself a cup of joe.

"Uh, careful," Steven warned.

"No. Talking. Before. Coffee." Mouse sipped the coffee, grimaced, and then, from the pocket of her robe, tipped a little booze from a silver flask into the cup. Another sip. A sigh. "Much better." Girlfriend had a definite drinking problem. They'd take care of that, but first things first.

"Breakfast!" Tessa yelled happily.

Mouse winced, clearly hungover.

They all helped Aria carry dishes to a long glass table facing the snowy mountainside descending to the streets of Golden.

Before they started, Steven raised his cup of chai tea, heavy on the heavy cream. "I'd like to thank you all, for helping me. We have a war coming up. But with you three on my team, well, I know nothing can stop us."

Every sauce was an explosion of flavor. Combined with the poori, it was the most exotic and yet the best breakfast Steven had ever eaten. He thought of where he'd come from, the Coffee Clutch, that normal day which had turned into the most abnormal of nights. The first of many to come.

After breakfast, Mouse disappeared into her room to sleep more, while Tessa and Aria snuggled into him on the couch. They watched the snow fall together in a tangle of warm bodies.

"Do you think we can really stand up against Mulk?" Aria asked. "Most of his vassals were with him in Cheyenne. We only fought his humans and some mentally ill Skinling."

"And that Warling," Steven said. "Kai Charon. The guy in the purple suit."

"Yes," Aria agreed. "As we saw in the tableaus, Mulk has Morphlings, Magicians, and other Warlings serving him. We are hopelessly outnumbered."

"There's also the yellow Dragonsoul that captured you," Tessa pointed out.

Aria nodded. A strange expression settled on her face. "Liam Strider. He's not exactly a vassal of Mulk's.

He was a Ronin, but the oddest Ronin Dragonsoul I've ever met. He said he is fleeing Denver because few Dragonsouls will survive the coming war. Yet I feel like we'll see him again."

"Which side will he be on?" Steven asked. He wondered if he could ever forgive the yellow dragon for stealing away Aria.

"Now that is a good question," Aria replied thoughtfully.

"Do you think he helped Mulk kill Steven's father?" Tessa asked.

Aria shook her head but furrowed her brow. "I don't believe so. Yet what happened to the Drokharis clan wasn't normal. We saw five full Dragonsoul males attacking him. They might've been part of Mulk's Primacy, but I can't see how. And normally, one Dragonsoul male will kill another and take his Prime. This all-out massacre is forbidden. I'm wondering what kind of deals Mulk made with the Primacies around him that they would turn a blind eye to the slaughter."

All this talk made Steven rage. "I don't know, but I'll get the truth out of Mulk. We still don't know everything about my father and what happened. Mulk's motive is the key. Why did he kill my parents and every single one of their vassals? If we know the answer to that, we'll know the answer to everything."

They went quiet. Steven slowly let go of his anger and banished any trace of worry from his mind. Everything would be fine, he told himself. His mom was safe, he had the Colorado Springs Hoard to finance them, and they'd done the impossible the night before. They'd broken into a penthouse Aerie, against all odds, and rescued one of their own.

Idly, he wondered if Aria would want to marry him, or if Tessa would, and he wondered about Mouse in the other room. How damaged was she?

He had no answers to his questions.

"Yeah," Tessa said finally. "We are outnumbered. Lucky for us, we have Bud."

They'd dropped the guy off at his apartment, leaving him thinking he'd had a wild Sunday night downtown.

All of them laughed, but Aria, true to her serious nature, pointed out something Steven hadn't considered. "Most Dragonsouls *do* have humans working for them— ambassadors to the normal world. Bud might be good to have. You never know."

"I'm human," Tessa insisted. "We already have one of those."

Aria snuggled into the barista. "You are, and yet you aren't. The power you wield is enormous. You're undoubtedly special."

Tessa closed her eyes. "Special, finally."

Steve let the peaceful morning flow into him. Yes. Special, finally.

But his uniqueness had come with a price. His birth parents had been murdered, along with all their vassals, Escort, and friends.

As the last scion of the Drokharis Dynasty, he had a responsibility to avenge them and to continue his father's work. What that was, he wasn't sure, but he was certain that like Tessa, the mysteries of their lives would come clear in time.

The battle for the Great Plains Primacy was only just beginning.

And Steven Drokharis swore he would win it so he could keep his Escort safe.

Special Thanks

For the readers all the readers out there who keep me in business! Thanks so much for offering me your time and for leaving the reviews!

And thanks to my brothers and sisters in arms. I've been loving spending Wednesday nights with the Denver Write Knights. We are mighty. And we eat pie. A good combination.

Thanks to James and Jeanette and Shadow Alley Press for letting me throw pages at you all. I love that way that you do books.

And let me toss more gratitude at Eden, Jeanette, and Tamara for the amazing editing experience. I love that you love words and ideas so much.

For my wife and my crazy daughters. I'd save the galaxy for you gals any time. And while cats play a special place in the galaxy, I love my dogs Rafi and Lolo.

A last shout out to those addicts and alcoholics who manage to stay clean and sober on a daily basis. You save the universe by what you don't do.

—Aaron Crash, July 2018

About the Author

Aaron Crash writes adrenaline-fueled odysseys into the extreme regions of speculative fiction. If you're looking for cyborg vampires or jellyfish centaurs, you've come to the right place. He is the co-author of the War God's Mantle series (Shadow Alley Press) and other over-the-top sci-fi/fantasy novels. He's been an Amazon All-Star and his books have broken into Amazon's Top 100. When he's not wrestling the word dragons, he mountain bikes, kills pixels dead, and has been known to watch a movie or three. He lives in Colorado where he does devilish things.

Books, Mailing List, and Reviews

If you enjoyed reading about Steven and his crew of badass ladies and want to stay in the loop about the latest book releases, promotional deals, and upcoming book giveaways be sure to subscribe to my email list:

www.ShadowAlleyPress.com

Word-of-mouth and book reviews are crazy helpful for the success of any writer. If you *really* enjoyed reading about Steven, please consider leaving a short, honest review—just a couple of lines about your overall reading experience. Thank you in advance!

Books from Shadow Alley Press

If you enjoyed Denver Fury: American Dragons Book One, you might also enjoy the other awesome stories from Shadow Alley Press, such as the Yancy Lazarus Series, Viridian Gate Online, War God's Mantle, Legend of the Treesinger, or the Jubal Van Zandt Series. You can find all of our books listed at www.ShadowAlleyPress.com

Aaron Crash

War God's Mantle: Ascension (Book 1)
War God's Mantle: Descent (Book 2)

⊥

Damnation Robot: Galactic Demon Hunters

Neutron Dragon Attack: Galactic Demon Hunters

Black Hole Werewolves: Galactic Demon Hunters

James A. Hunter

Viridian Gate Online: Cataclysm (Book 1)
315

Aaron Crash

Viridian Gate Online: Crimson Alliance (Book 2)
Viridian Gate Online: The Jade Lord (Book 3)
Viridian Gate Online: Imperial Legion (Book 4)
Viridian Gate Online: The Lich Priest (Book 5)
Viridian Gate Online: Doom Forge (Book 6)

⊥

Strange Magic: Yancy Lazarus Episode One
Cold Heatred: Yancy Lazarus Episode Two
Flashback: Siren Song (Episode 2.5)
Wendigo Rising: Yancy Lazarus Episode Three
Flashback: The Morrigan (Episode 3.5)
Savage Prophet: Yancy Lazarus Episode Four
Brimstone Blues: Yancy Lazarus Episode Five

⊥

MudMan: A Lazarus World Novel

⊥

Eden Hudson

Revenge of the Bloodslinger: A Jubal Van Zandt Novel
Beautiful Corpse: A Jubal Van Zandt Novel
Soul Jar: A Jubal Van Zandt Novel
Garden of Time: A Jubal Van Zandt Novel
Wasteside: A Jubal Van Zandt Novel

⊥

Two-Faced: Legend of the Treesinger Book 1
Soul Game: Legend of the Treesinger Book 2